THE (ANTI) WEDDING PARTY

THE (ANTI)
WEDDING PARTY

Lucy Knott

HEAD
ZEUS

An Aria Book

First published in the UK in 2024 by Head of Zeus,
part of Bloomsbury Publishing Plc

9 7 5 3 1 2 4 6 8

A catalogue record for this book is available from the British Library.

ISBN (PB): 9781837931712
ISBN (E): 9781837931699

Cover design: Meg Shepherd

Typeset by Siliconchips Services Ltd UK

Printed and bound in Great Britain by
CPI Group (UK) Ltd, Croydon CR0 4YY

Head of Zeus Ltd
First Floor East
5–8 Hardwick Street
London EC1R 4RG

WWW.HEADOFZEUS.COM

For Dan and for William

Prologue

'Typical,' I mutter under my breath as the British clouds decide to let loose and rain on my parade, quite literally if you count a wedding as a parade, which I'm going to say I do. I'm full of wedding puns today, apparently. Goosebumps prickle my skin and I'm beginning to lose all feelings in my pinkie toes, what with the draft in this over-the-top, dramatic and ancient room, and with the lack of circulation getting to them thanks to these too-tight and too-expensive heels, because according to my soon-to-be mother-in-law, I was under no circumstances allowed to walk down the aisle barefoot.

Nor was I able to buy a dress from a charity shop, have my best friend, Alex, as a photographer, or have McDonald's cater the wedding. Who knew there were so many wedding rules? I wasn't the kind of girl who swallowed the wedding handbook growing up or watched rom-coms. Romance was not a word commonly uttered in my house, with my own parents having only gotten married because my mum got pregnant with me three months into their relationship, which I'm sad to say, didn't last long. They managed a rough three years before my dad walked out, never to be heard from again.

I grew up with a ferociously independent mother who enforced that trait onto me, her only daughter. Marriage was not on my to-do list, not when it was consistently as long as my five-foot-five frame. No, marriage was not something I dreamt about nor had time for, but then as the saying goes, 'when you know, you know.'

'Ignore the weather; it's just a shower. How are you feeling? Are you all set?' Alex asks. I'm not quite sure which question to tackle first. 'Why are your lips blue?' She adds another question to the mix when she draws closer to me, stepping an inch away from my nose, her slim figure looking all rose-like in her blood-red bridesmaid dress.

I glance in the slightly smeared glass of the archaic mirror with a gold leaf border, and sure enough, my lips are blue. I think they add to the gloomy, cold aesthetic of the large stone room, to be honest.

'Because this place is freezing,' I tell Alex. I don't miss her slight grimace, the way her nose crinkles, making her freckles glisten and look like glitter in the dim light that the one creepy-looking lamp in the corner of the room is providing – the stained-glass window offering us nothing on this very conventional British day.

'OK, stand up. Come on, do some star jumps or something. We've got to go in five minutes,' she explains, rubbing my biceps and pulling me up. My feet wince as they bear my weight, toes squishing further into the rubber. My bandeau-style wedding dress is a little tight, but not so tight that I won't be able to have at least one bite of a cocktail sausage or whatever vegan sausage my future mother-in-law insisted my mother and I pay a little extra for.

Except there's no such thing as a little extra in our world;

it's all been extra. This whole wedding that my mum and I have bulldozed our savings for has all been beyond extra. But despite the looming threat of debt, and possibly IBS due to the artificial sausage meat on tonight's menu, I feel a tingle of excitement flutter in my belly.

Gripping onto Alex's shoulders, while my toes kick into gear that they are needed, I do a baby star jump, nearly going over on my ankle in these killer heels, but Alex grips my biceps harder.

'I've got you,' she says, beaming. My other bridesmaid, Alex's girlfriend, Charlie, is already lined up waiting for me to join the parade, I assume.

'I'm getting married,' I allow myself to squeal. Considering I never in a million years thought this day would come, nor wanted it to, it now all seems rather exciting and special, like someone actually wants to marry me.

And for a moment nothing, not the British weather, the blisters I'm bound to get in these monster shoes, the sleepless nights trying to choose between awfully similar fonts with my bride-to-be and ultimately just saying yes to everything she wanted – like getting married in a freaking castle – none of it matters when I think about Hannah and me at the altar in a few minutes, exchanging our vows. She no doubt looking effortlessly glam, her long, blonde waves sweeping the curve of her lower back; her dress, I'm guessing, will be skin-tight, hugging every gorgeous curve, and her lipstick will be the perfect shade of nude.

It won't matter that it's been a whirlwind romance, not when her family are taking up one side of the castle cathedral while Mum, Alex and Charlie are standing on the other side cheering us on. Mum with tears in her eyes, celebrating that I'm giving it a shot despite her and Dad's less than stellar modelling, or the pain and hurt of my previous relationships. Now I'm letting that all go. It doesn't matter anymore; what matters is that Hannah loves me enough to want to marry me, and how could I say no to that?

'You look beautiful,' Alex grins, 'and badass.' She winks. 'Tonight, we're partying in Casper's house.' She raises her arms above her head, the scent of peonies wafting around the room when she does so.

'Yes we are, we are not letting those fancy bottles of prosecco go to waste. But first I need to pee,' I note.

'Andi,' she sighs. 'Go, go, you've got three minutes,' she adds, swatting my bum with her bouquet as I shuffle past her. 'I'll meet you in the hallway,' she calls after me, closing the hefty wooden door of my dressing chamber behind us.

Gathering my mermaid tail into my fist so I don't stab the fabric with my dagger-like heels, I make my way into the dungeon – I mean, bathroom – my last wee before I'm a married woman. Is this what people do before they get married? Take account of all the things they'll do for the last time as a Miss.

I hike my dress up so high around my boobs, there is no chance in hell of any splash back going anywhere near it, and as I squat, I nearly jump out of my skin when I hear the loud *thwack* of a door slamming against the wall. When my heart settles, all I can hear is heavy breathing and panting outside of the cubicle, and suddenly my heart is once again erratic. For a moment, sweat builds on my bronzed brow as panic washes over me that someone is being murdered and can't catch their breath, like I'm at some sort of murder mystery party and not my own wedding. That is until the panting and grunting turns into heavy moans and breathy sighs.

My ears immediately prick up at the whimper; I've heard it before, a couple times over the last year.

'I have to have you now,' the voice is low, desperate and needy.

'You look so sexy in this dress,' the second voice matches the first in desire and filthy lust, and it's clear that the conversation is happening between kisses and is not the sound of murder.

Pain hits me as sharp as someone pouring a bucket of ice water over my head. My armpits feel clammy, my arms hot and cold at the same time, like I'm coming down with a sudden case of flu. I wipe hastily, my brain wanting me to burst through the cubicle door with a powerful, confident swing as I rage my worth, yet my fingers tremble as I go to even touch it, to push it lightly to see what's on the other side.

But I can't stay in the stall forever, not while the delicate whispers become more hurried. My hearing seems to have become hypersensitive as it hones in on every rustle of fabric.

With my eyes closed, I gently push the door open, and after one timid step forward, I slowly open them, so slow I have to blink to bring everything into focus.

'Hannah.' Her name is all I can muster as I take in the vintage lace-style wedding dress that is gathered around her hips, one long, lean leg resting over someone's hip, their mess of red curls draped over their bare shoulders, bridesmaid dress askew, breasts out for the world to see, except that Hannah's hand is cupped over one of them while her other is cupping the back of Ebony's head to stop it from bouncing off the stone wall in all their ravaged passion. I dare not look for Ebony's hands; Hannah's moan told me all I need to know.

In the exact moment I build up the courage to meet her deer-in-the-headlights gaze, the automatic toilet flushes and I stagger backwards, feeling a slight tug. It pulls my attention away from the free porn show I was getting, to my precious mermaid tail swirling around the toilet bowl.

'Oh, bloody hell,' I express.

'Is everything alright, Andi, I just wanted to check...' Alex's voice trails off when she registers the scene in front of her after bursting into the antique bathroom.

'What the actual fu—?'

'It's OK, Alex,' I cut her off. 'Will you just help me with this whole thing?' I ask, waving my hands over the lower part of my dress that's stuck in the toilet. She walks over to me, never taking her eyes off Hannah – that's when I notice Charlie behind her, the exact same protective, steely glare on her face.

No one speaks as we gather my dress from the toilet, its soggy weight making me more unsteady in my heels, the silence feeling haunting. I don't know if I want Hannah to say something or if I can stand to hear her voice right now. It's not like I have a choice either way, as she's very much choosing to remain a mime, a paused picture with Ebony's hands still in her knickers. I stumble, feeling sick and light-headed.

Charlie grabs my waist as Alex tries to carry the weight of the dress without actually touching the gross bits and trudge past the statue depicting my life crumbling.

'I don't recall that being in the maid of honour job description,' Charlie spits at my bride-to-be and her chief bridesmaid before we click, clack and squelch down the corridor.

'What's going on?' My mum's voice echoes down the long, grim hallway. 'Honey, where is everyone?' she asks, worry lines creasing her brow.

'Having sex in the bathroom,' I say, matter of fact, a laugh making the very edge of my lips tremble. It sounds utterly ridiculous when I say it out loud. I mean, sex on your wedding night is one thing, but sex in the bathroom two minutes before your wedding and not with your fiancée, well, it doesn't quite have the same ring to it.

I traipse through the castle – I mean really, a castle, it's a bit much – towards the banquet hall, past the lavishly decorated tables and grab a bottle of prosecco that's chilling in the ice bins. I struggle with the lid while I kick off my shoes, sending them flying across the room. One hits the back of an elegantly dressed chair with a bow tied around its back; the other makes a loud tinkle crashing down onto a plate.

Charlie grabs the bottle from me without a word and then mercifully deals with the lid.

'What on earth are you doing in here? Everyone's waiting.' Hannah's mum is marching towards me but is abruptly stopped when my mum steps in front of her. For a split second, I fear my mum might slap her.

'Why don't you go and ask your daughter and stay away from mine,' my mum all but shouts.

I take a large swig of prosecco straight from the bottle and plonk down on a chair as Hannah's mum storms out and Alex walks in. I hadn't realised she had gone anywhere, but she's carrying my favourite oversized hoodie and a pair of her Sweaty Betty quilted joggers that I would never be able to afford, and my eyes bulge when I see them. I love it when she lets me wear her clothes.

I'm in a prosecco-and-luxury-jogger fantasy dream as Alex and Charlie strip me down out of my sodden wedding dress and into the blissful comfies that I'm drooling over in my mind. I sit down on the deep burgundy carpet; Alex sits on the chair behind me as I nuzzle into her legs.

'Shall we go and get you a cheeseburger?' Alex says, loosening my low bun and playing with the baby hairs around it.

'I hate weddings,' I hiccup. 'I never want to go to another wedding for as long as I live,' I tell her, leaning my head into her thighs and looking up into her deep hazel eyes. 'But I would like to go to McDonald's, always. And Alex...' I pause.

'Yes,' she says simply.

'Please can I get five cheeseburgers?'

'Absolutely. You can have as many cheeseburgers as you want.'

'Maybe I'll have six,' I mumble into the bottle. 'Weddings are stupid, but chicken nuggets are not. Maybe I'll have some chicken nuggets too, but weddings, never again.'

I

'Chips and gravy in a tray, please.' I take the order with a nod of my head and get straight to work shovelling chips into a tray and ladling a generous amount of thick, brown gravy over the top of the crispy, golden potatoes. There's nowhere I can turn that doesn't send a scorching waft of steam in my direction. I place the metal lid back on the gravy and turn in the tight space to wrap up Jenny's order. In the good old days, Ned's Chippy was a hive of chatterboxes, the locals swarming here on a Friday evening for their end-of-week tea, but not today. All I can hear is the low buzz of a fluorescent light bulb above that I know is going to need replacing soon, and the whirring of a fan that Mum and I have placed on the other side of the counter so our customers don't deep fry themselves in the heat. No matter how little I believe the fan is actually working, this is truly a sacrifice, as each time I move, I can feel the sweat tickling my inner thighs on my side of the tin counter. Stockport has blessed us with a sizzling middle-of-July heatwave that has rendered everyone speechless (bar a mumbled takeaway order), sticky and sloth like.

Jenny and I exchange another, slightly less enthusiastic nod, in part saving our breaths for the air that keeps evaporating before it reaches my lungs. Next to me, Mum is ignoring the sweat that is pooling where her hair net meets her forehead, tossing chips into the fryer and dipping fish into the oil. Her face is not its usual welcoming greeting when we have actual customers; instead, it's wrinkled with confusion.

'Salt and vinegar, love?' I ask Dereck, my mind having blanked on a few of the regulars' orders. I'm working on autopilot, trying to ensure things run smoothly and I don't mess up, not while we're only just getting back on our feet, and I feel utterly holy that some of our regulars have returned. And who wants to get home after a long, arduous week, mouth drooling, ready to tuck into their delicious meal, a meal they haven't cooked which only makes it all the more luxurious and exciting, to find that there's vinegar on their curry and meat in their cheese and onion pie?

Ring, ring.

'Just salt please, Andi,' Dereck replies, dabbing at his forehead with a white handkerchief, bless him.

Ring, ring.

Salt and vinegar poised mid-shake, I momentarily forget what I'm doing.

'Sorry, salt and vinegar?' I repeat. I can feel a slippery tendril of hair trying to escape from my own attractive hair net. It feels like those times when you walk through a cobweb only to become adamant for the rest of the day that a spider is enjoying a pleasant stroll all over your body, scouting for new accommodation.

Ring, ring.

'Just salt.' I see Dereck's mouth move but between the whir of the fan, the buzz of the light, the phone ringing and my fear that a spider is weaving a web in my hair, my brain is not registering mine and Dereck's very simple and familiar interaction.

'Where's Jack?' Mum shouts over her shoulder, nose still scrunched as she lifts and dips the fish, like she's never done it before.

'You mean the Jack we had to let go three months ago?' I reply, wrinkles crinkling between my brows, causing my hair net to wriggle up half an inch.

'One more time just for the hell of it,' I say to Dereck, giving him my brightest smile as I stand looking as though I'm preparing for a ninja attack, but instead of nunchucks, I'm armed with a bottle of vinegar and a salt shaker.

Dereck wipes his top lip in clear frustration, the heat making us English far less polite.

'Just salt, please, Andi,' he says, moving closer to the counter, like he's about to reach over and attend to the salt himself. I can't say I'd stop him; I could clearly use the help. I nod and start shaking a generous amount over his order.

Ring, ring.

'Oh right, yes,' Mum says, clearly in another world, as Dereck waves a hurried goodbye at the same time as I send him an apologetic, tight-lipped, cheeks bulging smile.

Jack had been a helping hand when my nanna passed away. A hand that we couldn't really afford and one we could afford less and less as the customers dwindled down. Ned's Chip Shop had been my nanna and grandad's, and was my great nanna's and great grandad's before that. My mum, Kristen, has been working here since she was old enough to hand a can of Irn-Bru across the counter and dish out change.

Me, I started working with my mum and nanna around the age of thirteen, when Mum informed me that I would need to start earning my own money if I wanted to buy all S Club 7's singles from HMV and not simply wait for their album – which would have been the smarter, money-saving choice. I was a kid, what did I know? Witnessing this place go through its ups and downs, my mum knew how to save, knew how to stretch a pound. Now I'm thirty-four and have experienced recessions and pandemics through a grown-up eye, I get it. We scrimp and save in order to keep this place afloat. Ned's Chippy is our bloodline, passed down from generation to generation; when my mum retires, this place will be all mine.

Ring, ring.

'Sorry, did you say chips and gravy or curry and chips?' I mumble. Was it just me or was the phone getting louder?

'Curry and chips, please,' Connie replies, wafting a napkin in front of her face while smacking her six-year-old's reaching hands from stealing all our tiny wooden forks.

'Right, sorry.' I quickly wrap up Connie's parcel, add it to her bagged order and hand her the bag.

'You need to get some more staff in this place,' an unfamiliar customer notes as he steps forward. I smile gravely, bowing my head as he recites his order. I get it's as hot as the insides of a jalapeño pepper in here, but Mum and I are doing our best, and if he only knew how much of a fluke it was that he was currently standing in line with three other people and not on his tod.

'Honey, the phone really is being stubborn and I've got my hands full,' Mum says, not looking up from her deep frying. I shimmy around her and make haste, holding one finger up to the grumpy man while Mum cooks his food, and take a few steps towards the incessant phone. As I do, I nearly perform an Olympic-worthy gymnastics routine ending in the splits as I slide on the tiled floor, which seems to be wet.

'Won't be long, folks,' Mum shouts cheerily as I clamber upright, narrowly missing a shovel of chips to the face as she turns around and pours them onto a stack of newspaper layers, expertly balancing a fish on top with perfect precision. Except, not only does Mum not look pleased and enthusiastic in seeing to the grumpy man's order; she barely acknowledges her only child's near-death experience. Something's wrong.

I wipe my hands roughly on my old-fashioned white apron – the uniform hasn't changed since the days of my great grandad – and stretch and wriggle a little in an attempt to unstick my underwear from my butt cheeks, hoping I haven't just pulled a muscle. Of course, just when I'm about to pick it up, the phone stops ringing.

'For the love of—' I exhale.

'Andi, I think we have a problem,' Mum calls out, holding a hand up to the grumpy man which only furthers his grumpiness.

'Make that two then,' I say, placing the phone rather aggressively down on the receiver and walking as if eggshells littered the floor back to the counter. I need to get the mop asap, after I see to the next order. I try to blow a drip of sweat away from my top lip and position myself so I can get a draft from the open back door, but who am I kidding? Today, there is zero breeze, just a mind-and-body-melting ball of lava in the sky looming over us, making the fish and chip perfume I effortlessly wear each day more aromatic.

'I don't think the fryer is working properly,' Mum whispers under her breath and I dare not look at the man lest he see the fear in my eyes. A lump forms instantly in my throat.

'For how long, Mum?' I ask, needing to know the answer three hours ago. 'Have the orders that have gone out been cooked?'

'Oh, of course, Andi,' she says, frustration making her voice shake. 'That's why they were taking forever; I was cooking everything for longer,' she informs me, making my brain relax in the tiniest of ways. She then takes a giant breath that I know to mean it's time to suck it up and deal with it.

'I'm so sorry,' she starts, addressing the three people in the fish and chip shop. 'I'm afraid we're having difficulty with our equipment and therefore we are unable to serve for the rest of the evening. We're deeply sorry for the inconvenience.'

The man is out of the door before she's finished speaking, but it takes a moment for the lady on her phone to look up and register what is being said before she huffs and follows in the man's wake.

'Not to be the bearer of even more bad news, but I think the freezer is defrosting again,' I say, carefully stepping over the puddle to get the mop as Mum turns off the equipment at the sockets. Her brown eyes, which match mine, are glazed over and wet, the stress of the last couple of years suddenly vividly evident in the wrinkle of her nose, the grey circles under those eyes and the stern line of her lips.

'Mum, it's going to be OK,' I say, almost on autopilot, though this time, I'm not sure I truly believe it as I drain out the sludge from the mop. 'Things can't get any worse,' I add with a smile, trying to lighten the mood.

As soon as that sentence leaves my lips, the chip shop door bursts open and my best friend steps inside. Normally an exquisite sight to behold, she looks less sparkly and more green around the gills. The last thing I need tonight is something to be wrong with Alex, or sick on the chip shop floor.

I pause, mid-mop. 'Alex, what's wrong?' I ask immediately, as Charlie steps in behind her holding a beige box. Charlie's facial expression is far too gleeful for Alex to be ill.

'I'm fine, thank you, how are you, Andi? Have you had a good day? A lot of customers today?' Alex stammers through her barrage of unnerving questions, not taking her eyes off the wet floor, which clearly answered at least two out of three of her questions. My brows narrow.

'Is something wrong?' I push again, gripping the mop so hard, my knuckles have gone pale.

I step around the counter as Charlie nudges Alex and mutters, 'You forgot the box.'

Alex takes it, her delicate hands shaking, while Charlie's cheeks glow a proud red.

'It will be OK, you can tell her,' Charlie whispers, placing an encouraging hand around her petite waist.

'What's going to be OK? Is there something dead in that box? Did you kill something?' I ask nervously, ready to use my mop like a samurai should anything dead come towards me.

Charlie barks out a laugh and rolls her eyes at me, and I feel utterly bewildered as to why my usually chirpy, sunshiny, unicorns-poop-skittles best friend looks so meek.

'I'M GETTING MARRIED!!' she cries, her eyes closed, her voice so glass shatteringly high pitched, Shamu could have broken free from SeaWorld.

'I'M GETTING MARRIED!' she hollers again, in case I didn't catch it the first time. Believe you me, I would have heard it among a sold-out crowd at a Harry Styles concert. Despite the blazing heat, my skin prickles with an icy chill. I swallow hard but my throat is as sticky as my armpits.

'We're getting married,' my best friend then mutters in a barely there whisper, like she hasn't quite got control over her voice box. Her shoulders sag, like she finally ripped off the plaster. Her beautiful face looks pained, her button nose wrinkling. I force down the lump that formed in my throat rapidly after hearing the 'm' word.

'Oh my god,' the words fall out of my mouth as if she really has just told me she killed something and not that she's getting married. A droplet of sweat drips into my eyeball along with the vision of red hair and bare breasts. The mop falls to the floor with an unpleasant clatter that makes me flinch.

'Oh, honey.' Again, my words come out like she just informed me she's going in for major surgery tomorrow. Charlie is glaring at me, like if I don't buck up and be happy for my sweet-as-pie best friend in the next two seconds, her bejewelled knuckles are going to connect with my incredibly sweaty cheek.

Alex is a romantic and has been planning this wedding since the day she met Charlie some four and a half years ago. The same way Alex has been obsessively planning the wedding, Charlie has been zealously planning the proposal. This is not the happy moment she deserves right now.

Charlie takes a step towards the counter which makes me jump, as I think she's about to attack me for my lack of positive emotions. I promise I'm truly trying to coax my brain into action, but images of my dress whirling around a flushing toilet spin at the forefront of my mind. She leans on the counter as Mum appears from behind the shelves in the back, wiping her eyes with the back of her hand and then stretching her arms out to embrace both Alex and Charlie. My heart rips at the seams seeing my independent mum look so beaten, yet she's braving a smile as always.

'Congratulations, my beautiful girls,' Mum coos.

'OK, we won't keep you from work,' Alex then says hurriedly, once she's free from Mum's cuddles, clearly not noticing the state of the empty chip shop. 'Brunch tomorrow at the pub, we've got a wedding to plan,' she adds, like it was another thing she had prepared and planned to say, before turning towards the door.

'Ouch,' I let out with a duck as my mum swats the back of my head; both she and Charlie are looking at me with eyes as thin as slits.

'Of course, yes,' I choke before shaking my head and clearing my throat. 'And Alex, congratulations. I'm so, so happy for you, and you too, Charlie. Yay,' I manage and raise my arms. Immediately, Alex backsteps and skips into my outstretched arms with a squeal. My brain is already whizzing through the laundry list of tasks I need to complete tomorrow morning: hunt down a fluorescent light tube; research possible LED lighting; mop the floors; stock-take the fish, meat pies, cans; and call another repair person to check out the freezer and the fryer. Refill the tiny wooden forks.

'Congratulations again, this is the best news,' I whisper into her loose hair, the heat, her familiar scent and her giddy actions cracking a small piece of my armour and allowing genuine happiness to seep through for my best friend and her now fiancée.

'See you tomorrow,' she cheers, taking Charlie's hand, pulling the two of us in for a brief but tight cuddle huddle and then skipping towards the door.

Alex and Charlie are getting married, which means white dresses, wedding favours, vows, wedding cake and all kinds of romantic, fairy-tale faff. A large fly zooms past my eyeballs with no care or consideration for my personal space in my time of despair. I unhook the fly swatter from a nail on the wall as Alex and Charlie practically float out the door.

If there's one thing I strongly dislike more than an overcooked cod, it's weddings.

2

It's worse than I thought.

I'm sat in our usual spot at the back of the pub, tucked away in one of their deep brown leather booths across from Alex and Charlie. This is where Alex and I sat seventeen years ago, at the age of eighteen – Alex having just finished college, me having just finished a shift at the chip shop – when we confided in each other about our crush on the new girl that had just started working at the bookshop around the corner, which ultimately lead to coming out to each other as lesbian and bisexual. This is where I sat when Alex announced to me that she was going to university for photography and where I told Alex that my nanna was getting sick and I couldn't go on the girls' trip to Santorini. It's where we sat when Alex introduced me to Charlie four and a half years ago and where I expressed that dating was not for me and it was OK that Alex go off and have fun with Charlie – that I didn't need setting up with one of her friends and that I didn't feel left out.

Today, it's where I am sitting looking at an itinerary that could pass as Alex's debut novel, it's that thick and padded out. I try and flip it over in my hands to get a peek at the last page, but it's meatier than the meat pies we sell at the shop and I fear I might fracture my wrist.

'How?' I sort of mumble in shock. The book is colour co-ordinated and the font is not your typical hastily typed Times New Roman, it's fancy. It's been, what? Nine or ten hours since Alex and Charlie got engaged.

Alex is wearing a spaghetti strap white tank top, with her mousy blonde hair clipped back in a claw grip, wavy tendrils framing her heart-shaped face – forgive me for wondering what the clip is actually doing, it's barely containing any of her hair yet it looks purposefully messy and perfectly stylish. It's a shame my hair net doesn't have the same effect. Her face is dewy and bronzed, decorated with little makeup, just a dab of blush, a wave of mascara over her long lashes that are making her hazel eyes extra wide as she beams at me, a picture of 'I've ascended to heaven and I'm not coming down any time soon'. Her lips hold a touch of gloss and are grinning at me broadly, though I can see there's a slight twitch in her right eye.

Then there's Charlie, whose almond-shaped brown eyes are never far off Alex. Her shimmering black hair is grazing the top of her square-neck black tank, where her multitude of gold necklaces come to nestle too. Her signature distressed and oversized denim jacket rests just to the side of her, just as worn as the denim jeans she is choosing to wear in this ungodly British heatwave we are having, and yes, Charlie can pull off double denim – I'm not jealous at all. It's been a minute since I saw Charlie wear her famous jacket; these days, it can be found draped over Alex's elegant shoulders, and I'm certain that's the way Charlie likes it. Her expertly winged eyes and Vaseline-drenched lips are now turned in my direction, too, and offering me a grin as she takes in my shocked expression, which I'm apparently unable to hide.

'OK, so it's not like we didn't have any ideas before last night. There might have been a few elements already in the works,' Alex says, her cheeks blushing as her and Charlie's shoulders bump and they cast each other adoring, knowing glances. I stare at them both, trying to take it all in and will my stomach to stop gurgling with nerves, then I look back to the itinerary in my hands, my eyes darting across the page at all the pink-highlighted words, which once I read, send my gurgling stomach into overdrive.

I shift uncomfortably in my seat, making my thighs squelch against the leather fabric. I can feel my top lip beginning to clam up. Unlike Alex and Charlie, I do not smell like a fresh, clean, delicate puff of talcum powder; sweating only accentuates the vinegar that, after all my years working at Ned's, has absorbed into the very roots of my hair, and no amount of scrubbing with the finest Radox bath gel can extract from my pores.

It's not a smell that I despise by any means, quite the opposite really. For me, it's comfort. Fried golden batter and salt meeting sizzling hot chips is the smell that embodies my whole life. It smells like home and my mum, which to me are one and the same. It's been me and my mum since my dad walked out on us when I was three. That day, I didn't know what was going on; I'd been watching early-morning cartoons like a regular kid while my mum and dad were talking in the kitchen. I could see them chatting if I turned my head to the right as they'd left the kitchen door open. At one point, their voices had grown louder, like they were competing against my cartoon, and when I next twisted to my right, their wedding bands flickered at me from the dining table.

'Alex, this says Amalfi Coast for seven days,' I practically hiccup. My best friend isn't stupid and her smile visibly falters. I hate that I have punctured her wedding bubble, but seven days away from Ned's, I can't do it. Alex leans forward while Charlie rests a firm hand on my forearm.

'Andi, we're not twenty-one anymore, this is not some girls' trip to Santorini we have to scrape for, I've got your back, Kristen too. I want you there, I want your mum there. There's no way I can get married without you both,' Alex offers, her large hazel eyes pleading, the twitch speeding up, as the sweat on my neck turns cold and I shudder involuntarily.

'I can't ask you to do that,' and I won't, but the words create a stickiness in my throat. I've always been proud of Alex and what she has achieved as a freelance photographer. Between shooting travel shots all over the world for high-end magazines, selling prints on her very own website and her social media pages booming, she has done exceptionally well for herself since graduating uni. With Charlie and her small interior design company having taken off in recent months, the two of them are the successful girl bosses I could only dream of being. But it's times like these I feel so alienated from the lives they lead.

'You didn't ask,' Charlie says, pulling me out of my uneasy thoughts, her features less nervous than Alex's and more 'don't upset my fiancée, I'll kill you if you ruin this for her'. 'We can't have our wedding without our maid of honour. It's the bride's job to look after the maid of honour so the maid of honour can look after us. That's it, that's all there is to it, plus you finally get to meet my best friend,' she finishes, giving my forearm a little shake and offering me a firm, flirty wink. I look up at her from under my mascara-free lashes. With the steam that blasts at me from every angle in the shop, wearing mascara only makes my eyelashes stick together. There's very little point in wearing makeup at all, as it simply slips off my face or further clogs my pores.

If I was dead set on not attending this wedding before, Charlie's winking is the final nail in the coffin. Alex suddenly chokes on her chai latte and her right eye is barely staying open with the amount it's now twitching.

'Yes, erm, you and Owen will need to spend some time together,' Alex says, carefully placing her mug down and composing herself, exhaling a slight puff of air.

'Am I right in saying Owen, your "awesome" best friend, is the one that is extremely anti-wedding?' I ask, squinting my eyes together at my memories of Alex telling me all about Owen and how it broke her heart how cynical he was – though by all accounts an absolutely wonderful and good-hearted human being, she'd hastily add. 'Hmmm,' I say thoughtfully; maybe hanging out with Owen wouldn't be so bad. Though the winking from Charlie will have to stop. I have zero interest in a relationship, least of all a corny, sappy, wedding hook-up.

Alex looks like she would snap up any opportunity in a heartbeat to trade in best friends for her and Charlie for this wedding, and I can't say I'd be offended at the idea of being replaced.

'But look, it's not like we're doing this all on our own.' Alex starts waving her hands, brushing quickly past the topic of Owen, which suits me fine. 'My mum and dad are helping out and gifting us some spends, and it's Charlie's dad's villa that we're staying at, so we're all in this together, everyone is helping everyone,' she explains enthusiastically, her bubble filling up again as she sits up straighter like she's just vanquished all my money insecurities with her words. I love her for trying, and I wish that were the case, but while an all-expenses-paid trip to Italy sounds idyllic, extravagant and quite frankly out of my league (and something I will not be accepting), that and closing the shop for a week would put my mum and I at a huge loss.

With Alex and Charlie both grinning at me like they've solved all the world's problems, I find it hard to further state my case: that I can't make it to my best friend's wedding. I can't be her maid of honour. Wait, sugar. Had Charlie said maid of honour? As in, me being their maid of honour? Doesn't that involve action, performance, an organised individual who knows about this wedding malarky stuff and finds it all thrilling and magical? And if anything were to go wrong, I can't be there for Alex the way she was for me, not when I'm barely holding myself together from that trauma.

I grimace at the heavy wad of paper in my hands but quickly shift my features into a cheerful expression when I look up and find them both staring at me expectantly, waiting for my conclusion to this somewhat heavily rigged debate of two versus one.

'You never said anything about me being maid of honour,' I stutter. My skin crawls just saying the words out loud as images of hiked-up dresses and fingers in knickers come fast and furiously into my mind.

'Did you not open your box?' Charlie asks, with a slight eye roll.

'You mean this one?' I say, swallowing hard, as I pick the beige box up from the bench beside me and stare at it, terrified of its contents.

'You were supposed to open it,' Alex states with a nervous giggle as she nudges my hands to do so now.

'Wow, maid of honour,' I reiterate, precariously gripping onto the tiny ribbon that is delicately wrapped around the box, seemingly keeping it together. 'So I top up the Limoncello and organise the Italian strippers, right?' I chuckle at myself in hopes of steadying my breathing. Charlie laughs and leans back against the booth, shooting me another wink, while Alex gets hold of the wedding booklet and flicks to a page titled 'Maid of Honour' that I somehow missed. I'm not sure how, when my name is highlighted with turquoise highlighter. She starts waffling about bags of rainbow-coloured almonds as my brain runs through an entirely different script: possible last-minute excuses to ditch your best friend's wedding, as I give the ribbon a hearty tug and confetti explodes into the air and lands in my cappuccino.

'Owen is my best man,' Charlie notes, wiggling her eyebrows. I down my cappuccino, embracing the burning sensation that works its way from my tongue all the way down my throat, and kick her under the table.

'You're being an absolute sausage,' my Mum says, shaking her head at me as she finishes the last dregs of a cup of tea. How we're all still drinking hot drinks in the scorching heat

I don't know, but it's what we British do, I guess. I'm pacing the wooden floor of my apartment above Ned's, which my mum surprised me with for my twenty-first birthday. She'd kept the house in the divorce from my dad, a modest two-bedroom, one-tiny-bath home just up the road. This place had always been a dumping ground for my grandparents; they'd never really made use of it for anything other than storage, but when my grandad passed away, it had been the catalyst my nanna needed to sort through his things and have a good clear out.

Uncovering its potential had given my nanna and mum the rather brilliant idea of creating a space for me. It came in handy when my nanna started getting sick and moved in with my mum, no longer able to look after her house on her own once my grandad was gone.

I loved it then and I love it now. It could do with a bit of TLC and updating, but any spare money typically goes into the upkeep and maintenance of equipment in the fish and chip shop.

'We can't go, Mum, seriously,' I try again, my voice coming out strained as I graze my knee against the recycled wooden coffee table. 'Ouch,' I mutter rather pathetically.

'A complete sausage,' she says through a laugh as she stands up and starts busying herself with her apron.

'Mum!' I protest, snatching my own apron up off the arm of the well-worn couch. 'Closing for a wedding day would be one thing, but closing for a wedding week is bonkers.'

'You're bonkers if you think we're missing Alex and Charlie's wedding, Andrea,' my mum tuts, fussing her hair net over her bun, which is purely automatic, since it's not like we're doing any cooking today with our equipment malfunctioning.

'There's no way we can manage it.' I fiddle with my too-long hair, trying to twist it and make it behave under my unruly, tangled hair net. Like mother, like daughter.

'Not with that attitude,' she says firmly, marching towards the door. I follow, nearly tripping up over the doormat, my anxiety getting the best of me. This whole situation is making me itch all over. 'Honey, we'll make it work. It's a much happier occasion to close for than a pandemic, don't you think?' she adds, turning to face me halfway down the stairs.

'But I thought you hated weddings,' I moan. My mother looks at me aghast, like how did I possibly come to that conclusion, like she's oblivious to her scoffing every time we walk past a bridal shop, shaking her head and tutting at every rom-com trailer she watches, her eyes rolling into the back of her head whenever she hears the words 'happily ever after'. I stumble on the stairs. Her face suddenly falls serious, her brown eyes drooping.

'Oh, I'm so silly, this isn't about me,' she says, as though just registering my childhood trauma. 'Oh, sweetheart,' she begins and takes a step up towards me. We both sit down in the middle of the stairwell. 'Andi, I know I haven't been the best role model when it comes to love and dating, but my divorce, I've told you this before, my divorce, my opinion on "the one" is mine alone. You've seen first-hand how happy Charlie makes Alex; they're nothing like me and your dad, hey,' she tilts my chin up gently with her fingertips to meet her warm gaze, 'no two relationships are alike, you know that. I'm sorry if I've made you fear love, but love gave me the most incredible gift of all, maybe not some fairy-tale romance that lasted forever, but the most precious daughter that a mum could ever wish upon a star for.'

I snort, having tried to scoff and laugh while my throat feels tight and my nostrils are tingling. I squeeze the bridge of my nose, trying to stem the sensation of tears brimming. Since Alex entered the chip shop last night, my brain has been nothing but a barrage of unpleasant images of a wedding that never happened, images that I thought I'd laid to rest some time ago. Now, they're all rearing their ugly heads once more, and there's a massive part of me that's angry at Alex for putting me through this. Why not just elope or something?

'Honey, as harsh as this might sound, this week isn't about you. I know being reminded of the past isn't enjoyable and I'm sorry, but you're choosing to focus on that. Try and shift gears and focus on Alex,' she says, trying to stroke my cheek, but I jerk back.

'Mum, I'm not choosing to focus on my cheating ex. I'm not stupid, they're not exactly images I want in my head, thank you very much,' I snap, standing abruptly, ripping off my itchy hair net and smashing my elbow into the wall in the process. 'Aargh,' I huff, rubbing the pointy bit and looking towards the ceiling to stop the tears from trickling down my face.

'I didn't say you were stupid, I simply expressed that this is a wedding and the similarities end there. Not every wedding will end up like yours, in the same way every marriage does not share the same outcome as mine, though I'd still take mine as a win,' she continues, making me jump down a few steps, wanting to get away.

'What exactly am I supposed to take as a win, Mum? The mounting debt the wedding put us in, the feeling of worthlessness, the pure embarrassment, being unlovable?' I shout, reaching the door at the bottom of the stairs.

'Andrea,' my mum says sternly, causing me to pause and turn around instead of storming through the back door. My hand rests against it, shaking.

'You are not unlovable or worthless because of what Hannah did to you; you have a mother that loves you more than anything in the world and a best friend who looked like she was passing kidney stones when trying to tell you that she just got engaged because she was putting your feelings before hers. I think it's only fair that you do the same for her on this big occasion,' she tells me, standing up now, too.

'Well, life isn't fair, Mum,' I stammer before pushing open the door and raging into the shop.

3

Five days later and my knee is bouncing up and down in the only joggers I could find that seemed appropriate given Alex and Charlie's speech on comfortable plane clothes. The two of them are dressed in beige (Alex) and black (Charlie) wide-fit, linen trousers and breezy shirts with open-toe sliders, while I can feel my feet swelling and sweating considerably in the slipper socks that are digging into the tongue of my old Adidas trainers, which are neither clean nor in fashion anymore. So much for 'your feet will get cold on the flight'.

My bank account is drained and my mind keeps running down the list of everything I had to do before we left. Turn off the mains, drain the oils, lock the fridge and freezers, place towels across the floor in case of more leakage, secure the back door and pull down the shutter, turn the sign to closed. Once I tick all the boxes, I go back to the beginning. Check. Check. Check. Check. Repeat. I bloody hope the chip shop will still be there when we get back. I can't be certain my mum feels the same as there was something fishy with how eager she was to get away.

'Andi, what are the chips going to do, start a revolution

and hoist the building onto their shoulders and scurry off like a colony of ants?'

Not realising I had said my prayer out loud, I turn to look at Alex, giving her my best eye roll for her cheek. Charlie's sarcasm must be rubbing off on her. I appreciate her prosecco-infused, laid-back demeanour, but the last thing the chip shop needs is ants, full stop.

'I love you times a gazillion and I'm so unbelievably thankful you are here,' she adds, her eyes growing misty.

My leg begins jerking more violently than I thought possible, and I very nearly add a red wine stain – Alex insisted on getting me a glass to apparently calm my nerves (see: leg) – to my white jumper. 'I wouldn't have missed it for the world,' I find myself saying through gritted teeth.

Since my argument with Mum, I've kept my head down and buried myself in cleaning, trying to ignore as much wedding faff as possible, which was incredibly difficult to do. With Alex and Charlie having been a whirlwind of excitement and activity over the last few days, I was swept up in their glamourous chaos and never got around to having 'the talk' with Alex. And by talk, I mean the 'I know I'm your very best friend but I can't be at your wedding' talk. So here I am. Am I dreading the maid of honour speech? Yes. Is my right eye twitching over getting the ten-pound box of multi-coloured almonds that I was tasked to source through customs? Yes. Is the idea of spending seven days surrounded by Italians, the most romantic people in the world, at a wedding, making me want to itch? Yes. Is there anything I can do about it now? No.

'Now, look, about Owen.' Alex suddenly goes from being

fun and cheeky, ignoring my grumpy mood, to hushed and twitchy. 'I'm not sure who's worse, you or him, but I really need you to take charge and keep everything in line, and don't listen to Charlie, please; he's not good for you.' She looks so small and scared, and I fear for a moment that I'm some sort of monster and that my mum was right about everything. Burying my feelings is no easy feat, but I got the almonds, didn't I? I'm on the plane, aren't I?

My stomach knots at the fact that Alex has never been afraid to talk to me about anything except this flipping wedding. Between her words, the red wine, my ridiculous plane attire and the fact that I've had to protest my stance on relationships more than once in the last few days, I'm extremely close to overheating and having a panic attack, which I really don't want to do. The last thing I need is to cause a scene, it's just not my style. Actually, maybe that's exactly what I need: get the captain to turn this plane around.

'OK, so, one: when do I ever listen to Charlie, you know how I feel about relationships, and two: I'm good at being in control and in charge, I'm here for you, I've got this,' I tell her, giving myself a small pep talk in the process and still feeling in no way, shape or form like I'm in control or that I have indeed got any part of this.

Once we secured all our luggage – almonds intact, thank god, because who doesn't want a tiny bag of candy almonds moulding away in their junk draw to remember one day by – and walk through arrivals, Charlie instantly spots her dads. It's not a difficult feat. In a crowd of black and white suits holding A4 pieces of paper, the occasional white board or scrap of card, with black scrawled names where you can see the previous name seeping through from the other side, her dad, Will, is waving a cream A1 poster board covered in gold glitter, the silver marker reading 'soon to be Mrs and Mrs Walker-Moretti', while her papa, Gio, snaps pictures with his vintage Polaroid camera. I can see how Alex fits into their family. I watch as her eyes catch sight of the Polaroid and check my joggers for a spare tissue to mop up the drool forming at the corners of her mouth.

I've met Mr and Mr Moretti over Zoom many times in the past four years and they are honestly beautiful humans inside and out. Charlie took after Will, whose interior design company took him all over Europe where he met Gio in Italy. The two of them travelled back and forth from Manchester to Amalfi, mostly raising Charlie in the former but whisking her off to the stunning coast during school holidays. Now, Will prefers to spend more time in Positano, where they bought a villa and like to host guests and hold the most gorgeous events.

'Ciao, *ragazze*,' Gio shouts above the chatter in the airport, wrapping his arms around his daughter and soon-to-be daughter-in-law.

'Ciao, *bella*,' Will says, pulling me into him.

'Ciao, Will,' I say, slightly muffled as my face squishes against his firm chest. The poster board presses tightly against the back of my head as he cups it, giving me a rib-crunching hug. I'm going to be washing glitter out of my hair for days. When he releases me, I introduce my mum, who receives a double squeeze from both Will and Gio before they take her hands and ferry us away from the chaos indoors and into the chaos outdoors.

If I wasn't cursing Alex and Charlie for the joggers and slipper socks before, I am now. If I was, now I'm cursing them more explicitly. As I step into Naples' July sun, all the wind gets knocked out of me. I immediately begin to shrivel, going from a plump, juicy green olive to one of those dehydrated, wrinkly purple ones. I thought the chip shop was like a sauna on a hot British day, but Italy is something else entirely.

We make quick work of packing into Gio's small but roomy van, which gratefully has air conditioning that comes alive when he turns on the ignition. The chatter, mostly between Mum, Gio and Will, distracts me from the pools in which my feet are swimming, as we pull away from the crystal blue – the sky reflecting in the large glass windows and doors – and brown brick blur of Naples airport. Though it's only early afternoon, the travel is teasing my eyes closed, but I'm not one for naps. Rather dangerously, we manoeuvre away from the city, past Vesuvius, leave the motorway behind and venture through the backstreets of tiny Italian villages and come out onto the SS163 towards Positano, there is absolutely no way I can let my tired eyes close.

'Beautiful, isn't it?' Charlie says, turning around to face me with a bright smile, classic black sunglasses atop her head. Her and Alex are sat in the middle of the van with Mum and Will up front, Gio driving. I'm tucked away in the back with the bags. I choke, literally at a loss of breath, which I'm certain isn't due to my jumper slowly suffocating me in the heat and more to do with the panoramic view of the sea that sparkles so confidently, I'm unsurprised in the least that millions flock to it and fall in love with it every day.

'I think beautiful is an understatement, Charlie,' I splutter, pressing my nose up against the glass so I can take it all in. It feels like I should be able to reach out and touch the sea, but with my face against the glass, I can suddenly see the sheer drop of the cliffs we are winding ourselves around, the houses that adorn the mountain, the vegetable gardens and the rows and rows of olive, lemon and orange trees and a beach below where a cluster of brown and cream houses appear. Gio mentions something about Sorrento, and when we round the next bend, I know we are close to our destination as the famous multi-coloured mountainside that is Positano comes into view.

'Wait till you see the villa,' Alex squeals, her whole face glowing with happiness, not sweat. Mine is definitely a mixture of both.

When the van comes to a stop and we all start piling out, I completely forget about the blistering sun and how my joggers instantly stick to my inner thighs under its villainous rays. I live in a flat above a chip shop, I wouldn't call myself high maintenance in the slightest and I'll be the first person to put my hand up and say, 'Sorry, Tinkerbell, I don't believe in fairies,' but good lord if this place isn't something straight out of *Cinderella*. And I can't say I hate it.

My mum clutches Gio's hands and lets out a dreamy sigh. 'Gio, it's stunning.'

Gio smiles adoringly at her and it occurs to me that my mum needs this holiday. Besides me, I can't recall the last time she had people fussing over her or a time in recent years when she has let her hair down. The way Gio is holding her hands, Will coming up beside her and placing a caring arm over her shoulder as he says, 'Ahh, Kristen, this is just the entrance. Please, let us show you to your room,' makes my heart stutter for a moment. He doesn't sound cocky or boastful, but humble and excited to share his wealth.

I stare dumbfounded at the pink-washed, brick-and-mortar building which, from where I'm standing, has a large, rounded archway, at least three stories and five gorgeous windows lining the top floor, which look like something out of architectural digest with their ornamental white cornices that exude eighteenth-century history. The trees and their bountiful green leaves pop against the pink, and everywhere I look, there are ceramic pots large and small hosting the most exquisite purple and yellow flowers.

Suddenly, arms wrap around my waist from behind, jostling my heavy backpack and knocking over my suitcase filled with rainbow almonds. I snap to attention, blinking away the castle in the sky, and for a second, I wonder if it will still be there when my eyes flutter open again.

The arms belong to Alex and the villa is not an apparition.

'So, what do you think?' she says, nuzzling her chin into my shoulder, her breath tickling my ear.

'The almonds!' I shout, bending down to ensure the protection of the wedding favours at all costs. Jutting my bottom out in the process, I catch Alex off guard as my soft derriere thrusts into her stomach. She lets out a winded breath. Charlie lets out a howl of laughter.

'If this is what she's like with almonds, I definitely think we can trust her with our firstborn,' she comments when her laughter subsides. I straighten up, tugging at the collar of my jumper, and rub Alex's stomach.

'Sure, if you want your kid bathing in curry and drinking

Irn-Bru,' I tease. 'Sorry,' I add, draping my arm over Alex's shoulder. She playfully pouts and tugs at my cotton jumper.

'Should we take you for the grand tour and get you out of these clothes?' she asks as Charlie takes the suitcase from me, tugging my backpack so she can carry that too. All the other luggage seems to have made its way inside while the villa and I were caught in a magical meet-cute.

'I'd like that,' I reply. 'Thanks, Charlie,' I add as Charlie steps in front, leading the way. Alex tucks her arm into the nook of my elbow as we follow. We walk under the concrete archway, its subtle cracks that peek through the white paint making me smile at its strength and endurance, the marble floor gleaming in the sunlight that you can't possibly escape, even on this low level, thanks to the small windows that are carved out of the wall. The citrus scent that delights my nostrils as we ascend a set of stairs is a gift from the open terrace doors. The terrace looks out across the whole of Positano and is bursting with lemons. Trees meander over the trellises, branches wrapping around the white pillars; the lemons, as big as my hand, if not bigger, so rich and vibrant in their yellow skin, acquire all my senses. I can't look away from them; I can smell them and I have to touch them.

There will be time for that later though, I'm sure, as we continue to keep up with Charlie.

'Alex,' I say, nudging her as we walk. Though she has been here on vacation with Charlie several times over their time together, her eyes drift around the rooms as if it's her first.

'Mmm hmm,' she mumbles, captivated by the intricate

pattern in the blue and red tiles along the wall and the sweet aroma of espresso that wafts through a door which is slightly ajar. I sense that's the kitchen and it's a place I'm most eager to experience, besides the pool. Before I let my mind wander, I focus on what I wanted to say to Alex.

'I think this is the most beautiful place for the most beautiful bride,' I say, squeezing her hand. She turns to me, eyes suddenly wet. I think I have heat stroke, as my words even shock me.

'Thank you for being my maid of honour,' she says. Light bounces off the tiles, making her hazel eyes even more striking.

'Thank you for being my best friend,' I say, very much caught up in the moment.

She chuckles, blinking a few times, 'Who knew it would just take a trip to Italy and a luxury villa to unlock those mushy feelings in you.'

'OK, alright.' I shove her forward, but I'm grinning and wondering why I ever second-guessed coming.

A wedding in Italy, so far so good.

4

I awake the next morning sometime around six thanks to the sharp cry from a rooster that nests in one of the five long levels of garden that Gio owns on the mountainside to the right of the villa. Once it's done its morning duty, there's nothing. Complete and utter silence. No cars honking, no leaky boiler dripping and no postman knocking on the chip shop window trying to figure out where to slot the mail.

My heels sink into the silky linens that cover the mattress, their crisp, clean scent makes my toes curl and my limbs want to stretch out longer so I can bury down deeper into their warmth. The thin duvet is lush and inviting as it snuggles against my cheeks. It had taken me mere seconds to fall asleep last night.

Yesterday, I had a quick change of clothes after Charlie's brief tour of the magnificent compound and then spent the late afternoon into the evening sat around a large, rectangular table, eating everything that was put in front of me. Gio being a fifth-generation bread maker – a celebrity in the south of Italy – he'd cooked up a feast the likes of which I have never known before. I've never eaten garlic so fragrant nor a tomato so red and succulent, and the basil leaves are the largest, most mouth-watering I have ever had the pleasure of delighting my tongue with. I couldn't stop eating, thanks to Gio's mum, Roberta for encouraging my healthy appetite. The wine flowed and with no one in a rush to move away from the table, it felt lovely to relax and savour every morsel. Late lunch had blurred into dinner with happy conversations, words never slowing down. Gio and Will asked my mum about the chip shop and her life. Mum quizzed Gio on who was the most famous person he'd baked bread for, and Will which A-lister has the most extravagant toilet, while Alex and Charlie had their heads pressed together, deep in wedding talk.

I'd drifted off to my room somewhere around eleven-thirty in a lemon gelato haze to find Alex and Charlie had snuck in a goodie bag of silk pyjamas with 'Maid of Honour' inscribed in white cursive on the back and a box full of face masks, eye creams, body butters and spritzes that were a far cry from my usual salt and vinegar perfume. I'd gone to bed feeling like a much more optimistic, lighter and less cynical version of myself, but that might just have been the shot of sambuca I'd had after dinner.

I finally make a move and resist the rather unfamiliar urge to take a long soak in the white clawfoot bath – I'm usually a shower kind of woman; it's quick, easy, wastes less water and gives me more time to see to my to-do list in the mornings before work. I pull on a pair of denim-look linen shorts that I also found in my goodie bag last night – my thighs rejoice – team them with my loose-fitting, cropped white blouse that I've had since the nineties and spot a beautiful pair of white sliders by the door. My toes wiggle in celebration and pull me towards their new friends. A smile tugs at my lips at how well Alex knows me. Sorting my wardrobe out has always been a dream, but it's last on my list of priorities after Mum, Ned's and bills. I'm grateful for her practical gifts and feel more prepared for Italy's unapologetic summer heat.

I emerge from my quarters on the third floor and follow the strong aroma of coffee and a vanilla so sweet, I lick my lips, my tongue searching for the sugary crystals that surely have to be close; I can almost taste them. The saccharine scent powers me forward along with the early-morning breeze that drifts in from the terrace. The plants that line the window ledges shine with dew, their thick, green leaves catching the first golden rays, soaking up their breakfast. As I make my way up a small set of stairs and under a dusty pink archway, I can hear the hum of people talking.

My stomach performs an almighty somersault, and my steps become a touch smaller. I take a deep breath in and wrap my fingers around my messy low bun, checking if it's secure, but really in desperation to stretch out my fingers and calm my nerves. This is it: day one of maid of honour duties begins today and the world's least likely candidate for maid of honour, yours truly, has an agenda to follow and can't let anyone down.

'Morning, honey.' I practically jump out of my skin and very nearly karate chop a gorgeous purple and yellow ceramic vase as my mum comes to stand next to me. She gently pats my shoulder in greeting. 'You look lovely and summery. Did you sleep well?' she asks, completely unaware she just came out of nowhere and gave me a fright. One night in a luxury four-poster bed and the bags under my mother's eyes don't seem as dark. I take another steadying breath, remove my hand from its vice-like grip against my chest, move a stray grey hair away from my mum's bright eyes and can't help but smile, a little wobbly one at first – but I don't mention the scare because she looks like a flower blooming in the sunshine.

'Morning, Mum,' I reply, my smile more steady and confident now. 'I had a wonderful sleep, thank you. Did you?'

She places a soft hand on my elbow and starts walking. 'I did indeed after I indulged in a bubble bath and then slathered myself in cream.' Her cheeks turn a rosy hue, her shoulders inch up closer to her ears like she's a little embarrassed that she spent an evening relaxing for once in her life. My heart gives a tug for Alex and Charlie and their generosity and love towards my mum.

'Mum, that sounds incredible. You deserve to relax, you know,' I say, and she tilts her head as if to say 'maybe'. I pause for a moment when we reach the kitchen, the chatter becoming more lively and ferocious. 'You're not worried at all about the chip shop?' I ask with a small grimace, not wanting to ask and make her think she has reason to worry when she seems so happy, but at the same time unable to help myself. There are seconds in between the thrill of juicy lemons and opulent white sliders that make me feel as though I'm walking on clouds where my heartbeat becomes erratic and I panic about how much damage a week away is going to cause on top of the damage that's already been done.

'Sweetheart, this is a new experience for the both of us. I was never able to take you on holiday when you were growing up, so you enjoy this, OK? Ned's will still be there when we get back; it's always there,' she replies, bopping a finger on the tip of my nose with a smile on her face, though the darkness under her eyes seems to reappear when she talks about the shop. However, when the door to the kitchen swings open and a rather glamourous-looking woman, in an extremely pretty, flowing, yellow-and-blue print dress that matches many of the ceramic pots, throws her arms in the air and shouts, '*Buongiorno, signore,*' into the hallway, the darkness is replaced by awe and a glowing intrigue that lights up her eyes once more.

'*Venire, venire,*' the woman bellows, waving her arms so the billowing sleeves of her dress send a gust of wind in my direction and upon it, that lip-tingling smell of vanilla that dances out of the kitchen. Mum and I follow her into the large, square room that is home to a kitchen island thrice the size of my actual kitchen. Atop of which sits an earth-shatteringly appetising spread. I gaze at the food for a beat too long before the woman taps me on the shoulder and points a neatly manicured nail towards the terrace. I smile and offer a nod of understanding and follow her, only glancing longingly back once at the croissants that are the size of at least two Tesco bakery croissants combined.

My disappointment in being ushered away from the food doesn't last long. This morning, the long, rectangular table out on the terrace is decorated in vibrant ceramic bowls filled to the brim with oranges, grapefruits, apples and bananas so abundant in their colour, you wouldn't be amiss to think they were glass works of art from Venice. Large, ceramic serving dishes, again all polished to perfection, are piled high with almond croissants, what looks like Madeira cake, mini pizzas, focaccia and layers of different types of ham. There are at least four cafetières, three jugs of orange juice and an array of smaller jugs full of milk and cream.

'Andi, you're up,' Alex squeals and races towards me, dragging my attention away from the breakfast display. She embraces me in a warm hug, our various sun cream-laced body parts sticking together, and pulls me towards the chair next to her.

The woman sees to it that my mum is seated and starts to build her plate with toast and boiled eggs. '*Mangia, mangia*,' she cries at my mother as she continues to add to mum's plate while Gio fills up her coffee mug.

'Zia, Zia, *basta*, let her eat that first,' Charlie shouts over to the woman, who immediately freezes in her attempt to balance a custard tart on top of the mountain of breads on my mum's plate.

Alex chuckles and mouths to me, 'Charlie's auntie.' Ahh. My stomach does another nervous flip and the wedding jitters I had before getting on the plane, during the flight and right up until they were ambushed by this magical villa, come firing back with a vengeance. Italians don't miss a single detail; I have to keep up.

'Today's the day,' Alex says with a clap of her hands as I take a generous bite of an almond croissant. It makes a ridiculously satisfying crunch sound, small flakes of pastry falling gracefully onto my plate, some not so gracefully sticking to my cheeks. It's heaven on my tongue. I'm pretty certain I groan and close my eyes, getting lost in its flavour as Alex runs down the plan for wedding dress shopping, which is taking place before tonight's party to welcome all the guests to this week-long Amalfi Coast extravaganza. I've read the manual, I've memorised the program.

'That sounds great,' I say with a nod, trying to squash my nerves with buttery pastry.

'There are a few boutiques in Amalfi; Charlie has the list, don't you, Charlie?' Alex says, turning briefly away from me and pointing at her fiancée. Charlie nods casually, raising her espresso cup.

'It's just us girls today; Kristen, Zia Allegra and Nonna Roberta are coming too. We're booked into the first place at eleven,' Charlie responds and Alex practically swoons over her efficient rundown of the first group outing. I can't say I blame her; Charlie has clearly been paying attention and is keeping up with Alex's schedule and excitement. I imagine for a moment how pleasant it would be to have someone know me well enough to know I like things organised and that I'm fond of a plan or two. I shake away the thought hastily; this croissant knows me well enough, it just keeps giving and giving and that is more than enough for me.

'Wait until you see these places, Andi; they're going to make even the likes of Ebenezer Wedding Scrooge believe in fairy tales,' Charlie then adds, shooting me a wink. I swallow a bite of custard tart – that I'm now guzzling to keep words at bay – and squint my eyes in her direction, brows furrowing to express my annoyance at her comment. I get it. Just like my mum, I've not always been great at hiding my distaste, or should I say lack of belief, in romance. It was only several days ago that I tried to back out of my best friend's wedding; maybe Alex and Charlie won't let that go quite so easily and I deserve Charlie comparing me to one of literature's grumpiest characters of all time. But life is full of those that love rom-coms and those that can't get enough of horror. I just happen to fall on neither side nor anywhere in the middle of that spectrum. My life is chip sandwiches and the occasional battered sausage, and I'm OK with that.

'How much?' I splutter on the wine that I have been given in a glass so delicate, I'm scared it's going to crack at any moment.

'Andi, if you say that one more time,' Alex hisses under her breath as Mum slaps me across my bicep. I mimic zipping my lips to Alex and give Charlie an apologetic nod for stressing out her fiancé. I'm not sure what I'm more frightened of: Charlie's death glare or the fact that Alex actually sounds angry at me.

Leaving her to agonise over the pros and cons of the sixth dress she has tried on – in this shop alone – I wander over to the racks, moving away from my mum, and start having a nosy myself, to the utter fright of one of the sales assistants, who steps a little closer to me and eyes me up and down.

There's row upon row of ivory and white lace and silk, beading and no beading, long trains, short trains and traditional monstrosities that I can't fathom how one would even walk in. Flashbacks of my hideous mermaid tail come flooding back, the money spent and the look on the dry cleaner's face when I'd explained where it had been – from boutique to toilet bowl – and begged her to clean it so I could sell it.

'I mean, I can sort of understand spending thousands on a designer bag if it's sturdy and in good form; it could last you an age. It's practical, useful and you use it more than once, but a dress, designed for one day and costing this much, so help me lord, do you not think it's preposterous?'

The words are trickling out of my mouth as I sip on the fancy wine, swaying in and out of the racks; it's not until I hear a foot tapping behind me that I turn around and come face to face with the assistant that was giving me the once-over earlier. I hiccup at her venomous eyes, accidentally sloshing wine over the rim of my glass. The world suddenly moves in slow motion as we both lean forward in some sort of attempt at catching, swatting, magicking, kicking, licking away the tiny droplets of wine that are hurtling towards the train of a six-thousand-euro dress.

Though my eyes might be seeing things in slow motion, the droplets are in fact going at lightning speed and there is nothing either one of us can do.

Honestly, Horton the Elephant would be impressed with how teeny weeny the speck of wine that lands on the brim of the lace is, but the way the sales assistant's face blooms a beetroot red, I don't think she would care for me to start explaining the fact that you would need a microscope to see the drip.

'OUT!' she booms, her thick, Italian accent bouncing off the walls. I quickly hand her my glass with a small bow, and in my mind, I see it shatter within her vice-like grip.

Walking towards the changing rooms, Mum's ashen face is the first I see, but I don't look in Alex's direction.

'I'm just going to get some air,' I say and make haste for the door.

Outside, I pace up and down, praying for two things: that Alex and Charlie find their dresses in this shop and spend loads of money, making up my slight faux pas to the sales assistant, and that this is the last shop – I really don't think I can handle a seventh shop of the day.

My stomach is too anxious to take in the sights and sounds of Amalfi, though it does rumble at the numerous bakery and gelato offerings that surround me.

As the clock above the Duomo di Amalfi strikes three, I realise I have been burning a hole in the ground for twenty minutes and there is no movement at the boutique's front door. I can't wander off; if I get lost and miss the wedding, that truly will be the end of me. I just hope that by the time Alex and Charlie emerge, they are too overjoyed with their purchases to even remember my little mishap.

Considering they have a party this evening, I'm positive I'll luck out and this will be the last stop. Just as my brain is thinking such a selfish thing, the door chimes open and my group spill out into the piazza.

'I'm not talking to you for at least another hour,' Alex tells me, striding past me towards the buses, garment bag over her shoulder. I let out a small exhale and receive a shake of the head from Charlie while my mum grabs me by the elbow and in a hushed tone tells me to behave.

The coach ride back to Positano is a peaceful one, to say the least, bar the gasps, odd hitch of breath and murmurings of prayer as, on two occasions, the coach squeezes past another coach so very, very close to the cliff side.

'Ma Zia, stop now,' Charlie says in a stern, Italian tone as she looks back over her shoulder and gives Zia Allegra a pointed look. 'You'll only rile her up,' she adds, disappointment in her gaze when she looks over at me. I am still not forgiven from earlier, but we're coming up to around fifty minutes, so I'll give it another ten. Since we started the ascent up the two hundred or so rocky steps combined with a few steep slopes towards the villa, Zia Allegra has decided to berate me with intrusive questioning on why I didn't buy a dress, like she didn't hear or understand my 'hatred for wedding dresses' rant.

'Ma, why you no buy a dress for your turn; all the many beautiful dresses. You no find dresses like that in England,' she goes on, ignoring Charlie's plea. It's hard to concentrate on the icy shiver that those words send over my body when I'm preoccupied with my ragged breath and the small doses of oxygen I am just about managing to get into my lungs – I'm gasping ridiculously hard. The Italian landscape is not for the faint hearted. Nonna Roberta practically bounced up the steps like a young goat while Zia Allegra is talking for all the mountainside to hear without a hint of fatigue in her voice. Part of me wishes she would listen to Charlie's fifth attempt at getting her to drop this subject, but the other part of me is pretty impressed with her stamina to walk and talk at the same time – and the other, other part of me is thrilled that at least someone is talking to me.

'I'm OK, thank you,' I manage as I rest my hand against a stone wall, disrupting a small gecko. It darts from a crack in the stone up into the electric-purple wisteria that decorates the pathway.

'Eh, what about you, Kristen? A beautiful young woman like you should have a lover,' Zia Allegra says, turning her focus to my mum after giving me a small, saddened shake of her head.

'I've been married once, never again,' my mother informs her. From my position in the line, behind Zia Allegra and Mum – Alex and Charlie are in front and Nonna Roberta,

I place a guess, is already back at the villa, whipping up a batch of freshly squeezed orange juice – I can see Zia Allegra's lips stick out in a sort of pursed pout as she swats the air dramatically, causing the bangles on her right arm to jangle and nearly blind me when they catch the sunlight. I stumble on the uneven ground.

'You must be joking. Why not? You get married twice, three times, six times, love is love, honey.'

I can't help the smile that surprises my face at her optimism and matter-of-fact tone, like she wouldn't judge anyone for having that many marriages. That would certainly be refreshing compared to how some people turn up their noses at divorce, or how women get treated if they have children with more than one man. I swallow down the sudden horrible taste of inequality that settles on my tongue and shake away the negative images that pop up in my mind: the looks on people's faces that I bore witness to growing up, disgust at my Mum being a single mother, like it was all her fault my dad left. I pause for a moment at the next crooked step and gaze at the overflowing bunches of wisteria that drape over the high walls, their small, rounded petals cute and enchanting, the ombre of purples holding my attention as I will my smile to come back.

I take the step and am well and truly jolted out of my wandering thoughts when I hear yet another high-pitched squeal from Alex, the hundredth of the morning.

But when I follow the vibrations of her squeal and finally make it onto the terrace, her noise makes sense and is perfectly acceptable.

5

The long, rectangular table that usually sits in the middle of the terrace has been pushed towards the railings and is festooned with a delectable-looking buffet. Colours pop everywhere I look from the Caprese salads with their lush, red, beef tomatoes and Christmas-green basil, to the golden custard pastries with their juicy yellow lemon slices nestled in the middle.

The railings themselves have been decorated with strings of fairy lights that are wrapped around fruit garlands and the lemon trees that create the terrace's canopy have been given a slight makeover with the addition of roses dotted in between the beautiful fruit.

A couple of round tables have been placed on the terrace, but there's enough space for people to mingle with the wedding party hosting around forty guests. I'm stood at the entrance of the terrace, not the one where you enter from the kitchen, but the one reached by a short flight of stairs at the side of the villa's main driveway. After this afternoon's disaster at the bridal boutique and Alex having rushed off to get ready as soon as we got home, the next task of welcoming the guests this evening feels like redemption. I need to do an exceptional job considering we've got way past the hour mark and my best friend has yet to utter a word to me. I've been doing great so far with knowing a handful of both Alex and Charlie's friends. I've engaged in a little small talk and several catch-ups. The shared topic of 'isn't Italy gorgeous?', which only requires nods of agreement, has been easy. The smiling tightly at a few 'oh Andrea, we didn't think you would be able to make it with the chip shop and all' proved trickier. But I'm doing this for my friendship, I remind myself.

'Hello,' I say as two people come into view up the steps.

'Don't you just love weddings?' a young woman I don't recognise says with a megawatt smile that makes her bright rouge lipstick glisten under the twinkly lights. Her hand rests on the man's chest next to her, a large rock sparkling on her wedding finger. 'It's the most magical day in a woman's life,' she adds with jazz hands, snapping my eyes away from roaming around the party. I take a small step backwards, afraid that glitter might explode from the woman's fingers or that I'll be knocked out by her engagement ring.

Taking a sip of wine, I hope the sarcasm that is creeping up my throat will follow the wine back down. It doesn't.

'Sure, but have you ever made a perfectly even-coated, lightly battered fish or successfully changed a fluorescent neon light tube or independently fixed cracked tiles with filler?' I can't help myself; the words tumble out when greeting this rather perfect-looking couple.

The woman's smile doesn't falter at my differing views, though; her mouth only stretches wider as she waves away my words with a laugh. It seems she is not to be deterred and I'm only slightly relieved. I don't want her reporting me to Alex or Charlie for maid of honour misconduct.

'Oh now, come on, that can't beat the man or woman you love dropping down on one knee and declaring that they want to be with you forever. That you're the only girl in the world for them,' the woman says and practically swoons on the spot. She takes her eyes off me for a moment and gazes into the eyes of who I can only assume is her fiancé; we haven't been properly introduced. I splutter on my drink and start to think Italian wine might be a whole lot stronger than cheap British wine. Who was this woman, sounding like she'd just stepped out of a Disney Princess commercial?

'You know forever doesn't exist, right? There's actually no such thing. Everyone dies in the end,' comes a deep voice from somewhere behind me. I don't turn round, but if I was wondering what could possibly shatter this woman's wedding illusion – not that I was, maid of honour and all – death and the theory that there's no such thing as 'happily ever after' certainly does the trick.

Without another word, she elbows her fiancé and nods towards the buffet table. I smile innocently, as those words didn't actually come out of my mouth. I may have been thinking them, but I was polite enough not to say them. They walk away, mouths small, eyes somewhat wide and also wilting, like they want to hug me but also run away from me. I'm not sure if it's me they pity or Alex and Charlie for their choice of best friend.

I'm about to turn around to see who the voice belongs to when the air fills with the scent of warm honey and vanilla and Charlie glides over to me. She's wearing a beautiful cream shorts and shirt combo with her signature gold necklaces and her black hair is loosely curled. After finding their wedding dresses this morning, the two of them were glowing, and the highlight in her cheeks has not dimmed into the evening; it only shimmers brighter for which I am inherently grateful.

'Oh goody, you two found each other, what a treat,' she says with a bouncing flourish and a ridiculously over-the-top wink in my direction. For a second, I'm at a loss for what she's talking about, until I feel I flutter of fabric brush against my elbow which makes me jolt and I turn to my left. I come eye level with a man's bicep; it's large but subtly defined where his light denim shirt sleeve rests. Before I can glance up and get a good look, Charlie snaps my attention away.

'Now, I'm not going to try and convince you that weddings are the only thing to live and breathe for but please try and have a little fun,' she says, waving her arm across the stunning view of the Positano beach below. 'And remember, you're doing this for your very best friend who loves you dearly, so try not to scare off her guests or do anything else to ruin her day.' Her eyes bore into mine when she says 'anything else', and then she directs her next words at the man beside me.

'And Owen, if I see you roll your eyes at one more flower arrangement or happy couple, I'm going to put you in charge of finding the perfect garters.'

A chuckle emits from Owen's lips; it's slightly higher than his deep voice from earlier would have suggested and the wine in my stomach sloshes from side to side. I place my palm against my stomach, resting it against the simple black fabric of my skater dress. I know, who wears black to a wedding? But it's the only casual/formal dress I own. Charlie seems to pause to make sure Owen processes her words, then flits her attention back to me, then Owen, then back to me until it's understood that she is now addressing us both.

'There's a moment in every wedding that connects with a person,' she says, her tone softer now. 'Try and channel that or something,' she adds, more blasé and with a slight scrunch of her nose as if she's registering who she's talking to. She then waves her wine-free hand in a 'whatever' kind of way before kissing me on the forehead and walking off.

'The moment it ends,' Owen and I say at the same time when Charlie is a safe distance away.

I take another sip of wine as my laughter settles in my chest, and then glance down the stairs and back at my guest list to see if there is anyone left to welcome; there is not. I feel a slight tingle in my elbow and I know Owen is still by my side. Neither one of us have moved besides my twisting and turning to check if I am free to abandon my post for the night. Once I'm satisfied that this is the case, I finally look up to greet the man that had my back earlier when facing the Disney Princess, to find that Owen is looking at me.

His eyes are a blue-grey that pick up the light from every angle, creating a gorgeous halo around his pupils, which are large and catching the gold flecks that bounce off the fairy lights. His sandy brown hair reaches his chin and is heavier on his right as it flicks and flops over to that side in a bouncy, messy wave.

'I personally don't think there's anything better than a lightly battered fish,' he says, his eyes crinkling at the edges, no hint of teasing in his tone, like this is something he is serious about.

'Really? I thought of you more as a chips and sausage

kind of person,' I reply, the words flowing from my mouth with ease. Owen's thin lips curve into a smile under his scruffy facial hair – not quite enough to call it a beard, yet not exactly barely there hair to call it stubble, somewhere in between – and something dances behind his eyes.

'I'd say you're a chips and gravy kind of person,' he responds.

I tilt my head from side to side, my low knotted bun swishing across the top of my back, not wanting to give away if he's right or wrong; he's right and I'm certain I was right too.

'Owen,' he then says, putting his hand out, those blue-grey eyes looking straight into my brown ones.

'Andrea,' I reply, shaking his hand, which I can't help but notice could do with some hand cream. My mum is forever reminding me to use hand cream for all the washing and powdery gloves we wear; I should ask her for recommendations for Owen. For the minute we have been talking, I feel as though Owen's eyes have cancelled out the terrace, the people and the noise around me, so when someone cuts the cheese – literally cuts the cheese in the good kind of way – and I get a fragrant waft of caciocavallo, a cheese Gio introduced me to only yesterday, I'm pulled away from Owen's beautiful features and the two of us fall into step with my feet carrying me in the direction of the buffet.

'You're making a cheese board; what cheeses do you require?' I ask, loading my plate with a dry bread called taralli and thick slices of caciocavallo. Owen is loading up on prosciutto and artichoke hearts.

'Are cheese boards a staple on your dinner menu?' he

asks, and though the words come out serious and interested, there's a definite twinkle in his eyes this time.

My lips quirk with a side smile as I pop a whole taralli in my mouth. 'I wish, but humour me,' I shrug once I swallow the majority of my bite.

'I'm a blue cheese kind of guy, there's a cheese called dolcelatte that I could eat on crackers any day of the week, but I could sprinkle a mild cheddar on just about everything. Of course the burrata and Parmigiano Reggiano here are to die for.'

The smile he gives me reaches his eyes and causes dimples to pop either side of his now-glistening lips thanks to the juicy artichokes. I notice, having finished his small plate of prosciutto and artichokes, he is now eyeing up the desserts.

'What about you?' he asks, acquiring a slice of cheesecake.

'Does yellow cheese from a packet count?' I reply honestly; I can taste the disgust in the caciocavallo and imagine it rolling over in my mouth that it dare lay upon a tongue with such disregard for taste.

Owen lets out a wholesome laugh, his broad shoulders bouncing a little as he tries not to spray cheesecake crumbs on me.

'Oh goody, you two found each other.' This time it's Alex, and her tone is in no way bouncy but filled more with dread. I startle and turn away from Owen to Alex's rosy cheeks and happy eyes.

'Owen, I'm to report that Charlie needs you for best man duties,' she adds, blinking like she's trying to remember her message but the possible one-too-many shots of sambuca I can smell on her warm breath are making it difficult.

'On it, boss,' Owen nods at Alex before awkwardly

looking around for a place to put his empty plate. Not quite sure of himself, he keeps hold of the plate and then bends his six-foot-one frame to give me a sort of bow before he walks away.

I watch Owen leave with this strange feeling of loss in the pit of my stomach, like I've just eaten a doughnut but my stomach is growling like it's yet to have food. I don't like the feeling, and shove another bite of something that isn't quite a doughnut but looks like one into my mouth.

'Now, don't go getting any ideas. I've seen the kind of hijinks that can occur when two people come together to smash the patriarchy. I've been to enough Pride parades to understand that look – we're all in this together to fight the system. I don't know whose idea it was, thinking that the two of you would make a good pairing as best man and maid of honour.' She lets out a small sigh while grabbing hold of the crook of my elbow to rest her head on my shoulder. 'But don't let Owen give you any ideas. I love her,' she says with a yawn. She's going to have to slow down on the wine if she wants to last a couple more hours; wine makes us both sleepy.

I smile at the cuteness in her voice, the sweet and innocent way she says 'I love her' like it's nothing short of simple and a long stretch from scary. I sniff, clearing the sharp tickle in my nose.

'Are you suggesting I've got it in me to sabotage your wedding in protest of the commercialised, old-fashioned, outdated system that it is?' I ask, a small smirk at the edge of my lips as I say it.

'Andi, you have the ability to do anything if you put

your mind to it; I feel the boutique lady was about to call the police this morning,' she replies. The tickle in my nose strikes again. I cough to clear my troubling sinuses.

'Thank you for your belief in me and for talking to me again,' I add in a playful tone, though her words hit me somewhere deep in my chest.

'You're welcome.' Alex burrows her head a little tighter into my collarbone and I savour the feeling of her being so close. It's been a minute since it's just been me and her.

'And for the record, I wouldn't dream of doing such a thing. I told you on the plane, you have nothing to worry about with me and Owen.' I confirm, just to be sure she knows and is not harbouring a worry that me and my marriage views are planning on disrupting any part of her special day. I kiss the top of her head for good measure. This morning had simply been an accident.

'I know,' she says softly into my armpit. 'I love you, that's why you're my best friend.'

'I love you too, and besides, as your best friend, who am I to stop you conforming to capitalism; I'm here to support you in all your endeavours.' At this, Alex lifts her head up and shoves me playfully. I smile broadly and flutter my lashes at her.

'Could we not have just had a nice moment? Would that have been too much to ask?' she adds, swatting me across the top of my head with a napkin.

'What? I've got to save the mushy things for the maid of honour speech,' I protest.

'Oh wow, well please do get this all out of your system now,' she says, laughter dancing behind her eyes as she grabs the rest of my not-quite-a-doughnut doughnut and pops it into her mouth before disappearing into the small crowd. I raise my wine glass at her as she backs away.

Her vanilla scent lingers and the rollercoaster in my belly comes to stop until my ears pick up to the sound of my mum's voice, her laughter reverberating off the large lemons.

'It does make me sound typically British, it does, it does, owning a fish and chip shop, oh gosh. Mind, it won't be forever. I've only got a couple more months left in me. There's more to life.'

I feel as though I'm back on a rollercoaster that I didn't sign up for, that I'm too small to ride. What does she mean it won't be forever? The chip shop is our livelihood; it's all I know. What does she mean she's only got a couple more months left in her? Suddenly, wedding sabotage is the last thing on my mind.

6

The next morning, I'm the first awake; I even beat the caw of the rooster. Dawn is yet to crack, the sun is absent from the sky, and as I shuffle along the stone corridor in my fluffy slippers and pyjamas, I'm momentarily freed from my thoughts as the horizon soaks up all my attention. The sky is a warm, vivid purple that swirls into a grapefruit pink, and where it meets the water, it looks to be a phoenix rising, the orange and red feathers tickling the blue sea.

The stillness of the large villa and the calmness of the water tricks my mind into a peacefulness that I don't quite feel. I didn't see Owen for the rest of the evening as I was ambushed by *Zias* and *Zios*, all asking where my partner was and if I had children, and then by the odd old school friend who was suddenly very interested in my life story, why I didn't go to college or university and if we had any new items on the menu at Ned's. In my slight wine haze, I couldn't tell if they were genuinely intrigued or they were having a laugh at my expense and my having stayed in the same place while their lives had seen them travelling, building careers, getting married and having kids.

On more than one occasion, I found myself looking for Owen, desperate for him to save me with his 'we all die in the end' speech, and then I'd remind myself that I didn't need saving and indulge in another sip of wine.

The kitchen is cool when I enter, bar a little heat emanating off the stove where I see a red moka pot. The coffee welcomes me over and upon moving closer, I hear a small voice. It's not the coffee talking to me but Owen, though he's not talking to me. Through the crack in the kitchen door I can make him out chatting on the phone that's pulled up to his ear, peeking out from under his hair. Not one to eavesdrop, I busy myself with pouring a small espresso.

'Not everyone goes to weddings looking for love. No, I'm not going to look.'

I'm not trying to listen in but Owen's words carry on a gentle breeze.

'I'll pop back for a visit soon.' There's a short pause as I stir sugar into my coffee. The espresso here is so strong that I'm sure I end up drinking more sugar than actual espresso. 'Right, yes, you too, bro.'

Once I'm sure Owen is off the phone, I cough subtly, so as not to scare him with my sudden appearance, and make my way onto the terrace. He's sitting at one of the round tables – the terrace is still set out like it was last night with a few tables dotted around and the long table pushed against the railings – with a tiny cup of espresso and a plate of custard fruit tarts, his phone now turning over in one hand.

'I hope you don't mind,' I say, holding my cup a little higher.

'Not at all, please,' he replies, gesturing to the chair opposite him.

'I should have asked you about a dessert board, not a

cheese platter. Sweet tooth?' I ask, smiling at the thought, weirdly. As much as I love cheese, I'd pick dessert over it every time.

'Always,' he replies with a warm grin.

'From one yellow liquid to another, though I'm sure they don't make these with packet custard,' I say, which makes Owen laugh. I can't help but notice that his laugh is rather adorable and causes his stomach to move up and down under his loose, white t-shirt.

'You can't go wrong with a bit of Bird's Eye custard,' he says, causing me to snort on my sugary espresso as I take a seat.

'No, you can't but I think it's just Bird's. Bird's Eye make fish fingers,' I inform him, unable to stop another chuckle escaping my lips. I used to get the two mixed up when I was a kid and ask my mum for Bird's Eye custard all the time.

'No way, that can't be right. I've referred to Bird's Eye custard my whole life. Are you sure?' he asks, a slow blush creeping up his neck and into his cheeks. I nod and he relaxes back into his chair with a shake of his head, making his hair fall into his face. He brushes it back in a slow movement before pushing the plate of pastries closer to me with his other hand.

I help myself to one that has a flower of strawberries in the centre and take a bite as I look out across Positano. The place is more breath-taking than photos can possibly convey. Especially at this time of the morning, there is a magic that makes you feel like you're special. Getting to witness Italy's beauty like this, so raw and unfiltered, it's as if Italy is letting you in, showing you that you are somehow worth it, that you deserve to witness this gift. My throat catches on the swell of a cry. I swallow it down with a strawberry. I've worked in a chip shop my whole life; it's my destiny. I suddenly feel like an imposter on the Amalfi Coast, yet simultaneously like I'm meant to be here, like Italy is letting me in on a secret that I'm not just Andrea that works in a fish and chip shop – I'm Andrea and I can be whatever I want to be. Had Italy shared this secret with my mum last night? Is that what she had felt? She no longer wants to run the chip shop, she wants to leave me, leave it all behind, leave it all to me? At thirty-four, I wasn't expecting that yet: more responsibility than I already have. Life set and settled.

The lump in my throat turns to a tiny, angry crick in my neck. I can't do it all on my own. Do I want to? Do I even have a choice?

'Pastry for your thoughts?'

I blink, Owen cutting through my mind fog. His voice is gentle, his smile like that first sip of coffee in the morning.

I lick away a stray crumb from my lips, adjusting my eyes from the palate of purple and pinks to the blue and grey of his eyes and smile. A part of me feels like I could unload on Owen, tell him all of it, and that he'd get it, but the other part of me reminds myself that life doesn't work like that; no one can ever truly know what's going on in someone's brain – or maybe they pretend they do. They pretend to care for a little while, like my dad, and then they get bored or fed up of pretending and so they leave. So, I narrow my eyes and take another bite of custard tart, which is delicious and wakes me up with its creaminess and sweetness.

'What do you do, Owen?' I ask instead. Charlie has mentioned Owen many times over the years. His name is always accompanied with a brilliant smile, fond chuckle and happy memory, but I've not made his acquaintance until now.

'I'm not sure if I should be offended, as Charlie's dearest best friend, that she hasn't bored you to death with my bio,' he replies, eyes twinkling.

'Oh, she's told me and Alex all about you, but I'm fact checking. Making sure everything checks out. As maid of honour and all that, I have to do some snooping,' I say, giving Owen a playful wink.

Owen considers me for a moment. 'Oh, I see, that makes perfect sense. But you made one mistake. You're giving away your tactics. As best man, I might have to return the favour.' He returns my wink and the sugar in my belly decides to spin, creating a whirlwind of delicate golden threads in my stomach. I break my gaze from his and check if I have any coffee left in my tiny cup. I don't. It was gone in two sips. Maybe the sugar was too much, too early; the last thing I want is to be sick and let Alex down. I might need to hold off on any more pastries today. The thought upsets me but I will do anything for Alex.

'I run a small business out here and I work for Will creating pieces for his clients from time to time,' Owen continues. Once the sugar has caramelised and I'm certain it's set and is at crème brûlée status: hard, I look up. 'Does that check out?' he adds, his chin tilted low, his forearm resting casually on the edge of the table. I play with a pastry crumb to alleviate any queasiness in my stomach and then take a deep breath before I speak.

'This "business",' I start, using air quotes. 'What does it trade in?' I lean back like you see those cocky police officers do in movies when they think they've stumped the criminal.

'I'm a carpenter, so bespoke pieces, furniture, anything that can be crafted out of wood for Will, and I make clay, sometimes wood, ornaments for tourists and locals for my own business,' Owen answers before taking a bite out of an orange-dressed custard tart. His eyes never stray from my face, I notice. There are moments when his eyes are too hypnotic, and I have to glance at his lips or hair so I don't miss what he's saying.

'Where is this wood sourced from?' I query, wriggling in my chair and leaning forwards again, locking my hands around my empty cup of once sugary black liquid.

Owen dabs a napkin over his lips and clears his throat. 'All recycled. Old palettes, off-cuts from construction sites and workshops, broken skateboards, used bookshelves, dressers. Everything I use was once something else. It has a history and is ready for its next chapter, a new life. The clay is also local and sustainable.'

I cross my legs, then uncross them, suddenly feeling uncomfortable in my chair. Is that what my mum wants? A new life? Is she that unhappy? A dew drop from a large lemon shakes me from my travelling thoughts, only to replace them with another curious and scary one.

Owen follows my gaze to the lemon above my head which is about the size of a teacup Yorkshire Terrier and is hanging on to a thin branch by an even thinner stalk. It looks precarious to say the least. 'That sounds amazing,' I say, my eyes still staring at the lemon. A beat passes by and when I'm 50 per cent certain the lemon isn't about to fall any time soon, I turn my full attention back to Owen, who is watching my every move with what I assume is concern for my sanity.

'Thank you,' he replies, his soft lips curving up at one side with a smile. 'And I'd estimate one in every twelve people dies from a lemon attack,' he adds, flipping his hand from side to side, the wrinkle between his eyebrows deepening while he hypothesises. It takes me a second to understand that he's answering the question bobbing around in my brain about the lemon hanging above me. The sugar melts fast in my belly, threatening a tornado, and I worry that I really did overdo it with the espresso this morning.

'Specific,' I reply with a smirk as I gently rest a hand on top of the band of my pyjama shorts. Owen is wearing grey sweatpants with his loose, white tee; his large frame fills the chair, his feet stretched out in front of him, compared to mine, which I have tucked underneath me. He matches my smirk and wipes at his brow with a napkin, and for the first time he looks away first. I notice his hands, too, are large with thick fingers, his nails trimmed neatly, his palms worn and bearing callouses. The sun is halfway to its destination now so I can understand Owen getting hot – I suddenly wish I had my own handkerchief or there was a spare napkin going. The ceramic table has gone from light and cool to refulgent and toasty and is reflecting its heat onto the two of us.

Another comfortable silence washes over us. My thoughts move away from images of Owen putting his strong and sturdy hands to work each day, and onto the sun as it entertains us, ascending an inch or two. Owen clears his throat.

'What's the most unique piece of furniture you own?' he asks, head tilting with interest.

My brain scans over my apartment and through the chip

shop. It glosses over industrial deep fryers, though would that count? Over-worn side tables that were salvaged from our local charity shop and my tatty wardrobe that has seen better days, and comes to rest on my coffee table, which causes my bottom lip to vibrate and my fists to squeeze together.

'My mum and nanna did up the apartment above our chip shop for my twenty-first. They rehomed a lot of furniture from charity shops but for the coffee table, the two of them used a few dusty palettes from the sacks of potatoes and handcrafted it themselves. It's a mix of muted creams and beige, beautifully wonky – you can only place your coffee on the right-hand corner closest to my couch – but I love it,' I reply, thinking about how excited my nanna had been to present me with their pièce de résistance.

'That sounds perfect,' Owen says quietly, allowing me to get lost for a few moments in memories of my nanna. The women in my family truly were fierce and independent; if they set their minds to something, they would absolutely achieve it, wobbly leg or not.

'I have no doubt,' Owen says with a soft smile that sparkles a diamond grade or two brighter than his previous smile. I readjust my seating position to stop my neck heating from the angle of the sun, stretching one leg out and resting my bottom on my other ankle. I hadn't realised I'd spoken those last words aloud and suddenly, it feels too hot outside, but I know the sun has a way to travel before it reaches its destination for the day. There is still a pleasant breeze in the flavourful air.

I smile in response to Owen's kindness; my eyes flicker across the multicoloured houses, avoiding his contemplation.

I can feel the heat spread to my cheeks as they tingle ever so gently, and I hold my head a little higher to catch the breeze, wondering what that's about. If I'm hot now, I'm sure going to struggle today.

'What's the most exquisite thing you've made?' I ask, trying to distract myself from the weather and my body temperature, and because I'm genuinely intrigued. I'm not bad when it comes to DIY. I know my way around a hammer and nail, an electrical socket doesn't scare me, but that's all been a means to an end, to cut costs and save money; I had to do it. To take your time or have the patience to revamp a dresser – that I see people do on Instagram – or build something from absolute scratch, that would be a dream. I want to hear and see more of what Owen can do.

As though he just read my thoughts, Owen takes a quick bite of his custard tart, wipes his hands, picks up his phone and scoots his chair closer to mine. His beefy frame comes alive with clear excitement, the muscles in his soft biceps twitch, his fingers work fast pulling up his photo gallery and his hair blows in the wind like it, too, is dancing with anticipated glee.

'The pieces for Will are good for a challenge, his clients ask for all sorts of things, though this was a personal favourite.' He pulls up a picture of a coffee table with a stream of blue resin – I've scrolled Pinterest more than once to know of resin – meandering alongside two pieces of gorgeous knotted natural oak.

'It's stunning,' I gasp, being completely taken in by a piece of bark.

'But when it's just me and I get to work on the smaller pieces, that's what I live for.' The way he's so animated, enthusiasm coating his voice, my cheeks start to ache from grinning so broadly.

My grin gives Owen all the reassurance to keep going and next, I'm looking at a coffee machine with the most attractive knobs on it that I ever did see. The layers of colour, the shades of wood, the thick grains, it's striking. The same goes for a vintage-looking dresser where no handle looks identical, then a fruit bowl that rivals Italy's ceramic beauties.

'But what wood is that made from? How do you get so many layers and colours?' I ask, all the questions buzzing through my brain.

'Ahh, those are recycled from broken skateboards or old skateboards that have been donated to us. Most skateboards are made from seven layers of Canadian maple. When stacked, shaved, cut down and sanded in different ways, the results are brilliant – extremely pleasing to the eye,' Owen replies with a small, satisfied nod of his head; he's revelling in talking about his work.

Heat rushes to my cheeks once more when I look up and take in his scruffy, morning kind of stubble. Spending most sunny days in the UK holed up in a white kitchen under fluorescent tubes instead of the actual sun certainly didn't prepare me for this Mediterranean heat. I waft a hand in front of my face and look back at the picture, cooling down a touch. 'No way, skateboards, who knew? I've never seen anything like that before.'

Owen continues to show me examples on his phone and they only get more and more beautiful. The large designs are impressive but the small items made from clay are impossible not to gawp at. I'm definitely gawping and instantly envisioning how my tatty dresser would look with custom-built handles and a coat of paint, or how my apartment would look like an art gallery with wonderful clay fish dotted about.

'I know that dreamy look,' Owen states, making me blink back into focus.

'Oh yeah, what am I thinking?' I say with a chuckle, feeling the warmth of the sun graze the tip of my nose. The sugar in my belly seems to have settled, though I'm still aware of its presence but it's more comfortable now.

'You're thinking about your dresser, the handles, how you'd change them up,' he says, causing me to let out a genuine snort as I whack his arm in disbelief. He barks a rich laugh and rubs his bicep playfully, shaking his head. I pat his arm where I caught him with my knee-jerk reaction and we both smirk. I roll my shoulders back fully, finally easing into this lovely and unexpected sunshiny morning and letting my worries melt away with each swipe of Owen's phone. Each sophisticated piece of hand-crafted furniture replaces a worry with a thought of creation. Who knew furniture could be so swoon-worthy and inspiring? The pictures alone could be in an art gallery.

I can see the joy on Owen's features, etched into the creases around his eyes and the dimples around his thin lips that deepen when he speaks. There isn't a piece that doesn't come with a bio, be it where the wood was sourced or found, or what it was before it came to be what it is in the picture. I start to feel envious of the people who have these in their homes; the tin, grey and white interior of the chip shop feels all the more suffocating and cold.

Before I can allow myself to think too much about Ned's,

a message pings up on Owen's phone. I catch a glimpse of 'bro' and 'it's time' and 'out there', but I don't have time to analyse the text when I'm alerted to the time. It has somehow become seven thirty-five. I jump out of my chair as if a rogue cushion spring just propelled me skyward.

'Owen, it's seven thirty-five, where is everyone?' I panic, looking around. Then I dash into the kitchen, where only the remains of mine and Owen's coffee shows signs of life.

Like it took him a moment to register my panic, Owen strides into the room a couple of seconds after me.

'What time is the bus?' he asks, raking a hand through his breeze-swept hair while taking giant steps towards the door. I follow, bouncing to keep up.

'It's 8.14 at the bottom of the hill, about a fifteen-to-twenty-minute walk,' I reply, recalling the itinerary. 'Oh god, what kind of maid of honour am I? I'm supposed to keep everyone on task. We can't miss this bus; we're booked at the gardens at nine-thirty.' I wipe yet more sweat from my brow with the back of my hand, hopelessly flustered.

'It's not your fault, Andrea; I'm the bloody best man. Are we the only ones that didn't overdo the drinking last night?' Owen asks, though it seems obvious, so I believe it to be a rhetorical question based on the exasperated look on his face. We fly up the first flight of stairs and Owen hammers on Alex and Charlie's door.

I'm behind him stepping from side to side, like a lemon swaying in the Italian breeze, a fifty-fifty chance of me staying afloat or dropping loose. I'm usually more organised than this.

'Andrea, do you want to go and wake your mum and Nonna Roberta? I'll fetch Zia Allegra and Will and Gio,'

Owen says in a gentle tone as he turns and looks down at me from his six-foot-one view.

'Oh god, sorry, yes. I'm on it,' I reply, charging in the direction of my mum's room. It's only the second full day of this trip, what am I doing? I'm in charge of getting the brides to the altar and apparently, I can't even get them to a garden tour on time. I got distracted talking to Owen and basking in the glorious sunshine, what was I thinking? I can't have distractions. I can't relax.

When had I last lost track of the time? Maybe Owen was a distraction. A bad one. The best man and maid of honour were supposed to make for a great team. Being late for a cooking class and tour of the prestigious Amalfi Luxury Gardens didn't add up to making a great team in my book, and I didn't think it would in Alex's either. Alex and I may have joked about wedding sabotage but that was most definitely a joke; she had to know that. Even so, my clammy hands are anxious this faux pas will paint me in a harsh light, especially considering Amalfi Luxury Gardens are the caterers for the wedding.

7

Just over two hours later and the nine of us are stood in the entryway of the Amalfi Luxury Gardens. Against the lush green backdrop of the umbrella pine trees and blooming red flowers, we look a sight to behold. Only Nonna Roberta managed to put herself together and race down three flights of stairs and two steep slopes with all the grace of a gazelle. Her simple navy trousers and long-sleeved, light-cream t-shirt, styled with her wispy, white hair, make her look effortlessly elegant. Not even Zia Allegra could pull off a miracle with less than ten minutes to spare. She chose makeup over fashion and is wearing a pouty red lip and a delicate rose blush, with gorgeously long lashes that at least take the attention away from her leopard-print blouse and sailor-striped wrap skirt.

Will, Gio and my mother are all wearing last night's ensembles and I'm certain Alex and Charlie are still in their pyjama shorts teamed with baggy denim shirts that don't match the seasonal weather. Owen is still sporting his grey sweatpants but with a smarter button-down shirt that makes for an interesting and confused-looking combo. As for me, I think I'm the resounding cherry on the top of the profiterole tier. By the time I burst through my bedroom door with a literal minute on the clock, I grabbed the nearest things to me that I had sprawled out across the ottoman at the end of the bed, which happened to be my airport hoodie – yes, it's got that smelly, sweaty airport musk – and my capri pants that have snowflakes printed all over them, which were a last-minute addition to my suitcase for those days when you just want to be cosy and comfortable in private.

Pools of sweat are forming under my breasts, and I have half a mind to strip down to my t-shirt bra, feeling like it might go unnoticed in our sea of fashion disasters. I pinch the fabric of my hoodie and pull it away from my body, searching for a breeze to cool my appendages, when Alex looks over at me with an excited raise of her eyebrows as our tour guide introduces himself.

After the initial shock and chaotic start to their morning, Alex and Charlie had been kind enough to take some of the blame, though that did little to alleviate my nerves for there had been some slight tension in both their eyes at not having received a more prompt wake-up call. I spent the entire forty-minute bus ride unable to look at Owen and trying to stem the queasiness in my stomach every time a tiny car attempted to squeeze past our bus on the narrow Amalfi roads. Often the bus would come to a halt because a tourist wasn't quite sure they could get past, and all while the bus driver shouted, '*Mamma mia, vai vai*, you got the room.' A couple of times, I prayed we weren't about to topple over the side of the cliff.

We'd made the bus by a hair which meant, though we looked like we'd all dressed in the dark for some kind of fancy dress party, we had made it to the gardens on time.

No apologies were needed, bar our far from attractive and professional ensembles.

Our host had waved us off with a chuckle. 'It make it interesting, no? It's not about the fashion, eh, it's about the food.'

My shoulders loosened ever so slightly as I tightened the already tight bun I had wrapped my hair into.

Once our tour guide has finished running down this morning's agenda, we start moving through the reception area, which is a simple cream stone structure with a wooden desk surrounded by two potted lemon trees on one side and a wall of picture frames of famous guests and stunning shots of the gardens and its produce on the other. There is a small, glass cabinet bearing bottles of olive oil and aprons, which I assume is like a mini gift shop.

The sun immediately heats my ankles when we make it through the entryway and onto the first terrace. Alfonso, our guide, may as well be Willy Wonka holding the key to the chocolate factory, but the adult version is succulent green plants as far as the eye can see, bursting with plump, bright-red beef tomatoes, plum tomatoes and tiny chillies. Voluptuous leaves sprouting from rich soil, potatoes cosy underneath. Towering canopies of trees boasting large lemons and juicy oranges, grapefruits and olives, just starting to sprout. It's heaven.

Alex catches my eye, her small silver hooped earrings reflecting the sun's rays, making me look her way. A wide smile is spread across her dewy face, which I know this morning is due to sweat and not her down-to-earth stroke of makeup. Her cheeks hold a peachy hue as she mouths 'wow' to me before turning her attention back to Alfonso.

My neck cracks and my shoulders creak, finally relieving some of the tension from this morning. I squeeze my bun and let out a breath.

Tomatoes, Alfonso said something about tomatoes. My concentration zeroes in on the task at hand: we get to pick our own ingredients from this magnificent crop. I fall in line with my mum, who nudges me and wiggles her eyebrows over the landscape, and stay close to her while filling a basket with the most aromatic chillies, spinach and basil my nostrils have ever had the pleasure of smelling.

'Now, in twos, maybe *tre*. We get together and you do as I do,' Chef Maria tells us, waving a hand around our group and then pointing at herself. Under a beautifully crafted wooden structure, covered in luscious purple bougainvillea, stand four large wooden surface areas, each accessorised with chopping boards, knifes, pots, pans, bowls and a stovetop. Maria stands behind a larger platform that also hosts a woodfire oven.

Heeding Maria's instructions, we all start shuffling into pairs. I make towards my mum but Will and Gio get to her first – Alex and Charlie are a given and Nonna Roberta is already shouting orders at Zia Allegra on where to place her basket.

I look over at Owen, who has his eyes on the wooden worktop in front of him. After this morning's mishap, I feel a slight trepidation pairing up with him. My fingers grip around my basket a touch tighter as I take the four steps to where he has acquainted himself with a station. He moves his confident hands over the wood, exploring the texture, causing his lips to curve up on one side and making the glow in his cheeks more prominent.

'We've not started cooking yet and you're already drooling.' The nerves in my stomach melt away watching Owen in his element, though I take a tentative look around, checking if anyone needs me for anything, but they all seem preoccupied discussing ingredients. I think I'm OK to talk, to team up with him.

'Ahh, ha.' Owen makes a noise. 'It's so simple yet incredibly detailed and well crafted. It's sturdy without being heavy or weighted,' he tells me.

'It's pretty,' I agree, thinking how inviting this would look in a home with rustic vibes. I dare to dream of having a cosy kitchen one day. Owen smiles, meeting my gaze when I place my basket next to his on the worktop. He takes a step to one side, making room for me by his side.

'This would look outstanding in an old-fashioned-meets-modern kitchen with a rustic touch,' Owen says. I chuckle and he winks at me, as if he knew he just read my mind.

'This morning, we make gnocchi,' Maria informs the group, and in doing so snapping mine and Owen's attention away from kitchen design and onto food. I glance around one more time; everyone's on task, listening to our head chef, which gives my mind permission to tune in to her broken English too, while Owen picks up the flour and pulls potatoes from our baskets.

Rolling up the sleeves of my hoodie, I'm grateful for the fragrant perfumes emitting from this kitchen, distracting from the scent of said stinky hoodie that I still have to wear for the next handful of hours, and see to peeling and chopping potatoes while Owen brings two pans of water to boil on the stove. Then he's retrieving the plum tomatoes from our baskets and placing them in a large bowl before pouring one of the pans of boiling water over the top of them. The makeshift outdoor kitchen is quiet while we concentrate, but I'm enjoying the clatter of pans and peeking at everyone while they work. It's usually just me and Mum in the chip shop kitchen, where it was once chaotic, busy and nonstop, and now it's merely a deserted wild west. Cooking with patience, love and time hasn't been something I have partaken in for an awfully long time. My fingertips stretch and relax over the knife and slice with a comfortable ease.

'Do you enjoy cooking?' I ask Owen as he drains the water from the bowl, then sticks his hand into it to squeeze and squash the tomatoes, in a way that suggests he's done it before. I add my chopped potatoes to the other pan of boiling water along with a dash of salt and leave them to boil.

'I do. I enjoy getting my hands dirty,' he says, innocence all over his face, brows furrowed as his focus is on the tomatoes. Charlie chokes and snorts behind us and my cheeks immediately grow hotter than the sun that is roasting my calves.

'What's your favourite meal to cook?' I ask, ignoring the dryness in my throat. I send a scowl Charlie's way, unable to help myself, as I stick my hand into the bowl of tomatoes just to make sure Owen is squeezing them all right.

'How long has it been since you got dirty?' Charlie overrides my question and is promptly given a nudge and a soft but definite warning look from Alex. Owen shakes his head and I take a sip of the wine we have been given. I'm not afraid of Charlie's teasing, I'm used to it by now, but today, I'm not taking the bait. I already feel ruffled after this morning; the rest of the week needs to go smoothly. Besides, Owen doesn't need to know my business. I don't need anyone to please me when I can quite happily please myself. That doesn't, however, seem to stop my reddening cheeks.

'I love a good seafood dish,' he answers my question and flicks water at Charlie. 'I think I'm good with the tomatoes, if you want to do the chillies.' I look down at our hands overcrowding the bowl and my cheeks turn molten-level hot. Did I offend him with my need to check on the job he was doing? I collect the chillies and carefully dice them, along with an onion and two cloves of garlic. While I wash my hands thoroughly, Owen sees to a saucepan, adding olive oil, the onion, chillies and garlic over a medium heat. I tell myself to breathe; he looks at ease in the kitchen, he's doing a good job.

'Great and bold choice. Seafood can be a hard one to get right, but when it's cooked well, it's luxurious. I love a flour-dusted basa with slices of lemon, grilled tomatoes on the vine and a buttery garlic and lemon mashed potato,' I tell him, my mouth watering.

'That sounds divine,' he says, stirring the onions before adding the squashed tomatoes and turning to a low heat.

I nod my head wistfully. 'I haven't made that dish in a minute or two.'

It had been a favourite of my nanna's, and without her around to enjoy it, I felt less than enthusiastic to whip the meal up.

'Take the potatoes out of *l'acqua*, put on your board like this and press with your fork.' Maria shows our group.

Owen and I each work with a fork; I notice my presses are much rougher than his more delicate ones.

'Do you talk to your brother every day?' I ask Owen at the same time as he asks, 'Do you get to relax much?'

'You first,' he suggests gently, adding a spoon of flour to our now mashed potatoes. Without oil, salt or pepper, it's a wonder that these potatoes smell unbelievable and full of flavour.

'I do...' I start, tilting my head in thought. 'I mean, yes. I see Alex and Charlie as often as I can, maybe once a week, which helps me unwind. Other than that, there always seems to be a lot to do.'

His hands work through the flour and potato mix, kneading it into a dough. I dust flour onto a section of the surface. Owen doesn't speak, just smiles kindly like he's processing the information.

'Your brother?' I lightly prod.

'He's two years younger than me but somehow thinks he knows it all,' Owen replies with an affectionate chuckle. 'He likes to tell me what to do, and yes, when we're not around each other, we check in frequently. That's who I was on the phone with this morning.'

I nod in understanding, or at least in comparable understanding; when I'm not around Mum or Alex, we check in hourly. I think of Alex as the sibling I never had, and with it having been my mum and me for so long, before Alex, Mum is my best friend. I don't know what I'd do without her, what I'll do if she gives up the chip shop and I don't get to work with her every day. I swallow down the lump that threatens to get in the way of me enjoying the delicious food we are preparing.

'You don't always agree on everything?' I query, remembering their conversation from this morning and hoping Owen doesn't mind the thought of me having heard. His first response is a slight grimace; his eyes crinkle around the edges.

'Hmm, he's got an unhealthy investment in my love life and a habit of highlighting my flaws and pointing them out at any given moment,' he shrugs. 'He keeps me on my toes.'

'Have you not given him the infamous "everyone dies at the end" speech?' I smile, picking at the basil in my basket.

'It has yet to deter him; he's pretty insistent on me changing my ways and trying harder.' Another shrug.

'You mean to say that potential partners don't like the "no such thing as forever" mantra? I'm shocked.' I place a hand on my chest, faux aghast. The basil falls from my fingertips into the simmering sauce. Owen works the dough into long sausage shapes, per Maria's demonstration, his mouth forming an 'o'.

'How often does your "love doesn't compare to a lightly battered fish" chat up line work?'

I let out a bark of laughter before I have time to be offended, amused that he remembered my speech and impressed that he fired back. His shoulders move up and down with laughter while he passes me the circles of gnocchi he has cut the sausage into. I place a light thumb print in the middle of each one.

'It works brilliantly, I'll have you know. Keeps everyone away. I'm good on my own; I don't need, nor do I want, a relationship.'

'Way too much hassle, way too much work,' Owen agrees.

We clink glasses before each plonking a handful of our homemade gnocchi into a pan of boiling water and watch it rise to the top in under five minutes. Owen then ladles big spoonfuls into our fresh tomato sauce. Maria makes her way around the room with a large block of Parmesan cheese and a grater. There's no need for bowls as she grates the Parmesan straight over the bubbling pan and points at the spoons, giving us all the go-ahead to dig in.

The next minute is filled with the sound of nine people groaning and moaning, and the odd Vespa straining to climb a steep hill. The taste on my tongue is like Christmas morning had a baby with a warm summer's day; it's excitement mixed with utter pleasure. My taste buds demand more. I take another spoonful and close my eyes.

'I think this gnocchi agrees with us. I don't believe a human could ever make me feel this good,' I proclaim, to which, when I open my eyes, Owen nods, Charlie chokes and snorts for the second time and Alex tilts her head sweetly in contemplation. With the devilish look on Charlie's gorgeous, bronzed face, I don't take a second to muse what she is thinking, and instead take a larger spoonful and dissolve into food ecstasy.

8

'These bouquets are stunning, Will.' The terrace currently resembles a florist's workshop. I look around, taking in the beauty that surrounds me. Lemons and bunches of lavender lie along the long table, and the round tables are being put to use by experimental cosmos, dahlias and cream roses. Owen is cutting strips of brown twine and Will is scouring the lemons above our heads for the juiciest, yellowest fruit to add to our collection.

Gio is seeing to work at the family's bakery while the rest of our group, Nonna, Zia Allegra, Mum, Alex and Charlie, are lounging by the pool on the second terrace, unable to move anything but slowly after the gnocchi we devoured and velvety wine we had sipped all morning at the gardens.

I'm currently alongside the best man and Will, the two craftsmen of this ensemble, aiding with the flower arrangements for the wedding, which is now only an evening and two days away. I'm warming to the idea of celebrating love – being here with my mum and surrounded by good people, people who feel like family, makes the upcoming nuptials feel less daunting. I nod my head, proud of my own achievement in the short time that we have been here. As long as I don't cause a repeat of this morning's frenzied adventure, I think I can actually enjoy this Amalfi Coast extravaganza.

'Did you always want to work at Ned's with your mum?' Owen's voice cuts through the one-person celebration happening in my head, and I look up to see him wrapping twine around delicate bunches of lavender mixed with a single cream rose.

I feel the moment my shoulders stiffen as my brain scans memories from my life, choices I made and didn't make. I scratch my neck below my too-tight bun and can't help myself from taking the bunch he's holding so he can wrap the twine around my finger to tie the knot.

'Yes and no,' I start honestly. 'When I was younger, I'm talking seven or eight, I wanted to be a builder; I thought if I could just build a house for me and Mum, it would be perfect.' It feels like a giant lemon is crushing my sternum, my body not quite feeling lighter for having spoken these words, yet I continue, noticing Owen has stopped fiddling with the twine.

'At the same time, the place where I got to spend the most time with my grandparents was Ned's, and so I didn't believe I would ever venture far.' I finish with a rough chuckle and rub at my sternum.

Owen and Will seem to give me a moment to recollect, as neither of them jump to comment right away. I'm grateful for the second to compose my jumbled thoughts; the grief that still springs to life every once in a while over missing my grandparents, the curiosity of what would have been if I'd followed Alex to college and university and the more recent thought: what will I do if my mum decides to leave or give up the fish and chip shop?

'I believe that what's meant for us will find us and that we will always be exactly where we need to be at the right time,' Will tells us, as my nose delights in a sweet, flowery scent. I turn slightly to my left to find Owen holding out a rose. I take it off him and shake my head, waving it in the air, then clear my throat.

'Have you always done carpentry, always wanted to do what you are doing now? I mean, the way you swoon over furniture, I couldn't imagine you doing anything else,' I tease and get back to tying twine around a rather robust lemon.

Owen chuckles, securing twine effortlessly around fragile stems, clearly able to do it without me. I'm having difficulty with the lemon and Owen's hands are much larger than mine.

'I haven't always done carpentry, no. My mum was less than enthusiastic about me going into the same trade as my dad; she didn't want us following in his footsteps, to remind her of him. I scraped by in school – all that sitting still and lack of creative freedom wasn't for me – and so I ended up bouncing around retail jobs when I left. Dad would send emails and texts about crafting courses, woodwork shops, but not wanting to disgruntle my mother, I put them aside, tried not to think about them,' he explains casually, moving on to another bunch of lavender. 'Eventually, it was Charlie and Will here who saved the day. Will took me under his wing with an internship. Mum trusted Will and so I watched and learnt, very much enthralled by the design process, but it sort of clicked and I knew that I wanted to be the one building the furniture for the rooms that Will was creating.'

'He's got an eye for design though,' Will noted, his basket of lemons overflowing, his eyes crinkling with a loving smile.

'That's wonderful, I'm happy you found your dream and that you are getting to live it,' I say, smiling over a bouquet of cream roses and lavender.

'Yeah, me too.' Owen replies. Will's smile broadens before he turns his back and attends to a runaway lemon that fell from its stalk, narrowly missing his head. Owen and I exchange a nervous and knowing glance. No lemon attacks before this wedding, please, I pray.

'So, it's the age-old, clichéd question but I'm going to ask it anyway,' Owen starts with a slight scrunch of his nose, already cringing. 'What would you be doing if you weren't doing what you are doing now?' he asks before making a face, opening his mouth and flicking his tongue.

'Bit of a tongue twister that one?' I note with a playful smirk. His shoulders bounce with laughter and I pass a cream-coloured rose back and forth over my palm, allowing the feather-light petals to float over my skin. 'I've never known anything else,' I pause, debating whether or not I would like my brain to dig up old thoughts, but Owen's deep blue-grey eyes lure them out of me. 'I guess when I waved Alex off to college, there was a part of me that mulled over the idea of what it would be like to be joining her, to acquire a skill – in what, I wasn't exactly sure back then. I do love to cook, but making fish and chips every day can get a bit tedious. Anyway, it's too late for all that now.' The words come out slow, my mind thoughtful, remembering the nanoseconds that I let my brain consider working somewhere other than Ned's – but they were never realistic thoughts. I sniff a lemon to bring me back to the present and catch Will giving Owen a look from under hooded lids, his features soft with sympathy. But I don't need sympathy; my life is good.

'It's pretty special that you looked after and helped your grandparents so much, that each day, you are keeping their legacy going,' Owen tells me kindly.

'Yeah, yeah,' I brush him off. Was it special or had I just done the safest thing? Locked the door to my comfort zone and thrown away the key? 'What would you two be doing?' I ask, hastily taking the attention away from myself.

'You know, Andi, it's not just you that fell into the family business. I don't think I was built for anything other than interior design. My mum had me designing my own bedroom at five and called on my help to design the kitchen by ten. I was making coffee at her small business by fourteen. I can only imagine her thrill at seeing Charlie follow in both our footsteps,' Will replies, a watery sheen making his blue eyes glisten under the slowly fading sun. The late afternoon is drawing in but the weather remains toasty. I smile, feeling comforted by Will's words.

'Oh, I don't know, I'd probably be a rockstar or something,' Owen chimes in, causing both Will and I to burst out laughing. Somehow, the image of Owen as a rockstar doesn't quite fit; he's too calm and in no way in your face enough, though I'm sure his skilled fingers would be a dab hand on a guitar or keyboard. Suddenly, my belly is as warm as the tomato sauce we devoured at lunch time, and I quickly shake my head. My stomach has been awash with nerves since finding out about this trip; it needs to get a grip.

'Andi, do you have the almonds we can package? I have the small organza bags here and thought we could fill them tonight if you two were up for it?' Will asks, freeing me from thoughts of my troubling stomach issues.

'Yes, sure, absolutely. They're in my room; I'll just go and get them,' I reply.

Ahh, the precious almonds. One must take home a token of the wedding day – a rather narcissistic tradition if you think about it. Here, think of us when you look at this mini bottle of alcohol with our names on it, or this pebble engraved with the date. You don't want to forget such a special day in our lives, that it must now be a special day in yours, too.

'I can help you,' Owen offers, as I put down my bunch of lavender.

'No, no, it's OK. I can get them myself,' I reply, knowing I'm more than capable of carrying a box of candy when I'm used to hauling the food shop up the steep, narrow stairs to my flat. Help is not needed. 'I got it,' I reaffirm and walk towards the kitchen.

'Ciao,' I greet Gio as he walks into the kitchen from the opposite side carrying two large brown paper bags with steam creeping out of the tops. The smell of the crisp, warm, freshly baked loaves is out of this world, and I momentarily forget what I came in here to do.

'*Pomeriggio*, Andrea.'

'Please say we get to tuck into that bread at dinner?' I eye the bags greedily. Gio lets out a hearty laugh, throwing his head back. His salt-and-pepper hair catches the light from the kitchen island. Then he shrugs and waves his hand, his thumb and index finger touching.

'You full from lunch, no? You ready to eat again?' he says, his tone full of joy and delight.

'I hadn't even thought about being hungry or not, Gio; I just know I need to eat that bread,' I reply honestly.

He shakes his head, soft laughter still rumbling.

'I'll be right back,' I inform him, remembering that Will and Owen are waiting for me. He nods as I excuse myself and quick-march out of the kitchen, down the corridor, up a flight of stone steps and into my bedroom.

The dimming sky casts shadows over the room, deepening creases and folds in the duvet, highlighting its plushness and making it all the more inviting. I skipped out on the siesta when we got back from the gardens in favour of being a dutiful bridesmaid and working on the flower arrangements, but now the bed is teasing. *Just think of the bread*, I tell myself and bypass the bed, heading towards the arched window where I reach for the box that's home to the large bag of rainbow-coloured almonds I sourced back in England.

I pull off the lid and brace myself to be dazzled by the vibrant prism of colour, but instead am greeted by a muted green and grey with white speckles.

'Oh my god,' I cry. My hand freezes on the plastic bag, holding the top in a death grip. 'What have I done?' I know it comes out in a whisper; I can feel my voice as it shakes, the words struggling to pass the lump in my throat. My grip tightens on the bag. I'm angry; whimpering is not something I do. Messing up like this is not something I do; I run a chip shop, for crying out loud.

'Honey, what's wrong?' My mum's voice cuts through the buzzing between my ears, but I don't move; I can't stop staring at the bag of melted almonds.

'What kind of idiot puts sugared almonds in direct sunlight?' My voice is barely audible, even to myself, but I know that's what I'm thinking and my mouth is muttering away uncontrollably.

'Sweetheart, don't be so hard on yourself; you're not an idiot.' My mum rubs a hand across my shoulder blades.

'Mum,' I stutter, 'what's wrong with me? I've cursed this wedding. I mocked the almonds and now I've killed the rainbow.' I let the bag drop back into the box.

I swear my mum chuckles. 'Sweetheart, you've not killed the rainbow. Melted it, sure, but we can fix this; we're great at fixing things,' she says softly, playing with wisps of hair at the base of my bun.

Only, her words don't calm me; instead, they make me think back over all the things we have fixed together at the chip shop. A broken fryer, no problem. A clogged sink, easy. A buzzing fridge-freezer, sorted. The anger towards myself that's bubbling inside me turns to anger towards my mum.

'Are you thinking of selling the shop, Mum?' I bark. My voice sounds strange to my own ears; it's rare that I shout.

'What ever gave you that idea?' Mum takes a step back, looking at me with her large, brown eyes that flash with concern.

'Mum?' I urge. My own eyes widen, pleading, no lies. Her shoulders sag. 'It's not your dream?' I question, turning my back to the box of almonds.

'Yes and no,' she sighs, reminiscent of my own words when Owen asked me if I was living my dream. She sits down on the edge of the bed. 'Honey, working alongside my mum and dad was precious, something I'll always treasure. The same as working with my daughter. What mum gets to say that she sees her daughter every day? But yes, I've been thinking…'

'Is everything OK in here? I heard a shout.' Alex bursts into the room, cutting Mum off.

I casually close the box behind my back.

'Everything's fine, hon,' I say as merrily as I can muster.

Mum nods enthusiastically.

'I was just telling Mum about the bread Gio brought home for dinner. Oh my god, do you think it will taste as good as it smells?' I ask, walking towards her and hooking a hand around her elbow.

'Better,' she replies, a smile knocking the worry off her pretty face. 'Will said you can leave wedding favours for tonight as dinner is nearly ready,' she adds merrily, completely oblivious to my major mess up.

'Oh my god,' I groan, which makes Alex laugh. 'That sounds great, I'm ready to eat.' My heart performs a triple backflip at this saving grace. I will fix the wedding favours, narcissism be damned. My best friend will have her piece of Pride on her wedding day if it's the last thing I do.

I try not to grimace that it very well could be the last thing I do. I don't know how much more of this wedding my stress levels can take.

9

I'm dressed and ready before the rooster wakes again the next morning. There's no need to rouse the villa, as today's workshop doesn't start until mid-afternoon, so I tiptoe through the deserted, silent hallways and out onto the gravelly front path, opting to have a coffee at a local bar so I can ask the residents about the best places in town for wedding favours and sugar-coated almonds. I try not to dwell on Italy being late to the Pride party and hope a bag of vividly coloured almonds – which they traditionally coat in whites and blush tone pinks – won't disgrace their culture or, more importantly, be hard to get a hold of.

'Hey,' a voice hisses from near the bougainvillea a few steps behind me, causing me to startle and skip a few breaths. With one hand on my hip and the other against my forehead, I remind myself to breathe.

'Who's there?' I utter cautiously. The dim purple hues in the sky mixing with my blurred vision from shock make it hard to see. The owner of the voice steps forward, looming large. 'Owen, what are you doing?' I say before he can speak. His light-brown hair is messy and for the first time, I notice the faintest streaks of grey in the wisps that frame his face as they glitter in the early signs of sunlight.

'I was on the terrace and saw you walk past and wondered if you wanted company,' he whispers, combing a hand through his hair when it falls over his eye as he takes a step closer to me. My fingers wrap around my hip a little tighter. I dab at my top lip gently, my heart rate returning to normal.

'Couldn't sleep?' I question.

'I'm an early riser. I like to watch the sunrise,' he replies, with that lazy shrug of his. My lips curl into an easy smile, though I don't miss the slight twitch in Owen's left eye and wonder what is on his mind that's keeping him up, but I don't push. I have to focus.

'It is stunning out here.' I glance around. From this high up the mountain, the violet sky is silhouetted by the citrus and olive trees and the large umbrella pines that decorate the gardens and roadsides. There's no way of looking at it without it stealing your breath for a few moments, but once I've taken my breath back, I swing my arms into gear and take a step towards the entryway to make my exit. 'Right, I best be off, but I'll see you later,' I tell Owen with a wave.

'Do you need help with whatever it is you are doing this early?' He tries a different tactic, other than asking if I would like company.

'Why would I need help?' I say, maybe a little firmly, but no one knows about the almond debacle but me and Mum. My speed increases.

'You were rather quiet and distracted at dinner, and you only groaned once when you took a bite of the bread – and it was a small groan at that,' he informs me, making me scratch the back of my neck where the tiny strands of hair pull away from my low bun. My brow furrows at his observation; it's sweet and incredibly inconvenient. I need to get on.

'No, I'm fine, thank you. I don't need assistance,' I reply, walking faster down the road now, Owen still beside me.

'OK,' he says simply, tracing his hand along a low stone wall and looking out towards the glistening sea that's to our left. I stop abruptly when we reach a sharp bend.

'Owen, please don't take this the wrong way, but I really am fine and I truly don't need your help,' I say, hoping that he will get the hint and turn back. I don't wish to be rude but my palms are starting to sweat, my stomach beginning to bubble with what I have to do today before the group outing this afternoon and I don't want a witness. I can't let Alex and Charlie know that I messed up, again.

However, Owen doesn't seem to take it any way and has continued walking, hands in his jogger pockets. 'Oh don't mind me, I'm not helping; I'm searching for coffee,' he says without looking back.

After a second or two, I follow, contemplating just slightly whether I believe him. From what I've witnessed and experienced so far of Owen – helping Will and Gio with the dishes, aiding Nonna Roberta in harvesting basil, offering an arm to my mum any time she meets a set of stairs – he comes across as a gentle giant and one who likes to help and fix things, which aligns perfectly with his job.

But I don't need fixing or helping; I'm the one who does the fixing and helping. Yet, as I walk, I realise I don't actually know which way the coffee bar is, or the shops, so I follow two steps behind Owen, tracing my eyes over the gorgeous greenery and hoping I'm going the right way towards the village.

By the fifth razor-sharp curve of the mountain, rows of shops, restaurants, cafés and hotels come into view and the sun has risen beautifully into a crisp, light-blue sky. I breathe out as Owen turns around and an elderly gentleman next to me lifts up the metal shutters of a small shopfront with gleaming ceramics in the window. I point to the shop and give Owen a courtesy nod and duck inside.

'*Buongiorno*,' I say to the gentleman as I look around, knowing full well that the items in this shop are not what I'm looking for, unless I want to send everyone home with a pristine ceramic espresso cup that buying forty of would put me in debt. I do not have that change to spare.

'Wedding favours, *per favore*?' I bow at the old man, ashamed by my little knowledge of the Italian language and my expecting that he will understand English. He nods in return and points at the salt and pepper shakers.

'*Bella*, but no, no, *grazie*,' I say with a bright smile and walk back onto the quiet street. I squint my eyes at the now glowing sun and push up the arms of my long-sleeved, plain white t-shirt. Similar to Amalfi, where we had been dress shopping, the Positano streets are lined with brightly coloured shops, mostly boutiques selling gorgeously patterned dresses and swimwear, and cafés boasting chocolates and the finest pastries. I've lost count of the number of ceramic shops dotted between the odd prestigious sandal parlour and handcrafted sunglasses made from wood.

There has to be something around here. My head thumps as I walk past another pastel gelato café, one half of the tiny space hosting the gelato counters and staff, and the other a thin runway for customers. While the other customers begin to file in, I see an elderly couple standing at the end of the rounded countertop, sipping tiny cups of espresso, and figure they must be locals. It's a tight squeeze, though appealing and quaint. I need coffee but I feel like I'm running against the clock: in an hour's time, these streets will be a hive of tourists and I don't want to get swept up.

The air fills with a delicious warm vanilla that smells promising. I step into the first chocolate shop I see. Elegant boxes wrapped with gold ribbon adorn the shelves, trays of speciality cakes fill the cabinets, clear bags full of crystallised candied peels sparkle in the sunlight and buttery croissants larger than my hands make my stomach grumble.

'Ciao.' I wave at the lady behind the counter. 'Do you have almonds?' I ask, hopeful as I make a small almond shape with my hands.

'*Mandorle*,' she nods before turning her back, and my shoulders sag. Then she turns around, producing a pretty bouquet of flowers made up of sugar-coated almonds. '*Ma*, just this one left from the Easter,' she says, her voice sweet, her face thoughtful like she's concentrating on getting the words right.

'*Ma*, no, no, *grazie*,' I nod gratefully and resist the pull of breakfast pastries to the irritation of my stomach. It lets out a deeper gurgle when I walk back onto the road.

'Pastry for your thoughts?' Owen's voice sings along a blinding ray of sunlight. I hold my hand up once again to shield my watery eyes – I do not know when I last owned a pair of sunglasses – and a wrapped croissant finds its way into my hand, nearly my face. 'Ooh sorry, couldn't see with the sun,' Owen apologises, making me snort at his knuckle brushing my nose.

'You are not making that a thing,' I tell him, referring to the second time he's used that phrase, a pastry for your thought, on me. I take a hungry bite of the still-warm pastry; it cracks and crunches, then melts on my tongue.

'Thank you,' I add. 'Thank you very much for this.' I wave the pastry as we fall in step towards the railings that overlook Positano's pebbly beach. Flowerpots nestle in the square bollards, their delicate but bold flowers popping against the colourful backdrop. We eat in silence. Once I finish my breakfast, I let out a sigh, partly because my breakfast is gone, which is a shame, and partly because my lips tingle with words they want to say.

I bite down on my lip then open up, 'I left the wedding favours by the window and the rainbow almonds are now mushy pea almonds.'

'Ironic,' Owen deadpans, though his face remains kind, his eyes free of judgement, only a slight flicker of teasing. He brushes a napkin over his lips.

'Not helpful,' I reply, my voice a little flat yet light. We both blink at each other in the intruding sunlight that is not backing down today and is determined to cause tears. Owen is not wearing sunglasses either, I notice, but ignore that fact and continue, 'Alex and Charlie currently don't have wedding favours because of me.'

Owen doesn't comment right away; he takes time with his reply while I squeeze the napkin in my hand.

'OK, so maybe we continue asking around about the almonds, but keep an eye out and our brains switched on in case there's something else we can think of. Surely there's something that stands out more than a bag of rainbow-coloured almonds to symbolise love and happily ever after from the bottom of everyone's junk drawers,' Owen suggests with just a hint of sarcasm at the end. I can't help that my lips tug up at the corners. I like that he didn't make me feel judged or stupid for what I did; instead, he simply came up with a solution.

'OK,' is all I can muster because I hadn't even thought about an alternate wedding favour. Right now, it's the best and only plan I have.

'That's it, this place is on my hit list,' I announce as we exit what has to be the fifteenth bakery/confection shop we have visited. My toes are screaming in the ancient single pair of sandals that I own and brought with me. I should have worn my gifted sliders, and the heat is being incredibly inconsiderate of British people not accustomed to the sun.

'Who or what is at the top of that hit list?' Owen inquires, his sunlit blue eyes widening when he looks at me.

'Anyone and everyone who created the absurd institution that is marriage,' I say, indignant. Owen hums in response, a small curve at the edge of his lip, like he's holding back a full-on grin considering our dire situation, or something else that I can't quite put my finger on. He gazes at me for a beat before looking away. I pat my hot, sweaty cheeks, fully regretting this 'lightweight' long-sleeved tee.

We've had no luck thus far, with most bakeries repeating what the one before them and the one before them had said: that they are out of almonds. If they did have any, they were made up into the flower arrangements, confetti, that I saw earlier, and when they did offer to order them in, it would take up to a week if not longer. I don't have a week; I have less than two days.

I scrape my throbbing toes along the path. 'How are

you doing on the second part of the plan? Any ideas?' I ask Owen gingerly. If anyone should be coming up with a backup favour, it should be me. Owen stops walking just outside another *pasticceria* and hovers a large palm over my forearm. My skin feels even more constricted now under my sleeves, too hot. I dare not tell Owen that two already sweaty people standing this close together with the wafting warmth of bakery ovens in blazing heat is a terrible place to stop, and is scrambling my mind. I try to take a small step backwards, for the roads are becoming more and more crowded as the minutes pass by.

'I'm not going to lie, I'm having a really hard time with the whole concept of wedding favours. Really, what is the point?' Owen asks, ducking down a little so I can see the beads of sweat under his floppy hair. When his eyes draw closer, the blue makes way for those grey flecks that make them appear darker and more intense. I grip the hem of my shirt and start wafting for cool air as my cheeks crease into a hopeless grin.

'So, you're telling me that the pair of us and our strong dislike for the "system" combined means that this is an entirely pointless venture and I should turn myself in?' I sigh, still wafting, still sweating, grin still very much digging into my cheeks.

'Not exactly, it was just a thought,' Owen notes, a hint of amusement behind the grey. Then he removes his hovering hand and sticks it in his pocket. I take my opportunity to nod towards a quieter spot where the buses meet and where there is more of a piazza of shops, people not so sardined together. Owen follows.

'Honestly, that's where my brain is at. It's not giving me

anything. Nothing quite compares to the love that was packed into those tiny little nuts.' When I hear myself, I truly think I've gone mad, but it's over two hours into this adventure and I'm worn out. Owen's laugh vibrates through my entire body, seemingly giving me permission to release my pent-up frustration and join him. My eyes water, my cheeks ache.

Then Owen stands up straight, towering over me. 'I've got it,' he declares. 'We're being too negative. The only way we are ever going to think of something is if we believe in it.'

'What? You're asking me to be positive?' I gasp, playfully clutching at my chest, pleased when Owen chuckles again.

'What would you want?' Owen then asks, surprising me a little; what would I want? It's not something I ever take much time to think about, least of all in relation to a wedding.

'To not have a wedding, that would solve everything' I shrug; the thought gives me the heebie-jeebies, and my mind stays stubbornly blank. I squeeze the bobble that's tight around my bun. Owen's eyelashes flutter, a gentle smile creeps across his face.

'Hmm, that's not always the case,' he muses, 'and it won't help us here.' He says it kindly but I don't miss the shadow that passes through his expressive eyes.

'What would you want?' I ask softly.

Owen is quiet for a moment. We sidestep a group of tourists and walk towards a tiny passageway when a bus beeps and requires our spot.

'I'd make something.' His voice is calm and assertive; something inside me softens.

'That's sweet,' I say out loud, then quickly clear my throat. 'But we've only got two days and little resources – I don't think I even have resources; no one wants a battered fish,' I ramble, trying to think of things that I would be capable of making and coming up extremely short.

Before I can continue, my thoughts turning to chips in a newspaper cone, a group of tourists decide to meander down our passageway and suddenly, Owen is taking a step closer to me. His hand hastily presses against the wall behind me to stop himself from squashing me, and my brain is no longer thinking about fried food but instead how warm Owen's body feels against mine and how comforting his scent is – it's not a perfume or deodorant or manufactured smell, it's just him – my anxious mind melts and though my heart rate has picked up speed, my breathing is steady. I feel as though I'm on a vacation from all of it.

'Well, we might cheat a bit,' he starts, remaining in the same position though the stampede of people has now gone. I feel as if I'm in a cosy bubble, some sort of safe space that I can't truly describe or understand. 'The bakeries bake cookies, biscuits, pastries fresh every morning. What if we ask if we can buy their first batch of forty, or fifty to be on the safe side. They don't have to bake anything specially made per se.'

'Oh, what about those macarons in that last bakery; they had pastel colours, a few different shades. Do you think Alex and Charlie would mind pastel colours?' I ask excitedly, the idea taking shape in my head.

'Not at all. We put each one in a bag and maybe we ask Will to design a tag, maybe a pastel rainbow to match, that we can tie around the close with twine.'

'I love that, but do you think Will might be mad at me?' I can't help but ask, fear creeping back into my stomach.

'I'm sure he would love to help.' Owen stamps out my fear with a bright smile. 'I'm sure he's already designed a label for the almonds so we might simply have to tweak the colour palette a touch,' he confirms.

Suddenly, I feel a vibration between the two of us, a buzzing between my thighs and Owen's. Owen realises how close he is to me and colour dashes to his cheeks.

'I'm so sorry,' he apologises, stepping back and waving his hands over me like he's trying to assess if he's done any damage or caused me any harm.

'It's OK,' I tell him; I hadn't felt uncomfortable or threatened. Now that he's moved away, it's like the noise of the outside world gets louder along with the ringing in Owen's pocket.

'I'll just get this,' he says, as I ask, 'Should we head back to the last bakery?'

We both nod at each other and start walking to the quaint pastel hole-in-the-wall bakery that doesn't look to be bigger than a broom closet. I pause when I reach it, with Owen being a few steps behind me.

'Nate, I'm fine, I'm not moody. It's been years. I'm good. Now get back to work.' Owen is all laughs and wrinkles when he talks to his brother except as he insists he's fine. A slight darkness deepens his eyes, but only briefly before he's back to his casual, laid-back demeanour.

'Everything alright?' I ask when he hangs up and we pop inside the bakery.

'All good,' he replies cheerily before scanning the confectionary collection, his sweet tooth taking over.

10

The lady behind the counter, Katia, is more than pleased with our request, and between her broken English and our broken Italian – or should I say mine; Owen's Italian is pretty good – we agree to pick up fifty pastel-coloured macarons tomorrow morning, before angel Katia gifts us each a macaron to try. We take them to the only small round table, situated at the back of the teeny café, and put up our feet.

'You're a life saver,' I breathe out, clinking my macaron against Owen's.

He smiles shyly and takes a nibble of his cappuccino macaron. I feel my own cheeks flush when I say, 'And thank you for paying for them. I owe you.'

'You don't owe me a thing, Andrea. I'm happy to do it,' he tells me, his voice a tad raspy from the crunchy biscuit. I study the pale lemon one in my fingers.

'Owen,' I say thoughtfully, eyes on my macaron, 'you know before when you said that not having a wedding wouldn't save the day? What did you mean?' My curiosity for where his dislike for the institution, which rivals mine, gets the better of me. When he doesn't speak straight away, I take a bite of macaron and wave away my nosiness.

'I was in a long-term relationship, about five years.' His words come out slow, matter of fact. 'I wasn't the most affectionate, doting boyfriend; I knew I didn't want to get married but I guess I never really thought about what she wanted. Her interests were always so different to mine, we had fun but when I look back, we barely spent any time together. She was all about parties and going out, shopping and fine dining – she tried to get me to eat pigeon once. I thought she was happy doing her own thing like I was doing mine, but that hadn't been the case. One day, she turned up to the house telling me she was leaving and that she was engaged, and that was that.'

Owen's shoulders visibly relax like he's been needing to get that off his chest for some time. He looks huge against the tiny backdrop of the café, yet vulnerable.

I swallow the delicious bite of lemon macaron that I was chewing but it goes down slightly rough.

'I'm sorry,' I offer. My hand hovers over his macaron-free hand – which I'm surprised he hasn't wolfed down by now – but I get a sense he doesn't want sympathy, since according to his phone call, it's been years and he's fine, and sometimes all you need is to vent. I actually appreciate his willingness to take responsibility for his own actions and own up to his mistakes.

'Jeez, pigeon. You dodged a bullet there, mate,' I joke, making a yuck face. Owen nearly spits out his last bite of biscuit but collects himself just in time to save me from a cappuccino-crumb shower.

'Maybe I did, we were certainly opposites, but I could have tried harder,' he tells me, and for some reason, that erratic heartbeat of mine is back. I chuckle to cover it up in case he can hear it. He's already saved me once today; I don't need him worrying about performing CPR.

'I don't know, forcing you to eat pigeon has evil villain written all over it. You probably got out in the nick of time, just before she recruited you to steal an island.'

'A whole island?' he questions, a grin deepening the dimple on his left cheek.

'A whole island,' I nod, smiling enthusiastically, enjoying my imagination running a little wild.

Owen shakes his head, giving me a soft look. Gold specks dance around his irises.

'Besides, I wouldn't feel too bad. You want to talk about differences? I once broke it off with a girl for not liking chips,' I reveal, much to Owen's clear delight; I get one and a half dimples this time.

A beat of giggles passes before it's my phone that makes my thighs dance across the plastic chair. I hold a finger up to Owen, still chuckling, and not wanting to be rude. He nods understanding.

It's a text from Alex, and this time, along with my manic heartbeat, my breathing becomes a little quicker. I shoot to my feet, nearly knocking over the chair in the process.

'Owen, we've got to go,' I urge, wafting my arms around like that will magically lift him from his chair and get him moving. 'We've got to run.'

Owen gets to his feet, slower than I require, and looks at me as if I've just asked him to chop down a perfectly healthy tree for a bedside table. 'Run? I'm not a runner, Andrea.' He smooths his t-shirt over the roundness of his stomach, which stirs all kinds of things in me that I literally don't have time to think about. My phone chimes again and now I'm pushing Owen out the door, aware that I wouldn't normally behave this way but panic has crept in and I seem to have lost all control.

'The minibus leaves in twenty minutes,' I explain. 'We've got to get back.' It's not lost on me that it took us a good hour or more to descend the mountaintop this morning, and that was without the lively crowds of tourists bumping our elbows. My toes are screaming as we race along the path.

'Do you need a piggyback?' I ask Owen genuinely, with only a hint of teasing. He's a few steps behind me but there's something about his lack of bravado in this situation that's making the creases in my forehead less severe than when I first read Alex's text. I'm not sure if being laid back in this case is a good thing but I like that he isn't pretending he goes to the gym seven days a week and lives off protein shakes and that he hates running as much as I do. I blow away the wayward strands of hair that have broken free of my bun, which doesn't feel so tight right now, and keep pushing up the hill.

'I'd squash you,' Owen calls back, making me stumble over a stone with the tingle that shoots through my thighs. What is wrong with me? My sturdy thighs are meant to thrive on a climb like this, granted they have had zero experience or training, but I thought thick thighs would shine at a time like this – more power and all.

I grumble in place of a proper response. 'Mmm hmm.'

Next time I need to remember sunglasses and a hat; the sun has seriously done something to my mind and I'm feeling all sorts of discombobulated.

'Are you doing alright, Andrea?' Another shout from behind.

I choose to keep forging ahead, my eyes focused on the uneven road before me instead of looking back at Owen and his hulk-like build powering up the Italian mountainside. In response, I send him a thumbs up, holding my arm above my head.

'Are you hitchhiking?' comes a voice, followed by an obnoxiously loud horn. I startle and grab the railing to my right.

'Alex, what are you doing?' I gasp, once I've collected myself. Stepping off the small footpath, I move towards the white minibus that pulls up alongside Owen and me.

'Alex, thank god,' Owen huffs, resting a hand on his hip.

'Jump in,' she orders enthusiastically, 'we're going to be late.' Her pep doesn't scream fake to me, which I find odd as my stomach immediately plummets to abyssal plains, thinking that I've let her down, that they had to come and find me because I wasn't where I was supposed to be, doing what I was supposed to be doing, which was organising the group and ensuring we were on schedule. All because I was dealing with a catastrophe of my own doing. I feel as if I'm single handedly causing this whole week to go awry.

Charlie shoves my shoulder as I take a seat in the bus, interrupting the pity party going on in my head. She wiggles her eyebrows at me, a broad grin on her glistening, tanned face, which I don't quite understand – shouldn't she be scowling? – until Owen squeezes in next to me and I connect the dots.

I narrow my eyes as narrow as they can go without closing them, warning Charlie not to comment on what she is currently concocting in her mind. With Owen's beefy forearms pressed against my more slight ones, I'm too frazzled to comprehend my feelings right now. Plus, I have no alibi as to what we were doing in Positano town at the first sign of light without putting my foot in it even more.

Thankfully, we're only fifteen minutes late for our limoncello workshop. As Italians are renowned for their laid-back attitudes, our host waves off our apologies and gets started – she'd been late to release the last party, having gotten carried away discussing the properties of lemons and why the Amalfi Coast is home to the finest lemons you will ever come across. I can't help smiling at her passion and pride.

When we are ushered through a small house-cum-reception area, I am once again in another disappointing outfit in a stunning Italian location. It's a good job I don't have one of those Instagram accounts. My joggers and long-sleeved tee are not worthy of the impressive landscape that surrounds me, which I guess would be more Dior suitable and Dolce & Gabbana affluent – I've seen the perfume adverts.

Alex and Charlie certainly look the part in their suave, casual yet put-together ensembles of black and white playsuits that complement each other just so. I glance at Owen and his joggers that aren't too dissimilar to mine, then make a beeline for Alex and Charlie as soon as our guide instructs us to team up.

'Well hello,' Charlie says, draping a cocky arm over my shoulders. 'Early bird gets the worm, I see.'

'Oh Charlie, really?' I scoff, not caring for her innuendo. I shrug her arm off me.

'Honey, be nice.' Alex comes to my rescue while at the

same time moving a soft wave of hair out of Charlie's face, so not quite the total punishment for her crudeness towards her best friend that I would have liked, but that's Alex – as sweet as a perfectly ripe peach and hopelessly in love. I give Charlie my own deep glare.

'But Andi, do tell us what's going on there apart from maid of honour and best man hijinks? I do hope the two of you won't be late for the big day,' Alex continues, and I can see that I've worried her even though she keeps her voice light. That doesn't sit well in my stomach; it feels as sour as the citrus scent that hits the air as everyone begins carefully peeling their lemon rinds.

'Nothing is going on.' As I say it, I find myself glancing at Owen, who is already looking my way. He offers a small smile before getting on with Zia Allegra. His cheeks are a touch rosy and Zia Allegra waves her lemon peeler in the air, her voice booming about girls and something about wining and dining and not letting the good ones get away. My chest expands like my heart is physically trying to reach for him to share the pain of the conversation I know must be anything but a delight for him.

'We were grabbing coffee and I'm sorry, I won't be late again, I promise. I got swallowed up by the tourists and lost track of time is all.' I try to reassure her that I'm taking this maid of honour business seriously, though I know I've not exactly proved it so far and she doesn't know the half of it. I don't look away from her until she has given me eye contact and can see how serious I am. When she does look up, she gives me a small nod.

'Do you like my best friend, Andi?' Charlie asks bluntly, not dropping the Owen topic. I don't miss Alex looking slightly bothered by this idea, until she sees Charlie's broad smile and then she smiles too.

'No. I mean yes, I like him, Charlie,' I stutter. 'He's a nice guy, a friend, you know. A good friend to work with.' Forget a rain cloud, it's like the sun is directly over my head. I'm roasting and can feel beads of sweat dancing all over my body as I add spoonfuls of sugar to our jar.

I sense three pairs of eyes on me. I ignore Owen's as he's probably just checking everyone's doing the right thing, keeping his head up, doing his own best man duties, but I can't ignore Alex and Charlie's glares that are teaming with the sun above my head and heating my neck.

'I've never seen you this flustered over a human before,' Alex informs me much to my chagrin.

'Alex, please, I'm not flustered. I'm British, it's a million degrees out here, and I'm trying to concentrate on making this limoncello with the precise amount of grappa so it doesn't kill us,' I huff.

'It's OK to like him,' she presses, though the twitch in her eye tells me otherwise.

'I don't like him like that. I'm not looking for a relationship,' I reply firmly, trying to keep my hand steady as I funnel in the grappa with Alex and Charlie's eyes studying me intensely. 'I don't need anyone.' I can feel my skin begin to prickle and the back of my neck tensing at the topic. I've relied on people before, for happiness, for stress relief, for comfort, but it always ends miserably. Either they break it off because of my workload or I find a way to break it off because they don't understand said workload.

When you're standing in the middle of a flooded chip shop and turn to someone who is apparently supposed to have your back in a crisis situation, and all they can yell down the phone is 'you should come out, stop stressing, come and dance, loosen up', while music blares in the background, you learn quickly that your mum is right: you do things yourself, you don't trust anyone to have your back or burden anyone with your problems.

Suddenly, all I can think about is how that workload is going to increase when I get back home if Mum decides she wants nothing to do with the shop anymore and leaves the legacy to me.

'Who helped you clean up that mess in the chip shop?' Alex asks, knowing exactly where my mind has drifted to. I close my eyes and place the bottle of grappa down, allowing Charlie to take over and finish the last few drops to fill our jar.

'You did,' I say, my voice quiet, reminiscent of her coming to Mum's and my rescue.

'Right, and while, no, you didn't need me, and you and your mum are badasses that had most of the mess cleaned up by the time I got to you, I wanted to be there. It got done even quicker then, and you definitely needed the chocolate fudge cake I brought with me,' she says with a warm smile, poking me on the tip of my nose.

'I still dream about that fudge cake,' I reply, enjoying the brief relief thinking about food gives my brain.

'Sometimes, we have to let people in and take the help, because chocolate cake is better than no chocolate cake.' Alex's eyes beam at me, their familiarity and warmth loosening a few of the smaller knots in the back of my neck.

'So what you're saying is, never say no to chocolate cake?' I raise my eyes and crinkle my nose in thought, trying to make sense of Alex's metaphor as images of Owen giving me pastries for my thoughts play like a movie trailer in my head – loud, vibrant, exciting – but the pop of Charlie fastening the lid onto our jar pulls me quickly from that silly theatre room and deposits me back into reality. Owen and me, we're on the same page, and croissants are not the same as chocolate fudge cake.

11

This evening, I'm slightly tipsy on limoncello, not the one that we made today, as that needs to proof for at least sixty days before Will and Gio can enjoy it, but the good stuff from Nonna Roberta's cabinet. I'd love to take our jar home to recreate nights like this one, but I doubt airport security would allow me to take a large jar of highly flammable liquid that contains 99.9 per cent alcohol, a sprinkle of sugar and a few lemon rinds, onto an aircraft.

The sky over the mountaintop acts like a blanket of twinkling lights, illuminating the terrace for our meal. Gio's family made a focaccia that melts on my tongue; it's fluffy, salty and rich, made with the purest olive oil with a hint of bitterness that is pleasant and works with the sun-dried tomatoes and olives embedded in the top. I can't stop eating it, even now after a large portion of mussels in white wine and garlic sauce, calamari with spaghetti and a generous bowl of profiteroles.

I'm munching the delectable bread as Owen tucks into a second helping of creamy, chocolatey 'roles courtesy of Nonna Roberta. There's a hint of pink in his cheeks that I'm guessing the shots of limoncello and full stomach has put there. I press the back of my hand against my own cheek and know they're flushing too.

'There's nowhere more beautiful than the Amalfi Coast,' Alex suddenly stands and cheers, causing my eyes to snap away from Owen and glance nervously around the table. A feeling of getting caught in I don't know what makes my chewing slow down until I'm sure all eyes are on Alex. 'In this villa, we celebrate all love and I can't believe I get to marry this incredible woman in just two more sleeps,' she yells.

We all raise our red wine and I sink back into my chair, letting the sounds of the evening wash over me. There's the low hum of crickets mixed with laughter from around our table and others in the distance – it's a common song in the Italian evenings, I've noticed. After my chat with Alex and Charlie earlier at the workshop, I've not had a chance to talk to Owen. When we got back to the villa, I went straight to my room to make the most of the luxury tub and bath products. With the morning's sweaty start, the scorching hot water and scented bubbles relaxed my aching muscles.

To avoid thinking about Ned's, about Mum or about Owen, I lit some candles – vanilla scented – and picked up the book that Alex insisted on buying for me at the airport. A book she said I needed and would suck me in.

For a while, it was bliss, and had done exactly as Alex intended, until the woman herself burst into my bathroom with a limoncello halo around her head – a bouncing light beam personified – her phone aloft, snapping pictures.

'Oh my god, Alex, what are you doing?' I'd screamed. 'Put your phone away.'

'I'm capturing this precious moment in time that you, Andrea Adams, are taking some me time,' she'd said. 'How's the book?'

I'd scowled until she put her phone down. 'Good, thanks,' I replied hesitantly.

'Now, come on, you can't hide away from Owen in here forever; you're a badass, we own our feelings,' she'd then said, grabbing me a towel and opening it up for me to step into.

'You were literally just taking pictures and praising me for relaxing! I'm not hiding from anyone,' I protested – my best friend had definitely been sipping the Aperol spritzes by the pool that afternoon.

Though I couldn't deny that I would have happily stayed in the bathroom all evening if I hadn't heard what was on the menu for dinner.

'Come on,' Alex wafted the towel encouragingly, 'I know I might not have liked the idea of you and Owen at first because he's a touch grumpy and sarcastic and you need someone that loves love and loves you because you're the best and I know how incredible you are, and if I wasn't marrying Charlie, I'd marry you. And Owen doesn't like marriage, and he's an enabler... but Charlie loves him, so I know you're safe.' Alex's words were sweet and unexpected, and only a little slurred as she explained all the thoughts drifting through her mind. I liked when Alex was happy and not mad at me, even if I was still mad at her for dragging me to Italy. My heart had tugged at her kind-of marriage proposal, while I couldn't help giggling that she thought Owen was grumpy.

I'd stepped into the towel. 'Come on, stop worrying about

me. I have lots of people around me who love me, and while I adore you for your offer to wed me, you can't, because you're marrying Charlie and it's going to be amazing,' I told her, towel-drying my hair while she sat on the edge of the bath.

'You don't think I'm stupid for getting married, for having a wedding?' Her tone was soft, a little vulnerable. I'd dropped my hair towel, a knot of guilt in my stomach at my own sarcastic ways and how they had made her feel. I'd been the only stupid one.

'Not at all, Alex.' I'd cupped her cheek. 'Nothing you do is stupid, nothing at all. This is right for you, this is what you want and you are doing it because of love, and when we do things for the right reasons, it's not silly at all. I'm sorry if I ever made you feel silly,' I'd told her, my mum's words reminiscent in my mind, and wanting to put Alex first, no matter the anxiety that still nestled heavily in my stomach.

'You don't make me feel silly, you keep me on my toes and I love you for it, but sometimes your venom towards love frightens me – love can be beautiful,' she'd said, messing with my damp, frizzy hair. I'd looked down at her sparkling white toenails, knots reforming in my neck that the bath had loosened for a while.

'I know, honey, it can be beautiful for you, it is beautiful for you, OK?'

'Where was my invite to the bubble bath party?' Charlie had interrupted, not one crinkle of worry or jealously across her features, just adoration in her eyes as she looked from Alex to me. 'My girls, is everything OK?' she'd then asked, walking over to sit next to Alex on the tub.

'Oh, don't you know?' I'd started with a grimace. 'Alex and I are getting married now; your wedding has been cancelled.'

Alex whipped a bath towel at my thigh, causing me to howl, before she pushed Charlie backwards into the chilly remains of my luxury bath.

Now, the chatter around the table picks up over espresso, biscotti and more limoncello. I'm content nibbling on the square of focaccia that I stopped Gio taking away from the table. I catch Owen's eye, having not realised I was looking his way, and he smiles. It's wholesome and makes me giggle as I think back to Alex calling him grumpy. Yes, he keeps to himself and might throw a sarcastic comment into the world every now and again, but if he lets you in, he's passionate and funny and kind.

Had he let me in? Why does that feel important when I know I can't return the favour? I don't want a relationship and I don't think Owen does either.

'Have you tried that citrus bubble bath?' Owen asks, cutting through my thoughts when he pulls up a seat next to me. I take it he had the same idea as me this afternoon for he's now wearing a fresh outfit – a crisp, large, white t-shirt and black cargo shorts – and smells like oranges and lemons. My crazy thoughts immediately vanish into the ether as I'm brought into the present by his eyes that glow grey under the soft bulbs.

'Yes, my skin has never felt so silky soft,' I say enthusiastically, rubbing a hand over my forearm. Owen watches my movements and chuckles.

'Right, I'm not usually a bath person but they seduced me with their goodie bag of soaps and bubble bath,' he tells me.

'Oh, don't get me started on my dream bathroom. Can you imagine a clawfoot tub, pretty turquoise tiles, shelves for plants and a wooden sink unit with deep porcelain sinks? I mean, plants in a bathroom, who knew, right?'

Owen's eyes stay locked on mine; they seem to twinkle a beat, flashes of green flicker around his dark irises before he speaks. 'That sounds fantastic.' His voice comes out rough, causing him to clear his throat and look away.

'Owen, I have an extremely important question for you,' I say boldly, the focaccia in my hand having been forgotten as I point it at him, excited by my question. Could you get drunk off of olive oil? 'Carpet or no carpet?' I say.

'I think someone needs to lay off the limoncello.' I hear Charlie's voice behind me, her hand on my shoulder. Alex is giggling like we're back in high school. I look at Owen, who rakes a hand through his wavy locks and narrows his eyes at me.

'I love the no carpet aesthetic because the more wood and natural pieces the house has, I think the better,' he replies, making me sit up straighter in my chair and put down my focaccia, only to pick up a profiterole.

'Yes, I love wood, the wood vibe is gorgeous,' I exclaim, much to Charlie and Alex's delight – their giggling increases. Owen ignores them, so I continue my happy questioning.

'What would you do in a bedroom?' I ask eagerly, popping the profiterole in my mouth, ready to listen to Owen's ideas. Alex and Charlie bark, making me jump a little.

'Please, Owen, do tell us what you like to do in the bedroom?' Charlie says, and that's when I hear it. My cheeks flush and the profiterole I just devoured rolls over in my stomach. I smack my hand to my forehead.

'Oh god, Owen, I didn't mean it like that!' I say quickly, shoving Charlie's hips, pushing her away from my chair.

Owen chuckles, which doesn't help calm the flipping profiterole in my stomach. I've got flashes of bedrooms, Owen, wood and candle-lit bathtubs in my head, and it's all making some sort of delicious, curious potion in my mind that I now can't shake. I close my eyes and breathe, trying to dispel the images but not entirely sure that I want to. They are pretty appealing and have caught me completely off guard. I'm never letting Alex and Charlie near limoncello again after this week.

'Come on, honey, let's give our maid of honour and our best man some privacy, I think they need it,' Charlie teases, and without opening my eyes, I can hear them shuffle away. When I think it's safe, I open one eye, only to find Owen leaning forward in his chair, his meaty hands clasped together, making the slight curve of his biceps pop, and a delicate smile on his face causing his left dimple to appear. How can Italy be so hot even when the sun has long since gone to sleep? It wasn't fair.

'I'd do...' Owen starts, simply dismissing Charlie's teasing and attempts at turning the conversation to wicked territory, which for some reason causes a warm flutter in my belly. Somehow, I don't think I can be as respectful as Owen is clearly being, because I don't think I can deal with him talking about interior design in the bedroom, innocent or not. I've suddenly become a woman who gets turned on at the idea of a man talking about how he fluffs his duvet.

I rudely, I admit, interrupt him talking.

'Profiterole?' I offer, practically shoving one in his face.

'No thank you,' he says with a gentle smirk and a slight

squint of his eyes, like my changing the subject is not lost on him. 'Andrea, can I ask you something?'

'Sure,' I croak, gulping down the huge bite of profiterole I had taken. He looks serious and there's a slight difference to the smirk on his face; it's bordering dangerous rather than its usual playfulness. Our usual easy, casual banter, saving-the-day missions and marriage-bashing has been replaced by a spark of something tempting, but I am not about to become a wedding weekend cliché of best man and maid of honour getting together. And I'm sure Owen would want no part of that either. What do they put in the focaccia here? I lick the cream from dessert off my finger and look nowhere near Owen's eyes when I do so.

'What do you like to do when you're not working?' Owen asks, sipping his wine slowly, his eyes intense as ever, and for a split second, I wish I could give him a sexy, playful answer – but that would be a total lie for appearances' sake, and I'm not about lies. The second passes and my brain returns to normal, my shoulders automatically move up and down as I huff.

'I like to pay the bills to keep things running, fix the mounting pile of things that need fixing in the chip shop. Ooh, I help my mum with jobs at her house, there are always things that need fixing there, it's an old house. Like I mentioned, I see Alex and Charlie over drinks when I can,' I pause and lean forward, my t-shirt dress scraping my ankles. 'You know what I dream about sometimes, Owen,' I whisper, this time looking into his undemanding eyes.

'What's that, Andrea?' he whispers back, his lips glistening from his wine.

'I used to really love cooking. Sometimes, I think about

how delightful it would be to pour myself a glass of wine, put some music on and cook for enjoyment.' I tell him, aware that my eyes have slipped away from his and glazed over, as the red wine in his glass looks blurry – a fuzzy, murky red.

There have been times – when I've declined pub invites and girls' holidays – that I've considered my life to be simple, maybe on the boring side, but in this day and age, how can one not be grateful for a roof over their head and a way to make ends meet?

I've seen cafés and pubs close down right next door to Mum and me, so if opening more days and working longer hours to claw back profits on what we lost during hard times is what we have to do to keep us from shutting down, then I'm going to do it. Mind, who would want to buy out a rundown chip shop? My grandad would come back to haunt me if we ever sold it. Is Mum prepared to live with that guilt if she turns her back?

Owen smiles softly, and as I've gotten used to, takes his time with a response like he's processing all the information I have given him. I feel as though I should find it unnerving the way he takes his time like that, like he's studying me, but instead, I find my skin warm.

'A spot of British TV always makes me feel at home,' he chirps, adopting a heavier British accent.

'How often do you get home these days?' I ask, feeling more relaxed now, the wine making me feel sleepy. I could curl up in a ball on this chair like a cat, if I'm not careful. I push my wine glass away from my tempted hands.

'I speak with my mum and dad most days and pop home a couple times a year. I'm due a visit after the wedding.

Neither of them can make it and both want a rundown and to see pictures,' he tells me, putting down his own wine glass, which contains one or two sips left.

The wine in my stomach swirls and sloshes at the thought of being that far away from my mum. I couldn't do it. I wonder if Owen finds it hard, but before I can ask him, a glass shatters somewhere near the end of the balcony and with it, a howl of merry laughter explodes into the night. Zia Allegra is wafting her shawl out to her sides, making her look like a bat, while Alex sways, moving through the crowd, trying to keep Charlie upright. It's the sound of 'party's over' in my ears.

Owen and I catch each other's eye for a second that unexpectedly appears to be free of loud noises and distraction. We hold each other's smile before standing at the same time. I narrowly miss cracking my head on his chin, which he seems to be aware of as he awkwardly hovers a bear-like paw over my forehead as I straighten up, uncurling my legs off the chair. The cool evening air suddenly feels gentle and warm around me, but I don't have time to spare to analyse the terrifying concoction of thoughts that have been going through my mind today, as Alex is suddenly stood tipsily by my side.

Immediately, Owen frees Alex of Charlie's light but swaying load by hooking his arm under her armpit and practically scooping her off her feet. Charlie makes a small groaning sound but she looks like she's sleep walking. When Owen notices her shirt dress shifting up her thighs, he carefully sweeps her into his arms, ensuring she's not flashing anyone, while Alex nuzzles her cheeks into my collarbone, faintly snoring.

Wrapping one arm around Alex's shoulder to steady her, I quickly clink a glass with my fork with the other.

'For anyone wanting to walk the Path of the Gods tomorrow, please be up early as we are meeting in the kitchen at eight forty-five,' I announce, unable to help myself from rolling my eyes at Owen with Alex softly snoring in my ear.

We manage the walk to Alex and Charlie's room, nodding our heads and saying goodnight to the rest of the guests that had joined us for dinner, Will and Gio kissing Alex and Charlie on the foreheads as we pass them, their fatherly expressions a mixture of amusement and endearment.

Once in their room, Owen places Charlie carefully on the bed and tucks her in, which causes me to wobble and nearly send Alex to her knees in a crumpled heap. I catch myself and her just in time and let out an exasperated sigh as Owen disappears into the bathroom.

'Come on, trouble,' I say to Alex as I nudge her into the bed. She flops onto the sheets and I pull the covers up to her chin so she looks like a cosy dumpling.

'I'm not trouble,' she murmurs, tugging and pulling her hand out the blanket, pointing her index finger in the air then side to side. 'But you two are,' she finishes with a barely there whisper.

I freeze, unable to look at Owen, as the sudden intimacy of this little endeavour washes over me. The room is dark except for a sliver of the silver moon that slips through the tall, arched window. It's night time. It's bedtime. Alex and Charlie are safely tucked in and now I'm going to go and tuck myself into bed, and no, I don't need Owen to do that for me.

I turn away and walk towards the door as I hear Owen

place glasses of water on either side of the bed, and then too quickly, his stacked frame is by my side.

Shutting the door quietly behind us, I'm extremely aware of his body heat and proximity.

'Thank you for that,' I croak and take a step back so my face isn't inches away from his broad chest.

'No, thank you,' he replies, voice coming out a little higher than I'm used to.

'OK, bedtime,' I say, daring to look up and praying his night time grey eyes don't swallow me whole. Whoever I was praying to clearly wasn't paying me any attention. I feel my lungs expand with a sharp intake of breath that I don't want to make obvious, but when I try and keep my breath quiet, it gets caught in my throat, making me splutter.

'Are you OK?' Owen asks, that hand hovering again, this time over my shoulder. Not touching, just hovering, causing my body to heat.

'I'm fine, thank you. Good job team,' I say hastily, nodding at the door and holding my hand up for a high five. I completely ignore the sizzle in my fingertips when Owen's hand engulfs mine, and skip backwards down the hall towards my room. 'Night, Owen,' I shout.

'Goodnight, Andrea,' I hear faintly down the corridor, and the way my heart feels feral rattling against the cage in my chest when he says Andrea and not Andi, I completely ignore that too.

12

It's eight-thirty the next morning and I've secured a megaphone from one of Will's renovation projects and am walking the halls ensuring everyone has enough time to get up and dressed. I haven't seen Owen yet, but I have squawked outside his door, reminding myself that the task of maid of honour is a sacred one and the quicker I get everything done and the smoother I achieve each chore, the sooner I will be back home and the happier Alex and Charlie will be. I don't need whatever wine-induced fuzzy feelings were messing with me last night.

Feeling more like my in-control self, I have coffee prepared for everyone on the stove, bottles of water at the ready and even a first aid kit full of supplies thanks to Nonna Roberta, who giggled at me when I had asked if she was coming on this excursion. Apparently, the Path of the Gods is not for the faint hearted or the elderly, who, in her words, have had their fill of outings already this week. *Tell me about it*, I had thought.

Under the duties scribbled in my notebook for Ned's, I made a to-do list of remaining jobs to get through today, concentrating hard on not letting my eyes drift across my list of impending errands back home when I wrote the new additions. My main goal of the day: getting a group of most likely hungover adults up and down the severe rocky paths, steep hills and narrow cliff edges of the *Sentiero degli Dei* safely, while sneaking off at some point to pick up the wedding favours without drawing attention to myself. So not that big a mission.

Slowly, the party begin to gather in the kitchen, Alex and Charlie looking a little worse for wear. Eyes barely open, still gripping onto the hope of sleep. I place croissants in front of them along with espresso and count the room, pleased that everything is running smoothly so far. I just need Owen to turn up.

'Charlie, please can you go shout Owen again for me,' I ask, before turning my attention to the group. 'If everyone would like to make sure they have a bottle of water and then make their way to the front driveway. You should all have a printed map with you that can be found on the breakfast table. You can pair up or walk in groups as it's not recommended you go at this alone,' I finish, taking a breath and feeling more like myself, more in control than I have in days. We have a few more people joining us for this expedition and I notice the woman from the party the other night glare at me, that blingtastic engagement ring narrowing its carats at me like it's mocking me and my last words.

It can't know of my one-woman plan of shimmying up and down the mountain on my own. Could it sense the hypocrisy in my voice, my plan to do everything alone, always? My wedding finger twitches, the phantom feel of where my own engagement ring used to sit making me shudder. No, I shake my head, I didn't need some expensive jewel back then and I sure as hell don't need one now. My plan is going to work today, I tell my brain as I look over my list. The thought of getting into my comfy bed tonight and being able to place a tick beside each line of my to-do list is enough to propel me forward.

I'm walking out the kitchen as Charlie, tortoise-like, meets me at the door.

'He's not in his room; he's probably already out watching the sunrise or pottering about his workshop or something,' she informs me, lazily.

An unpleasant dip occurs low in my stomach at the thought of not seeing Owen, his scruffy bed hair, light stubble and grey joggers, before starting the day, as I have grown accustomed to over the past few mornings, but I swiftly ignore it and march on. It's a good thing. With one day and one sleep in front of the wedding, there is no time for distractions.

'Right, OK, let's go,' I call out to the party and move into the morning light.

It doesn't take long for me to start sweating; every step is mismatched, requiring pure concentration and the use of pretty much every muscle in my body. My thighs and bottom twinge from the larger platforms and chunky stones and my ankles are screaming from the small skips and jumps the narrower paths and stairs make us do. With each swat of a fly, I wobble on the uneven ground, and have to remind myself a couple of times to pause and take note of the view. If I thought the villa had a view for an art gallery, this one would have private exhibition written all over it.

The sky bears but a few plumes of misty clouds, the sun illuminating the glistening navy sea that is far, far below us and the picturesque colours of Positano make it seem as if we are standing atop a rainbow that has nestled into the mountainside.

We are ascending higher and I still haven't been able to make a break for it from Alex and Charlie.

'What did you and Owen get up to when you left our room last night?' Charlie asks when we take another water break, the air around us growing choppier. I know water is supposed to help but I feel myself getting a stitch where it settles in my stomach. I dig my nails into the ridge over my hip.

'We made mad, passionate love on the balcony,' I retort, not wishing to be outdone by Charlie's taunts today. The heat, the sweat, my aching muscles and the fear that the lady from the bakery is going to sell my fifty macarons, are threatening a crankiness I am doing my best to keep under control.

Alex splutters on her water while Charlie raises her bottle, impressed, a smirk carved into her pretty face.

'Was I a gentleman?' Owen's voice makes my whole body jolt like I've just been electrocuted by an unexpected stray bolt of lightning on this sunny day. I grab my chest for fear that my heart is going to come crashing through it and squeeze my eyes shut tight to catch my breath. When I open them, he's in front of me, black cargo shorts, large white tee, sweat on his brow and hair flipped over just so, his pink lips bearing a cheeky smile. It's like the mountain is magic, the fog some sort of wedding week mist that sends people's emotions amok.

'Absolutely,' I say, mustering all the confidence I can so I don't die of embarrassment on this hill and get left for the mountain goats to consume.

'Good,' he mutters casually before brushing past me. When I think I'm safe, he leans into my ear, his warm, ragged breath grazing my neck. 'I've secured the macarons; they're safe in the villa,' he whispers and then continues walking ahead.

My stomach drops like a dead weight while simultaneously performing a pirouette. I don't know whether that was the start of an incredibly hot porno, an act of such kindness and thoughtfulness to wet anyone's whistle or that Owen just set back women's rights a hundred years and I should be mad at him for stepping in and helping when I didn't ask for it or need it.

I'm aware that I was having trouble breaking free from this endeavour and I clearly needed the help, but all rational thoughts have soared out of my brain, my contradicting emotions bubbling uncomfortably inside of me.

'Planning your next rendezvous?' Charlie chimes in, wiggling her natural, bushy brows at me.

'Drop it, Charlie, alright, just drop it, please,' I say, my mood turning sour. I'm fed up of her stupid teasing.

'Going to give the mountain goats a show?' She doesn't take the hint and I can't handle it.

'Charlie, give it a rest, we're not having sex. Owen and I are just friends, just friends so would you two stop pushing,' I say, stroppy and indignant.

'Hey, it's all OK, Andi,' Alex steps in, her wavy bob bouncing as she walks closer to me. 'You know she's just messing with you, but we can drop it, OK babe.' She looks from me to Charlie sternly.

I stare at a rock, my mind reeling; I can't catch up with the thoughts racing through it.

'I don't need anyone to do things for me. I can do things for myself. I don't need to be rescued.' I know I'm saying my thoughts out loud but most of the group have passed us now and are miles ahead, so it's just Alex, Charlie and me as far as I know. 'And I don't need to be teased constantly. I'm not having sex and I don't need sex.' Even to my own ears that very much sounded like a person in need and want of sex.

Charlie chuckles in response, obviously thinking the same thing I am, but it's enough to boil my already heated blood. 'You sound like you could do with a good taking care of.'

I don't know if Charlie is still drunk but she's truly pushing it.

'Are you going to let her talk to me like that? I don't need taking care of.' I can hear my voice growing louder. 'I don't need people to do things for me.'

'Come on, Andi, we all need people from time to time. What's this about? Do you want to talk about it?' Alex offers.

'No I don't want to talk about it,' I scoff, tugging at the bobble around my low bun, the sweat on my neck itching my skin. 'I shouldn't be here,' I mumble. 'I have a chip shop to run, and you know how much I hate weddings, and why.' I hear the words, I hear them but I have lost all control over what is coming out of my mouth.

'Andi, it was three years ago, the world doesn't revolve

around you and your aversion to all things love,' Alex says, her voice firm yet soft. I can't look at her, I can feel the hurt in her voice, I don't want to see it in her eyes too, but there's a part of me that can't drop it, can't let go of my own pain.

'When does the world ever revolve around me, Alex?' I laugh and it comes out a maniacal sound, but I can feel the tear that trickles down my cheek along with it. The moments with Owen these past few days have felt all-encompassing and I'm screwing it up as we speak but I can't stop talking.

'I didn't leave your side for a month after what Hannah did. I've listened to you berate love, trash rom-coms that you haven't even watched, disregard romance books I recommend that you won't give the time of day and I felt petrified to tell you my happy news – I'm tired of it, Andrea. I'm getting married tomorrow, I'm in love and it feels amazing. I'm sorry you got hurt but you can't stay closed off forever. It's not like Charlie and I have never been hurt or haven't kissed our fair share of frogs. Maybe you and Owen both need to grow up and drop this whole sarcastic, love sucks act.'

'Hey, come on, there's no need to bring Owen into it, babe,' Charlie comments, and I wish I had the power of laser eyes; I'm so mad at her for protecting Owen given how cruel she has been to me.

'I'm not having a go at him, Charlie, but all this brooding sarcasm. Look at this place...' She waves her arms out across the mesmerising vista, but my eyes are far too misty to appreciate it in this moment. 'It's unbelievable and I'm so freaking happy to be here and to be celebrating us,' Alex finishes and I know her eyes are wet, I can hear it in the slight wobble of her voice, though stoic is what she is leading with. She's angry with me and it makes all the hairs on the back of my neck stand to attention, but I'm angry with her too, with Charlie.

'Of course, celebrate it Alex, celebrate your day, your magical day of love but dragging it out for a whole bloody week. Don't you think it's too much, a little over the top?' The words are out of my mouth before I truly know what I'm saying in my foggy red rage.

'At least it's not a goddamn castle in the middle of nowhere,' Alex bellows this time and it hits me square in the chest, like she's just thrown a rock and it's shattered the glass box around my heart that has been protecting it all these years.

I stagger backwards – if she wanted to shut me up, that's certainly done the trick, and there's a part of me deep down in the splinters of glass that are now stabbing at my heart, uncomfortable and painfully tearing at the seams, that knows I'm wrong, that shutting me up was the right thing to do, but my god if it doesn't hurt.

Silence washes over the mountainside except for the buzzing in my ears and the rattle in my chest. My heart is wriggling like a freshly caught fish. I don't know whether to scream, shout, sit, stand or run as images of that day, images of what was meant to be the happiest day of my life, storm my brain like icy splatters of relentless rain that leave me drenched and there's nothing I can do about it.

Suddenly, there's Mum's words about the shop like a haunted whisper between my eardrums, the fear of the unknown, not being qualified for a life outside my comfort zone – and just like that, like the moment I saw Hannah and Ebony tangled up in each other, I feel like my world is crumbling and I've got nothing to hold on to.

I must be falling now because out of the corner of my eye, I see Alex lunge for me. I see the moment her ankle twists under itself with a loud pop as she trips over an unforgiving loose rock, and then she's on my level in a heap on the floor. Her scream catapults me out of my stupefied state.

'Alex, Alex, I'm so sorry, are you OK?' I say, cradling her head. Her hair is covered in grass and leaves, a light graze on her left cheek.

'Baby, hey, breathe, I'll get you down from here,' Charlie says, trying to scoop Alex up as she writhes around in pain, hands around her shin, ankle limp. I want to throw up.

'What's going on?' Owen's voice booms as he strides over to us, more assertive and confident than I have ever seen him.

'She tripped over that rock, I think she's twisted her ankle or broken it,' I'm rambling, bile rising up my throat as I speak. Charlie is standing now, Alex in her arms, but she's shaking with tears streaming down her cheeks. I try and take Alex off her, wanting to carry her myself; I did this, I can fix it.

'Let me get her, Charlie,' I say as Owen steps in.

'Andi, just stop, I've got her,' Charlie snaps.

'Charlie, she's my best friend, I can fix this. Let me fix it,' I shout.

'You've done enough, Andi,' she says, nudging me out of the way a little.

'Andrea, it's OK, just let me—' Owen starts but I don't let him finish.

'I don't need you to do anything, Owen, OK. I don't need your help with this, I can fix this,' I bark, causing him to step backwards. His grey eyes glisten, his lips part but he doesn't speak, he just moves closer to Charlie.

'Charlie, let me hold her and you keep me on the path, OK, no buts.' His voice is calm and gentle but decisive as he takes Alex from Charlie without waiting for a reply. Her slim thighs look extra demure against Owen's broad chest.

'You tell the rest of the group that we're heading back but they can carry on if they want to,' Charlie says to me as she starts walking. 'Tell my dads that we're going to the hospital, please, they can meet us there. I'll get Zia Allegra to meet us at the bottom of the mountain.'

'But I want to come, I want to help,' I splutter, wanting to hold Alex's hand like that time she held mine when we were six and I fell on my roller blades and sprained my wrist.

'That would be helping,' Charlie tells me firmly and starts guiding Owen down the path.

It takes a good five minutes before my Bambi-like legs listen to the cues my brain is trying to give them, and I turn around to face a steep climb in search of the rest of the party. With every step, I whimper and pant. Every breath like a razor-sharp dagger to my chest.

13

The villa is eerily quiet. It's gone 4 p.m. and I'm pacing Alex and Charlie's room, waiting for any news on their return. I've put fresh, fluffy towels on the bed, iced cucumber water by the bedsides and pulled all the foot masks and face creams from the bathroom as well as treats from the kitchen into baskets on the bed. That way, Alex and Charlie can both rest and be pampered tonight and not worry about a thing.

I lean over the bed to smooth out Alex's pillows, wincing as my knee brushes against the fabric, the cut I received when I tripped up in search of Will and Gio, stinging. It's nothing I don't deserve.

'Alex's parents just got in,' my mum tells me, stepping into the room. My knee jerks and creaks, bringing tears to my eyes.

'I am a terrible person,' I mumble. 'What am I supposed to tell them? Alex was so excited to greet them and show them round this evening and I haven't heard from anyone; I don't know what time they will be back. She gets married in the morning, what have I done?' The tears flow and there's no way I can stop them as I slide down the edge of the bed to the floor. Like fluffy towels are supposed to make up for what I did.

'Oh, honey,' my mum starts as she sits down next to me and places a hand on my unbattered knee. 'They were both happy to go and get freshened up in their room before the onslaught of excitement and greetings ensue. They're very much exhausted from their travels, so don't you worry about that. They know their daughter is in good hands. And Will said Alex is just getting casted up, so give them another hour or two and they'll be home safe.' She pats my knee softly as a gasp escapes my lips.

'A cast? She's going to be wearing a cast on her wedding day. Jesus, what kind of best friend am I?' I dig my knuckles into my eye sockets hard.

My mum chuckles and I have no idea what's funny right now. I've single handedly ruined my best friend's wedding. I'm a complete and utter monster of a human.

'Sweetheart, a wedding day is quite simply just that: a day. There's no magic potion to stop the rain, no secret serum to avoid breakouts, no crystal ball to predict if the marriage will last and you're making the right choice, no neon sign or winning buzzer to tell you you've got the right one.'

'Mum, that whole mentality is what got me in this mess. I appreciate you trying to make me feel better but I screwed up; I let my negativity ruin Alex's day and now she is going to be wearing a cast in all her wedding photos.' I can't hear my mum's views on the system right now.

'Oh, I'm not trying to make you feel better, honey, and I'm aware of your screw ups, but what I'm trying to say, if you will let me, is that it's all perspective. If all Alex and Charlie care about is wedding favours and photoshoot-style pictures, then yes, I guess you could say it's somewhat spoilt, but if I know Alex, it's about love and celebrating that love with family and friends. I don't think a cast is going to devastate this wedding,' Mum says softly, gently rubbing my knee.

'But what about all this fanfare, this whole "wedding week", all this emphasis on putting wedding in front of everything, wedding workshops, wedding crafts, wedding cooking, taking us away from the shop for a whole week, making it all about her,' I say with a slight huff. If Alex doesn't care about the commercialised wedding aspect, then why go through all the trouble of a weeklong wedding extravaganza in Italy?

'Hmmm,' my mum starts, then pauses. 'Honestly darling, I think that was an excuse. I mean, don't get me wrong, it's Alex, and the romance of Italy, the rom-com element of it all is most definitely her, and Charlie too, but she's not daft. When was the last time you took a break?'

'Mum, come on, we can't afford to take a break,' I try to argue.

Mum scoffs, 'I don't know about you but while that might be so, I've been gagging for a break.'

'You really are thinking about getting rid of Ned's, aren't you?' I ask, sitting up a little straighter.

'My point is, you put wedding in front of anything and people find it hard to say no. How often does Alex get to see her parents? How many girls' holidays have you missed – I'll answer that: all of them. So yes, maybe a part of it is selfish, but honey, can you honestly tell me that spending a week in Italy with your best friend, for once not missing out, is such a bad thing?' She turns to me and gently runs a delicate finger along my cheek as I try to process everything she has just said.

'No,' is what comes out, what says it all really. Besides all the wedding fluff – I know, but I still can't quite warm to that yet – I wouldn't call making pasta with luscious views, drinking the world's best limoncello and having wonderful conversations with a heart-stoppingly gorgeous man, a week ill spent. And yes, I said it, Owen is soul-achingly beautiful, and he probably hates me.

Before I can backpedal and ask my mum further questions about our chip shop, which she is being infuriatingly cryptic about, I hear a loud bang as what sounds like the heavy front door opens and closes.

I shoot up to my feet, the pain in my cut causing me to shriek as I straighten my stiffening leg.

'They're home,' I say, suddenly frozen to the spot.

'Maybe give them a minute or two, let Alex see her parents first,' my Mum suggests, wrapping a hand around my bicep.

'OK,' I whisper, tears threatening my eyes once more as my mum guides me down the hall to my room.

My body prickling with goosebumps and a sudden shiver stirs me awake, as apparently hiking mixed with emotional stress, arguing with your best friend and putting her in the hospital the night before her wedding day is enough to render one exhausted. I hadn't meant to fall asleep. I wipe the drool from the corner of my mouth and rub my arms as

I sit up. The moon is a pearly glow outside of my window which is letting in enough light evening breeze to make me chilly.

I need to find Alex and talk to her. The thought causes my stomach to gurgle and growl. It occurs to me that I haven't eaten since breakfast, but I can't eat and enjoy any such pleasure before I have fixed things with my best friend.

The hallway is quiet, though the eerie feel from earlier has disappeared and has been replaced by a warmth that only the laughter I can hear on the terrace and a full house can infuse into the walls, giving the large stone structure its cosy, inviting vibes.

I chance a peek into Alex and Charlie's bedroom, not quite sure I can face the whole party just yet and breathe a sigh of relief to find Alex curled up on the bed, snoring lightly.

At this point, I feel waking her up would be the least of my sins and I'm running out of time to make this right before her big day, so I tiptoe in, not wanting to scare her.

When I reach the bed, I slowly kneel onto it and go to reach for her shoulder to gently shake her, but I get a sudden cushion blow to the head and let out a wail of a scream.

'Have you snuck in to finish the job? Murder me before I can walk down the aisle?' Alex asks, placing the cushion back at her side and leaning on it to help sit herself up.

'I could never murder you. Just think of the mess,' I reply. We both laugh a barely there laugh and then sit in silence for a beat.

'I'm so sorry, Alex,' I say first. 'I'm sorry for making this week about me, about hate and painful pasts instead of love and your happiness. I'm sorry for never watching rom-coms with you and for disregarding your book recommendations when I know how much joy you get from them; what kind of best friend doesn't listen to their best friend talk about books? I'm a villain if there ever was one.' I hang my head.

'That is a very villainous thing to do,' she mutters under her breath.

'I know and I don't know how to express how incredibly sorry I am to have hurt you. I love you and Charlie so much and I'm truly happy for you. I didn't mean all those nasty things I said,' I explain, fiddling with the crinkles of the duvet.

'The thing is, you did, you did mean them, Andi,' she replies, and my heart feels too heavy for my body, like it's about to drop out of my foot any minute. 'And it's OK. I knew this would be a big ask and there were parts of me, with all the excitement, that just ignored it. I thought that if I wasn't thinking about the past then it wouldn't matter and you would forget about it too because we'd be having so much fun.' She reaches out and takes my hand that is anxiously faffing with the duvet and steadies it.

'It's not OK, Alex, none of it is OK. You brought us here, looked after us – my mum is having the time of her life and all I've done is complain and moan about wedding duties and cocked up at every opportunity,' I argue, embarrassed that I've treated her this way.

She squeezes my hand. 'You wouldn't be you if you weren't complaining or moaning about "the system".' She uses air quotes with her free hand when she says 'the system' and chuckles. It's music to my ears.

'I'm sorry that I sometimes dismiss your fears about Ned's, about money,' she then says, which causes my eyes to widen in surprise. Of course I tell her when I can't afford things, but I've never shared with her how it sometimes makes me feel when I can't do all the things she can, how on occasion, her ignorance of our two different worlds can make me feel so small, because I know she doesn't do it maliciously and her sorry just now is proof of that. I'm about to tell her it's OK when she continues.

'Sometimes I get angry with you when you don't let me help you. I get angry at the chip shop, that you say no to everything because of it when I could simply just help you, but I know while I think that may be kind, it makes you feel worthless, and I never mean to do that. I just want you to be happy and live your life and have all the things I have,' she admits.

I place my other hand on top of hers. 'Thank you,' I whisper, 'thank you, Alex. I appreciate you saying that. If I'm honest, Ned's makes me angry sometimes too. I feel so much pressure to keep my grandparents' legacy going, to provide for and help my mum, that I've made it my whole goddamn personality. And if a decent fish and chips in Manchester is one's whole personality, I can't imagine how dull it must be to be my best friend.'

She snorts at that. 'It's better than a decent fish and chips though,' she says with a smile that's warm and not icy as I was expecting.

'The point is, I need to find some form of balance with work and life and stop thinking I'm the only one with problems,' I confess.

'Is that what this is? You're offloading your problems, sharing them with others so you don't feel so alone?' She waves her hand over her casted ankle and I grimace.

'Now come on, that's not a problem, it's an exclusive accessory,' I say, shaking my head at the trouble I caused.

'You're not wrong. I imagine I'm the only bride who has one for her wedding day.'

I think back to what my mum said about what this wedding means to Alex but it's trumped by my own thoughts. 'I'm sorry I've ruined your wedding photos, Alex, and that you spent the day before your wedding in an Italian hospital.'

She tugs at my hand that's in hers.

'If anything, you've made the wedding photos more interesting and it will be a story to entertain us for years.'

'You're not mad that they're not going to be perfect?' I ask, looking up into her tired eyes.

'Andi, I've not been dreaming about the perfect wedding day; there's no such thing as perfect. I just want to marry Charlie; I want to wear the white dress and have snot bubbles when saying my vows. I want to watch my dad awkwardly wriggle around the dance floor, have my mum blinking in every perfect wedding shot and have my wedding-hating maid of honour forget where she put the rings seconds before I walk down the aisle.'

'I thought that's what this whole wedding week was about: you starring in your own rom-com?' I say, slightly shocked by her revelations and the accuracy of her predictions for the big day – except, yes, I do know where the rings are right now: safe in my bedside drawer.

'Of course I want the rom-com, but I don't want anyone else's rom-com, I want mine, Andrea. It's not about sticking wedding in front of everything, as you so eloquently put it; it's about taking time out of the whole rat race just for a second, and spending time together in spite of what the world can sometimes throw at us. It's about love. For the record, Hannah was a cheating mare but you can't let her ruin love for you. One bad rom-com does not define all rom-coms,' she finishes with a nod. Her cheeks are flushing red, which could be from the pain medicine, but she's becoming more animated and springy to the touch like my Alex.

It still stings, hearing Hannah's name, but deep down, I know Alex is right. I can't let Hannah or my dad dictate my life anymore. I can't keep carrying around that pain, that anger.

'If you threw all caution to the wind right now and just listened to your heart, what does it want?' she asks, clasping both my hands in hers now and fluttering her eyelashes at me.

Instantly, I see images of Owen in my mind. I see him smiling as he helps himself to another slice of cheesecake. I see him caressing random pieces of furniture. I see him, his intense grey eyes looking at me, really looking at me when I speak. I see him accepting my apology and I gulp hard.

'I need to apologise to Owen,' I tell her and her eager smile softens.

'I think he called it a night a little while ago; maybe let him sleep on it,' Alex offers, 'and Andi, don't think, just do, OK. Don't think about what will or won't happen, what might or might not happen, just let it be. You can't keep trying to protect your heart in case of what-ifs; unfortunately, life doesn't tend to work like that. We can't always plan and control everything, but that's OK because I've got you,' she says, tucking a wayward strand of hair behind my ear.

I smile at those words. The same words she said to me moments after Hannah ripped my heart to shreds.

'I've got you too,' I tell her. 'Tomorrow is going to be like Hallmark crashed the Amalfi Coast and are filming a brand new lesbian rom-com, I promise.'

'I don't think Hallmark do lesbians,' she retorts with a smile.

'More for me then,' Charlie cuts in, making Alex laugh. My eyes crinkle at the merry sound and simultaneously roll at Charlie's comment.

'You're bound to one lesbian for happily ever after,' I say, bouncing over to Charlie and wrapping my arms around her. 'I'm sorry for maiming your fiancée; I promise no more maid of Chucky and more maid of honour from here on out.'

Charlie squeezes me back. 'I promise no more teasing you about your clear desire to make out with my best friend from here on out,' she whispers in my ear, and strangely enough, I don't want to punch her.

'Deal,' I say, and this time, I truly can't ignore the way my stomach swirls like spun sugar at the sweet thought of what it would be like to kiss Owen.

14

By the time I wake the next morning, my stomach is grumbling angrily at me for having skipped lunch and dinner, and if the other gurgling sounds it's making are anything to go by, it's threatening to eat itself, but all I can think about is finding Owen so I can apologise. Before I can eat and appease my stomach, or look for Owen and lay all dignity to the side and grovel at his feet for my being so unkind yesterday, I check in with Will and Gio.

'Alex and Charlie are both up, having breakfast in their room,' Will informs me, smiling fondly at Gio who is cutting thick slices of homemade bread and adding it to a serving platter for the guests who are enjoying breakfast on the terrace. This morning, that includes my mum and Alex's mum and dad.

'That's perfect; the makeup artist will be here in just under an hour,' I say, glancing out of the patio doors. 'Will you excuse me a minute?' I add, staring longingly at the crusty bread before turning and walking out onto the terrace. The waking baby-blue sky instantly puts a smile on my face; the weather is set to be a toasty one but there's not a cloud in sight or a slight chance of rain and that's enough to make me relax a touch.

'Morning, sunshine.' Mum greets me with a kiss on the cheek; I lean into her, comforted by the fact that no matter my mistakes or mishaps, she always manages to love me and give me the benefit of the doubt. Then my eyes fall on Paula and Nick, Alex's parents, and I think my stomach is about to evacuate my body the way it spasms and groans. They are standing and I am panicking. Suddenly, Nick is pulling me in for a hug and slapping me on the back the way he's greeted me for the last twenty-something years. Tears sting my eyes.

'Alright, bruiser,' he chuckles, stepping back when Paula swats him to the side so she too can envelope me in a hug.

'Oh, come off it, Nick,' Paula says while her chin digs into my shoulder. 'How are you, honey?'

'I'm fine,' I stutter as they both take their seats again. 'You don't hate me?' I mumble with both shock and relief.

'Do you remember that time when you girls were maybe fourteen, fifteen,' Nick starts, tilting one hand from side to side. 'Alex wanted to join us for that photoshoot for the bridal boutique down in London? She begged us to let you come too.' My eyes squeeze shut, as if they can block out the sound of Nick's voice if they are closed. 'You got so mad at the owner for only stocking sizes six to eight and that the modelling agency only sent us models to suit. You demanded on-set that we boycott the whole thing.'

'It was an expensive shoot, top models, top designers, a substantial price tag for us,' Paula chimes in and I don't think I'm ever going to be able to open my eyes again.

'You tipped up the entire bowl of blushed pink almonds all over the shop,' Nick says and then his booming laugh causes my eyes to dart open as a gecko scurries into the nearest flowerpot so fast, its tiny legs are a blur across the hot stone.

'Almonds,' I mutter under my breath; what is it with me and almonds?

Nick is laughing but I remember when we got home early that weekend, Mum had scolded me for costing Paula and Nick a job while also praising me for standing up for what I believed in – it was a confusing time. I had been riddled with guilt knowing how hard my family worked to pay the bills but also a little bit proud of myself for sticking it to the man. Though I'd taken my nanna's apple pie and custard round to Paula and Nick's house every night for a week to apologise.

'What my dad is trying to say is that you shouldn't be allowed near weddings.' I snap around to see Alex in her cream silk bride robe, her hair pinned back with a claw grip ready for makeup. Her eyes twinkle at me as she hobbles to a seat which my mum helps her into. My face immediately heats. She's not wrong. My track record isn't exactly stellar.

Nick barks again as Paula reaches up and takes my hand. 'What Nick is trying to say,' she starts, giving her daughter a pointed look, 'is that we ended up hosting our own bridal shoot for all shapes and sizes and it was one of our most lucrative shoots, not just because of the money but because of what it gave us in terms of clientele and dignity. Sometimes, something may appear broken or lost but it's just a matter of perspective.' She smiles softly at me.

'I'm pretty sure whichever way I look at it, my ankle is definitely broken,' Alex says with a shrug, but her lips are curving upwards into a small grin which tells me she's teasing me. Honestly, my stomach doesn't know what to do with itself this morning. One minute, I feel as though I could eat an entire tray of croissants; the next, I feel as if it's already uncomfortably full of squirming noodles that I don't remember eating.

I nod at Paula. 'Can I get you anything?' I turn to ask Alex.

'Jewels to bedazzle my cast,' she replies in a dramatic voice as she waves her arms to the sky.

I'm unable to stop my eyes from rolling, but before I can curse her while simultaneously tunnelling the earth for its finest crystals, Gio walks in with the makeup artist and everything is a go.

I haven't seen Owen all morning. We're T-minus forty-five minutes until Alex and Charlie walk down the aisle and I have to stand at the altar opposite him, and I can't bear the thought without having apologised first. Unlike the dresses Hannah picked out for her bridesmaids and Alex – bold, blood-red numbers – my dress is champagne beige and floats over my body like a nightie. I can hardly complain; it is rather gorgeous and by far the prettiest thing I've ever worn.

Though its floaty-ness means I'm trying to hike it up as delicately as I can as I half run and skip down the corridors in two-inch cream heels in search of Owen. When I reach his door, I pause to catch my breath. For once, the thought of Hannah doesn't knock me off balance; it gives me a determined kick up the backside to make things right. She may have ruined our wedding but I'm not about to destroy this day for anyone. I take a deep breath and knock on Owen's door. No answer. I knock again.

Aware that I have very little time, I push the door open, not wanting to waste a second of it.

The room is messy, clothes adorning every surface, a sketchbook strewn here and there, and the scent that I can't put my finger on lingers in the air. Without permission, my nostrils inhale it, like they can't get enough, and my stomach reminds me that all it's eaten today is a bite of a custard pastry. *Don't faint*, I warn myself. *Don't do it, not now, of all times and places.*

While I'm debating on whether my level of wooziness is grounds for passing out, the bathroom door abruptly swings open and Owen charges into the room, definitely aware of the time. His laid-back manner has been replaced by knotted brows, his jaw strong and set, his grey-blue eyes hazy and desperate as they dart over the room looking for what I can only presume is his bow tie.

His champagne shirt has yet to be buttoned and his soft stomach is glistening from that recently showered glow.

'Owen,' I say, my voice coming out low and hoarse.

He freezes as though he's only just become aware of my presence.

'Oh, Jesus, Andrea,' he gasps, stepping back, large hand resting over his heart.

I blink once, then twice, then three times to pull myself together and draw my eyes away from Owen's palm and the thought of laying my head where it rests.

'Look, Owen,' I say, snapping into professional-me mode, the me that barters with suppliers and gets a twelve-pound tray of eggs for ten quid, and doesn't get distracted or bamboozled by a half-dressed man with floppy, towel-dried hair and intense eyes. 'I'm so ridiculously sorry for what happened yesterday,' I begin as I walk over to him and start buttoning up his shirt. 'I didn't mean for any of that to happen. Alex and I fight sometimes, we say mean things but we love each other. What I haven't told you before is that I was once engaged, had a wedding planned and everything but it turns out that my fiancée was screwing her maid of honour. It left a mark. Alex knew that all this would be hard for me but honestly, I'm a grown-ass woman, it's not my wedding, it's hers, and I shouldn't have let the past control my present, especially not when it's not really my present, it's Alex and Charlie's. I was hot and bothered trying to plan an escape route down the mountain to get the macarons. Oh shite, the macarons.' I'm deftly aware that my voice has gone from road runner-like speed to nothing. My hands that had been working over Owen's buttons slow down and start to shake when I reach his soft stomach and my knuckles graze his warm skin.

How can I feel so turned on and at the same time want to cry?

Suddenly, I can no longer see the trembling in my hands as Owen's large ones cloak them, putting a stop to my mission to dress him. What am I doing?

Before I can crumble, which I'm not amiss to doing at weddings, though it's usually my own, Owen is talking, his voice wrapping my entire chilled body in a warmth I don't believe I deserve.

'Andrea, the macarons are sorted, there's nothing left to do but get the rings to the officiant and enjoy this magical day.' The warmth heats up south of my navel as Owen leans ever so slightly forward so that his lips brush my ear. 'But if you stand here trying to dress me for much longer then

I think we may end up causing trouble that no amount of macarons could get us out of.'

I stumble backwards, scratching the back of my neck, hoping the distance from Owen's hot, bulky frame will cool me down. That or a blizzard from the open window would magically appear and clout some sense into me.

'OK, yes,' I shake my head, 'we've got to go.'

'One more thing,' Owen says softly, stepping forward into my space. Forget blizzard, I'd need an actual avalanche to take me out and cool me off. 'Do you trust me to help you?' His words come out on a slow breath, the dim light in the room making his blue eyes turn that devilish grey.

I can all but nod as my arms prickle with goosebumps.

'I need to hear you say it, Andrea.'

'Yes, yes I trust you,' I breathe, praying to the powers that be that I didn't just sound like a winded donkey.

Then Owen's arms are reaching over my shoulder up the base of my neck and into my hair. Now I know why it had to be hovering over the past week, why I could never touch him or him touch me, because his touch is setting my body aflame. Surely, he can't be about to kiss me, not when I made such a fool of myself yesterday. I owe him more than a rambly sorry and a rushed make-out session that would come with a looming fear of his best friend killing him if he's so much as a second late to her wedding.

But his lips never meet mine. One gentle tug of his wrist and my sandy blonde hair tumbles down my back. All the tension between my shoulder blades evaporates, as does the need to tug at my bun and scratch at the irritated skin pulled taught at the base of my neck.

'Thank you,' I whisper, meeting his deep gaze. The dimple

in his left cheek appears and I have an intense urge to kiss it, but something in his pocket lets out an almighty wail, alerting us to the time. He takes it out – his watch; he'd set an alarm – before he turns back to me and drops the quickest yet most thoughtful kiss on my forehead.

Grabbing his bow tie off the desk, Owen strides to the door and holds out a hand to me for I am not moving. I have apparently become nothing but a puddle on the floor. He'll have to mop me up and squeeze me into a bottle if I'm going to see any of this wedding.

Forehead kisses. Who knew? I don't think I'd ever let someone offer that form of care to me before. Of course Hannah and I kissed and we certainly didn't wait for marriage, but to be stood so close to someone, in their bubble, open to each other's vulnerabilities, allowing them to take care of me without words, how Owen's forehead kiss just made me feel – I'd always shut that down.

A large, calloused hand wraps around my much smaller, in need of hand cream (cleaning products can do that to a person) one and I'm being pulled towards the door, my hair soft against the bare skin on my back, flowing as free as I feel now that I've managed to speak to Owen – and maybe just a little bit because my insides now feel incredibly squishy to the point where I can't tell my emotions apart; they are kind of in a puddle of mush.

Hand in hand, Owen and I race up to the third-floor terrace that we haven't yet been privy to seeing since we arrived in Italy. Chatter sings through the morning's fresh and vibrant air as guests find their seats. We take a peek at the garden and I'm both shocked at how the sight before me is turning that puddle of mush into an extremely clear and strong, joyous emotion of wonder and happiness. Though that could be the fact that as soon as Owen's eyes fall upon the scene, he gives my hand a gentle squeeze and my heart seems to sizzle in my chest like it's about to explode into some magnificent firework display.

There are twenty white plastic chairs on either side of a lush, green lawn, a wooden sign encouraging guests to mingle rather than choosing a family side. To the left, the mismatched stone wall that leads to the next tier of olive trees is draped with Pride flag bunting, and to the right, where the ground dips to the second level of orange and lemon trees, makeshift wooden poles have been planted, allowing peaches and cream ribbons to blow in the steady subtle breeze.

At the end of the aisle is a rustic, handmade, wooden arch decorated in similar blush, champagne and peach tone flowers and ribbons. It's neither grand nor over the top, flashy nor gaudy; it's warm, welcoming and so exquisitely Alex and Charlie. The mush in my stomach makes room for a splodge of guilt when I think back to what I said to Alex on the mountain yesterday, calling this whole week too much, too over the top. This, this is anything but over the top; it's lovely.

'It's horrible,' Owen whispers, deadpan, pulling me back to the present.

'It's disgusting,' I concur.

'Owen, Andi.' I hear our names from somewhere to the left of the garden behind a small shrub and turn to acknowledge the voice, which sounds awfully like Alex's dad.

'Yes, oh wise mother nature,' I whisper and receive

another squeeze from Owen while he covers his mouth with his other hand, stunting a laugh, which sends that sizzle to my cheeks.

'Andi, you've not got time for jokes; you've got five minutes till my daughter walks down that aisle and she's waiting for you.'

Owen and I immediately pull apart and nod at each other in lieu of words. Then I sprint, faster than Alex's legs could currently sprint, towards her room, whizzing by Charlie, who is spending the final few minutes getting changed in Will and Gio's room. Through the crack in the door, I glimpse her shiny, black hair glistening in the orange glow of the sun as she has a quiet word with her dads. It looks like a precious family moment that I do not want to interrupt and so I keep running.

'Don't worry, I've seen Charlie, she is not currently engaging in any type of sex act with a member of the wedding party; she looks nothing but hopelessly devoted and ready to marry you,' I say as I burst into Alex's room.

'Really?' Alex says with a heavy sigh and an eye roll as Paula makes some final adjustments to her sequinned bodice.

'Sorry, it just came out,' I say, ducking my head and walking over to my best friend in the whole world.

'No, it's OK, it's good that you can joke about it,' she replies, taking my hand and flapping it around.

'It's about damn time really, don't you think?' I manage a smile and shrug.

'I'm nervous, Andi,' she then says.

'I couldn't tell,' I note, glaring at our flapping hands and then steadying them with my uncaptured hand. 'Alex, I don't know what happens next, I didn't quite get this far, but all I know is that you love Charlie and Charlie loves you, you both glow when you are with each other. I see it, and if for a moment I hang up my black-tinted glasses, I love it. You look like a goddess when you glow. Lord knows I could do with a bit of glow. Somehow, working over a greasy deep fryer does not permit that.' I squeeze our hands together. 'But also, I'm 1000 per cent sure Zia Allegra has connections to the mafia, and I'll get her to talk. If Charlie ever hurts you, she's a goner.' I wiggle my eyebrows and she snorts. Paula is shaking her head but there's a smirk on her rouge-red lips.

'You're not snuffing out my Charlie,' Alex says, giving me a firm glare, her lips curving upwards.

'Well, you don't want her dead. If that isn't grounds for marriage then I don't know what is,' I tell her, and she shoves me gently in my collarbone.

'Come on, honey, I sure as heck can't top that speech, so let's get you married,' Paula states, causing us all to release a mix of both nervous and happy giggles.

15

'I'm so glad that's over.' Owen is leaning into my shoulder, his warm breath tickling my collarbone, causing my chest to glitter with a delicate smattering of goosebumps. I don't know when the security guards to my brain decided to take a holiday, they definitely didn't run it by me, but there's certainly no one manning the doors, allowing every naughty, unacceptable thought without so much as a background check or payment. It's incredibly inconvenient.

'What a waste of a glorious morning,' I retort back to Owen, trying and failing not to make eye contact. Though I was really in a lose-lose situation. There had been a crumb, a small pang of tightness in my chest watching my beautiful best friend walk down the aisle in her sleeveless, jewel-trim bodice and tulle skirt that camouflages her cast. A hint of a tender pain in my heart at her accomplishing something that I failed to do, an experience that had once again tossed me aside, left me out. Then Owen had nodded at me from his side of the makeshift altar, made the subtlest gesture of pretending to check his watch and I was all in.

Replacing my own bruised ego with the happiness of my very best friend had taken over and my eyes had not once rolled back into my head as I stood and embraced the special ceremony.

'I mean, I could have been walking the ruins of Pompei, getting up close and personal with people who got turned to stone.' Owen's voice is low so only I can hear him as we walk back down the aisle following the newlyweds.

'Or we could have been taking a death-defying Vespa ride along the Amalfi cliff side in peak Italian traffic,' I suggest.

'Either or, would have been far more entertaining than this,' he states, making my nose fizz with laughter.

'I can't believe neither of you forgot the rings,' Charlie muses when we reach the edge of the garden, ready to make our way across the third-floor terrace.

'Or push either of us off the ledge during our vows,' Alex adds as the guests begin standing. She's leaning on Charlie just so, having opted for no crutches during the ceremony. She hadn't winced once walking down the aisle, though all her wedding photos are going to depict her with an easygoing lean while she stood opposite Charlie under the archway. Now, though, I see her wince as she tries to dispel a little weight off her foot and onto Charlie's shoulder.

I'm honestly surprised she hasn't attempted to cause me physical harm after the last few days.

My body seems to be inching closer to Owen's as the guests huddle at the end of the path where the four of us have congregated. A cold sweat breaks out on my brow for fear of Charlie Richter-graphing my heart rate.

'If everyone would like to make their way across to the terrace, please, just follow the garden round past the disgustingly loved up Mrs and Mrs,' I announce, taking a step away from Owen's towering frame as the swarm starts to move again. I can be useful and efficient; my brain can listen to instructions despite the Italian water trying to steer me astray since I arrived on its coast.

'All other brides will be jealous they don't have me for their maid of honour,' I tease.

'Maid of honour for hire,' Charlie suggests.

'Always the maid of honour, never the bride,' I chuckle, feeling somewhat lighter now that the ceremony is complete. A part of me feels like I've cracked it, like the hard shell that had formed over my heart to protect it from the evil known as love and weddings has been broken now that I have attended one and come out unscathed. Though I can't quite say the same for my poor Alex. But from the glow in her cheeks, that I believe has nothing to do with her Charlotte Tilbury highlighter, I would say her special ceremony was everything she dreamt it would be and more.

'Right, you two stay here,' Will says to Alex and Charlie as he comes up behind me, making me jump. Owen turns casually, hands in his trouser pockets, a lazy, wistful smile on his face. I ponder for a second what thoughts are racing through his mind – thoughts of his ex, proposals that never were – before I'm being rushed by Will to take my place on the terrace so the brides can make their grand entrance.

But before I leave her, I give Alex a quick kiss on the cheek; at the same time, Owen leans forward and drops a kiss on Charlie's nose. Did I say I had made it out of this wedding unscathed? My stomach would strongly disagree as a swarm of butterflies seem to come out of nowhere to inhabit it.

Alex rakes a hand gently through my wavy hair as it falls over my chest when I step away from her.

'I like your hair like this, Andi,' she smiles sweetly.

'Me too,' I reply without hesitation before Will is tugging on Owen's arm and Owen is tugging on mine towards the party.

The terrace is a slight exaggeration of the kitchen terrace and the ceremony décor amped up by one hundred. The flowers Will, Owen and I put together adorn the centre of each of the six tables. The lemons are illuminated by the gorgeous glow of the sun, bouncing golden rays are gleaming off the silky cream petals and the brown twine balances the sheen with a muted rustic, earthy presence.

More of the rainbow bunting is strung along the railing intertwined with a plump garland of a mixture of the roses, lavender and lemons. With the backdrop of Positano below, it's positively stunning. Of course, hibernating throughout the scene are enough twinkling lights to give Clark Griswold a run for his money, just waiting for the sun to show signs of weariness so they can steal the show.

As we draw closer to our seats, I spot them: there in the middle of each gleaming white placemat is an organza bag containing a pastel macaron, tied with a cute tag bearing a sweet pastel rainbow inscribed with Alex and Charlie's name and today's date. My heart performs a gold medal-worthy backflip, back handspring with a round-off to finish.

I glance up at Owen to find him already looking at me, his eyes more seafoam blue than grey now, with a slight sheen to them. I reach for his hand and give it a gentle squeeze, hoping that if his brain is fighting off any unlocked memories of the past he'd rather not have to revisit, like mine had done earlier, then he knows he's not fighting them on his own.

'Horrendous,' I mutter.

'Godawful,' he states, eyes crinkling around the edges.

We find our seats next to my mum, Paula and Nick, Zia Allegra, Nonna Roberta, Will and Gio and pick up the mini Pride flags, just as a low thrum of music begins to play from speakers that must be effortlessly hidden on the balcony.

Will is suddenly raising his arms in the air, giving us the signal to wave our flags as the song grows louder.

Then Alex and Charlie are entering the balcony through a glittering rainbow, a harmony of Adele's 'One and Only' and lots of loud cheering and woos.

Hand clasped in hand, Alex is grinning and bearing it while she sways and dances to their special table. I'm reminded that I forgot to ask the makeup artist what setting spray she used as there's not a single smudge of mascara or tear-streaked blush on Alex or Charlie's radiant faces. I hope the lady used it on me too, to seal the sweat in my pores and not because of tears. Crying is not happening. I'm certain she misted me with something, but I hadn't quite had the patience to sit still for as long as it was going to take to prettify me in my desperation to get to Owen.

Guests are joining in with the wiggling and dancing, meaning that every few sways, Alex and Charlie stop to say hellos and revel in congratulations and hugs. As they mingle, I notice waiters begin shuffling about and for me, the party is officially under way.

'The only good thing about weddings,' Owen says, doing that lean thing again, which sends a shiver dancing unapologetically down my spine without consent.

'Especially an Italian wedding,' I croak and subtly try and clear my throat. Owen doesn't seem to notice anything odd about my voice, of course – why would he? As the food is placed on the Mrs and Mrs table, we get a sneak peek of what's coming.

'It looks like some form of risotto,' Owen whispers, thoroughly distracted, his straight nose making his features look serious, which they most definitely are when it comes to food. I spy the waiter pouring red wine elegantly with one hand.

'There's no more trouble for us to get into, right?' I whisper back to Owen, eagerly awaiting my glass to be filled.

'Unless you were planning on giving Alex a broken arm to match her broken ankle?' Owen queries, deadpan, placing his napkin on his knee and moving his macaron off his placemat so there is room for the risotto to be set down. My heart does something unruly, watching his eyes grow wide with flecks of passion when his plate is placed in front of him. I can't believe I'm going to admit it, but I feel ridiculously jealous of a plate of risotto and find my mind wandering to what it would feel like if Owen looked at me like that, like he wanted to devour me just the same.

'Andrea, Andrea,' I hear Owen calling my name like he's already said it more than twice.

I attach my lips to my wine glass and take a large gulp as I turn to look at Owen, whose fork is aloft by his juicy lips.

'Andrea, it's artichoke risotto,' he tells me with so much excitement, you'd think Santa just shimmied down his chimney.

'I take it it's good,' I say, slowly putting my wine down and picking up my fork.

'It's incredible,' Owen enthuses, holding up a large bite on his fork. I chuckle.

'Owen, I have my own,' I say, stabbing at my bowl with my fork but he only grunts, lifting it closer to my lips like I needed to have tasted this risotto yesterday.

So I wrap my lips around his fork, I repeat, *his fork* and immediately let out a grunt of my own.

'This isn't food; it should be mounted in some artists hall of fame. That's insanely good,' I concur, rushing to load my own fork now with a healthy bite.

Mum is giggling next to me; I feel her gently put a hand on my fork-free hand before turning away and engaging with Paula and Nonna Roberta. Owen and I eat in a comfortable silence, savouring the dish before us.

'Do you think there's something wrong with us?' I ask Owen thoughtfully as my empty plate is taken away and my wine refilled. 'This food is to die for, Italy is magical, could you not just have a wedding for the party?'

Owen takes a lavish sip of his wine, his eyes narrowing in thought. I twist my shoulders a tad to face him, elbow on table, wine glass hovering over my lips.

'You mean to say, I should have proposed?' he asks.

'I mean there was always annulment, divorce, you had options,' I say, tilting my wine glass towards him then taking a drink.

'But do you really think pigeon would have been worth it?' he argues, mirroring my actions with his glass.

'You know, Hannah still went through with the party;

they ate all the vegan sausages and vegan carrot cake. What happens if I missed out?'

'On vegan sausages and vegan carrot cake? How do you make a vegan carrot cake? There's no replacing that traditional cream cheese; what would be the point?'

'She was a monster.' We both take another sip, emptying our second glasses.

'Take it easy, honey, don't forget your speech,' my mum's voice replaces Owen's and I nearly send a tsunami of red wine across our table as my last gulp threatens to escape both my nose and mouth. I cough and dribble a little before dabbing my napkin against my lips.

'Owen…' I start, but Owen has become an ice sculpture, fork poised at his lips, just hanging there as he stares straight ahead.

Only when the main course is placed in front of us does Owen turn to look at me. I don't feel nearly as hungry as I had been seconds ago and this time, Owen barely registers the food.

'Andrea, the speeches. We forgot about the speeches,' Owen mumbles so quietly, this time it's me doing the leaning in.

My nostrils are signalling to my stomach that if this course tastes as amazing as it smells then there is no question as to whether I am eating it or not. My limbs are taking action of their own accord, my hand is grabbing hold of my fork and scooping up one ravioli whole. There's no time to cut it. *Just get it in and forget about all your woes*, my brain encourages. On the other hand, if I eat it at a snail's pace, maybe there won't be time for speeches or moving tables for a makeshift dance floor.

I elbow Owen, causing a ravioli to fall back into his bowl. If looks could kill. I think he's opting for the same option as me: eat and forget about our woes.

'Sorry,' I mutter weakly. 'It's not like it fell on the floor, you can still eat it, but go slow, will you,' I add, nodding at his plate. For a moment, I worry that I don't have a plan B if Owen doesn't agree to my plan A, but then I watch as his currently blue eyes move from me back to his plate. He picks up his knife and ever so slowly cuts a ravioli into quarters. He then pricks one quarter with his fork and runs it at tortoise speed around the edge of his bowl, collecting sauce as it goes.

I'm staring at him unabashed, mouth wide open for how long I don't know, until a clash of cutlery draws my attention around the table as the others place spoons, knives and forks neatly across their empty bowls.

Copying Owen's clever actions, I start cutting up my ravioli, ignoring a confused look from my mum and a 'this woman is definitely not Italian' glare from Zia Allegra.

Fifteen minutes later, Owen has one ravioli left, I have two, everyone else's bowls were cleared long ago. I get the feeling of all eyes on me and Owen, and look up to see Gio nod at a server waiting in the wings. All at once, servers emerge, like a group of Victorians swanning onto the dance floor in synchronised twirling at a masquerade ball, bowls aloft, sending a rich espresso scent up into the air that is mixed with a heavy dose of an undeniable Italian vanilla cream.

I don't even have to look at Owen to know that he has swiftly inhaled his last raviolo. What's he playing at? We're both doomed.

16

I can't lie, there was no hesitation with dessert; the minute that bowl was put in front of me, I had to act fast so Owen wouldn't try and claim my tiramisu for his own and enjoy a second helping. I knew it was going to be delicious and it had been exceptionally good, but now I'm staring into the blood-red wine in my glass, twiddling the ends of my loose hair around my fingers, wondering why I hadn't thought to break my own ankle and skip out on this day by being laid up in hospital.

I'd seen the occasional YouTube video of dancing flower men, choreographed father and son dances, super talented maids of honour singing a song they'd written about their lifelong friendship with the bride, to receive a chorus of roaring laughter and applause. I had nothing. From day one of finding out I was to be maid of honour, this was the part I had been dreading the most. Granted, it's not like Alex had given me a large amount of time to put together a wedding flash mob but still.

Independent me had no skill that could either humour or bring this wedding crowd to heart-wrenching tears. I'd allowed myself to consider what I'd say just the once, and then I'd shoved it so hard to the back of my mind, I had completely forgotten about it. And I thought breaking Alex's ankle was the low point. I'd hit rock bottom.

A bold ray of sunshine suddenly bounces off Owen's glass, blinding me in my peripheral as he tips and swirls the stem before taking a sip.

Turning, I pull his wine glass gently away from his lips, ignoring the gloss that it leaves behind. His cheeks are slightly rosy and his eyes flicker with a hint of amusement at my being so bold.

'Owen, you can't just drown your mistake in tiramisu and wine; Charlie is expecting a best man speech, too. How many Harry Styles songs do you know?' My whole body seems to stiffen awaiting his answer. I know there is no such thing as a perfect person but not liking Harry Styles is definitely a marker for whether Santa puts you on the naughty or nice list, I am sure of it.

'Oh no, you're one of them,' Owen sighs. I gasp. We sit staring at each other, eyes narrowed for a minute before I kick my stubbornness in the shin and swallow my pride. Owen is going to hate this more than I am, so that's something.

'I need you to come with me,' I say, reaching for his hand and pulling him up and away from the table just as Will and Gio stand, along with Paula and Nick. They look to Owen and me as if to say, 'are you ready?', and head for the front of the table beside Alex and Charlie.

Shooting them a grave, brief smile, I nod, then start running towards the very end of the garden out of sight.

'We haven't got much time,' I tell Owen.

'Andrea, my speech is next; Charlie is going to kill me,' Owen says, a look of sheer panic on his face. I've never seen him so ruffled. I'm humming a tune in my head, trying to find the lyrics.

'But what if we join forces, give them a speech they will never forget,' I say, making sure to open my eyes wide rather than kneel on the floor to show I am practically begging. Owen's blue-grey eyes flicker with amber flecks under the yellow sun; I look away sharply to stop myself getting distracted trying to decipher their true shade.

'You said I need to be better at asking for help, so this is me asking for help and won't it be better than you winging it?' I say, knees buckling slightly, my chest constricting. Owen glares at me for a moment; I can feel his stare on my cheekbones as they heat.

'What did you have in mind?' he asks, only a slight hint of worry in his features when I finally look back to his face.

'Well, there's this song that Alex loves and I thought that maybe, maybe we could sing it for her? You know, this song makes me think of her and that way, we're not just up there rambling and talking out of our arses and screwing everything up like I have been doing all week.' The words rush out and I'm aware I don't pause for breath.

Suddenly, Owen's thumb is gently grazing my cheek, a barely there touch as if he's testing the water, unsure of even himself as to what he is doing and if he is allowed to be doing it. Strangely enough, no part of me wants to whack his hand away or kick him in the nuts. The way his rough skin is heating mine makes my body both relax and feel extremely alert at the same time.

'Are we choreographing this performance or keeping it strictly vocals?' he asks, making my lips split into a wide grin.

*

The magic fairy spray the makeup artist splashed onto my face this morning has failed me by the time Owen and I are walking back onto the terrace, glistening with sweat and a little wheezy, but just in time. Will, Gio, Paula and Nick are taking their seats and the floor is ours.

I look up at Owen, resisting the urge to wipe away a trickle of sweat making its way down his neck and disappearing behind his collar, and nod. His hand is resting, feather light, against the small of my back as he nods in return before moving to the other side of the terrace, where he is to walk on and meet me in the middle.

Both Alex and Charlie's faces are creasing with curiosity and I've no doubt a wrinkle or two of fear, but I push that to the back of my mind as Owen's phone begins to hum the first notes to 'Adore You'. Then the two of us are gliding towards the top table, arms outstretched like elegant ballet dancers performing an incredibly off the cuff version of *Swan Lake* – Owen's choreography, not mine.

When we reach the top table, we clasp our hands together – at my stomach, Owen's waist – lifting them up together, up over our heads and around where we let go of each other, pulling our arms back to our sides, twisting our bodies as they fall. I do my best to ignore the tingling sensation that Owen's strong grasp leaves behind, but my fingertips feel like sparklers, sparklers that if I'm not careful, are going to sizzle quickly and burn me if I don't let go. I display some extra-enthusiastic jazz hands to dispel the sensation. Now, we're facing our best friends. Taking in my gorgeous Alex, with a single tear shimmying down her face, my crooning grows louder as I pour my all into the song, hoping she knows just how much love I have for her.

We're skipping to the left, then jumping to the right, then spinning around in a circle, Owen's voice is booming over Harry's and I know when all this is over, I'll have to tell him, I'll have to let him down gently, be kind about it, that he should never, ever sing again in public, maybe not even the shower. But as his hulking frame squats low, then rises tall, as his thick forearm reaches over, his hand resting on my shoulder immediately heating the bare skin, as we start to cancan, laughter threatens to interrupt my tremendous vocals while tears are clogging the inner corners of my eyes.

He's helping me and I don't feel ashamed or useless, ripped of authority or weak; in this moment, I feel euphoric, though that might be the sheer magnitude of power zipping through my body as we're dancing like no one's watching. Whoever said it's good for the soul wasn't wrong.

The song is coming to an end and Owen stumbles a little over his two left feet, I catch him around his waist in an almost bear hug, his scent – that I still can't put my finger on – engulfs me, I'm smiling so bright the crinkles around my eyes actually hurt.

I'm saved from meeting his gaze, which I can feel burning my skull through the top of my head, as Alex and Charlie are standing up. For a moment, realisation of what we just did dawns on me; I should be embarrassed, I should have been more me, more organised, more put together, but somehow, here in Positano, here on this enchanting mountainside, I feel that this performance was the most me I've been in a while, the most raw and messy version, the most true speech I could gift Alex with.

And she's... she's clapping. I think my legs are moments away from buckling, Owen's weight suddenly feels a little too much but as Charlie bounds over to him, he stands up straighter to receive her hug, her pretty face disappearing in his broad chest.

'I pray with all manner of my being that someone caught that on camera,' Alex says when she reaches me, less bounding than Charlie, crutch now in one hand.

'And I pray to whichever Italian saint has the most power and sympathy that it wasn't,' I reply, wrapping my arms around her neck and squeezing her gently.

'That totally made me forget about the missing rainbow almonds and replacement macarons,' Charlie chimes in, throwing an amused wink my way as she steps away from Owen, whose cheeks are slightly red. When he sweeps a hand through his hair, it flips to the right and stays there, sweat acting as the perfect hair gel.

I offer a small smile, my eyes slightly fuzzy now, my head buzzing with adrenaline. I think the shot of sambuca we had for courage before our performance is kicking in.

'I think I need some air,' I tell our little group.

'You're standing on a balcony outside,' Charlie informs me.

My blurry eyes roll in her direction as Alex swats her bicep. My heart flutters at my best friend sticking up for me, her knowledge of my lack of exercise and my current need for rest.

'Go rest, we'll let everyone's food go down before our first dance,' Alex says sweetly, swiping another runaway tear from her face. I'm still mesmerised that not a dot of blush is smudged.

As guests start pulling Alex and Charlie away, chattering, mingling, the tremor of footsteps beginning to dance maybe earlier than Alex expected, Owen gently hovers a hand over my shoulder blades and guides me towards the garden where we were practising minutes ago. It's more sparse than the balcony which allows me to suck in a healthy breath of the crisp air.

When I see the grass, I fall onto the soft tufts and stare up at the baby-blue sky. My long, wavy hair splays out around me, enjoying the unusual freedom from its normal confines of a restricted bun. Owen seems to consider me for a moment, my own private parasol, keeping the sun from stinging my eyes. His own are currently an enchanting swirl of those blues and greens, with a hint of something dancing behind them that I can't place.

Not wanting to stare, I close my eyes for a breath. The ground suddenly feels warm, like lava is spreading underneath me, as Owen lies down too.

'Can I tell you something?' he croaks. I can't feel his eyes on me; he must be looking up as I am. Not an inch of us is touching but there's a static where our fingertips are millimetres apart. My throat instantly goes dry. Can he hear the thumping in my heart? The rattle of shivers that sweep my body when he's this close to me?

'Sure,' I say, and it comes out on an anxious, struggled wheeze.

'I really don't think you should sing in public again, ever,' he states, a small chuckle rumbling from his belly. I chance a glance at him, his broad chest is moving up and down, a large paw rests over his stomach, keeping his white shirt from lifting in the breeze. The fabric presses against his skin and I swear to the mother of god that I'm never mixing wine and sambuca again as my brain flashes with an image of Owen's hulk-like body being pressed up against mine, keeping me in my place.

I swat at his sides, as if swatting away my naughty thoughts, causing his knees to shoot up to protect himself.

'I was going to say the same to you,' I retort through a playful scoff, glad of the distraction.

'I don't believe you; my voice is like a choir of angels singing,' he states, laughter bubbling in his throat as he tries to stay serious.

'More like a choir of angels crying,' I tease and all of a sudden, the ridiculousness of what we both just did hits me and I burst out laughing, clutching my stomach, tears trickling down my ears. Owen is laughing too, and it sounds a lot more like heaven to my ears than his singing.

'That's a bit harsh; I'd never want to upset an angel,' he tells me with faux innocence, his voice turning from light to more of a rough whisper. Our eyes meet and something about the way he says those last words has my brain in bits; every cell locates images of Owen acting devilish, like those rugged men you see on the covers of spicy books that scream 'take me to the bedroom!'. Thankfully, before I have a chance to stray too far into the wood of no return, my mum appears in my peripheral.

'I'm sure I said lay off the wine,' she says, stepping onto the grass, her tone light, amusement etched on her glowing face.

'Speaking of drinks, can I get you anything, Kristen?' Owen asks kindly, getting up to his feet and wiping away his own tears. Mum rubs at his bicep.

'No thanks, honey,' she replies, and then Owen is walking away and she is sitting down next to me on the grass, her olive-green chiffon dress blanketing the ground in front of her as she tucks her legs to the side to avoid kicking me in the ribs.

'Well, that was certainly entertaining. You and Owen looked great up there,' she muses, a twinkle in her eye from today's rather happy sunshine.

'Well, I know that's an outright lie,' I reply, plucking at another blade of grass and chuckling.

'I'm telling the truth; you make a good-looking pair,' she adds, playing with a strand of my hair that's resting over my shoulder.

I snort, 'Mum, don't get all Disney on me; I've had enough fairy tale for one day.'

She prods at my shoulder. 'Alright, but Andrea, will you promise me one thing, just one thing?' she asks, placing a finger on my cheek and twisting my head to face her instead of the blue canvas above.

'What's that, Mum?' I reply, squinting as the sunlight behind her head catches me off guard. My eyes immediately begin streaming but she doesn't let go, only shifts her position a little to shield me better.

'Maybe swap the concrete wall for more of a wooden wall, maybe a few sticks. I taught you to be brave and independent, but sweetheart, don't dig your trench so deep that the good things can't get across, OK?' she says softly, still twirling my hair in her fingers.

'I don't want no big bad wolf blowing down my house, Mum,' I say.

Her eyes turn quizzical. 'What?' she retorts, the crease in her brow deepening.

'Wood and sticks are no good; the big bad wolf would just come barrelling in.'

'What are you talking about, Andrea?' I receive a swat to the top of my shoulder.

'You were literally just talking about a wall made of concrete and sticks?' I plead and hunch my shoulders to brace for any more attacks.

'Are you drunk, Andrea?' She starts swatting at my ribcage instead, causing me to curl up into a ball.

'Mum, stop it, no,' I laugh. 'I get it, I get it,' I say before she starts tickling me like she used to do when I was a child and got too cocky for my own good. When she settles down and stops trying to assault me, I uncurl and sit up slowly.

'Mum,' I start, then pause, waiting for her to look me in the eyes. When her own thoughtful gaze meets mine, I continue, 'Are you really thinking it's time to step away from the chip shop?'

She lets out a heavy sigh before giving a brief shake of her head. 'Yes, Andrea, I am. Now I haven't thought about all the ins and outs, and we definitely need to have a talk, honey, I'm not about to leave you high and dry, so why don't we enjoy the rest of the time we have here and then we can figure out a plan when we get home,' she explains, rubbing my forearm.

I don't speak for a moment; it's difficult to find the right words or vocalise them past the growing lump of fear in my throat that when we get home, everything is going to change and I have no idea what I'm going to do.

'OK,' is all I manage as Owen bounds back. Though he didn't ask me if I wanted a drink, he has brought me one anyway, like it was natural for him to just think of me and know exactly what I would like.

I stare at him for a second when he hands me the drink, unable to help the squint of curiosity in my eyes. My mum chuckling snaps me out of my little trance. She pecks me on the cheek and then it's just Owen and me again and an unusual fluttering sensation in my stomach.

17

Sipping on our drinks – a pleasant and fruity red wine – Owen and I make our way back to the balcony to witness Alex and Charlie's first dance and the father-daughter dances before the merry wedding guests take to the makeshift stage. Positano seems positively bolder, brighter and more alive than I've witnessed it these last few days behind us and the lemon, lavender and rose scent that perfumes the terrace spreads a joyful smile across my face.

Italy truly does have a way of distracting you from all your worries and woes if you let it. You dare not spoil the magical surroundings with a drop of pessimism or undesirable thoughts or someone ends up with a broken ankle.

Owen doesn't make to join in with the jiving and neither do I. I almost think we're getting away with it until Nick and his swinging hips start waltzing our way, hand outreached, poised to grab mine.

I raise my wine glass to let him know I'm busy and can't dance with wine in my hand but that doesn't stop him gliding with a grin that is getting broader the closer he gets to me.

'Owen, please will you help me find cake, I need cake,'

I say quickly, turning to look up at Owen, whose eyes go wide at my question, obviously, because Owen loves cake. Then his lips tilt into a tiny smirk and he's staring at me without a word but I can't make out what he's trying to convey as panic is rising at Nick's increasing proximity.

'Owen, please,' I practically beg.

'Oh, of course, yes, come on,' he stutters over his words a touch awkwardly and then waves at me to follow him. We meander down the third-floor steps and keep going until we're in our usual spot, the terrace off the kitchen. Today though, it's a hive of noise and energy as chefs mill around cleaning dishes and pots from the earlier sit-down meal and preparing the evening's buffet.

Owen and I duck and dive, nodding innocently at everyone we pass. I suddenly don't feel so innocent, though, when I see the elegant platters and carefully placed plated confectionary.

'Owen, are we allowed to just take these?' I ask in a hushed tone.

'Probably not,' is what he comes back with, not giving me much confidence at all, but the wine in my stomach is in desperate need of some soaking up. Surely, they won't miss a large bowl of tiramisu.

We're walking past the fridge and one minute, Owen is like Goliath, two heads bigger than the kitchen's occupants; the next, he's hunched down low like some prowling lion about to attack its prey.

'Quick,' he says before rushing past the stovetop and out the kitchen door. Once on the other side, I straighten up, hand on my lower back circling it as it creaks. I hadn't realised I'd copied Owen's stance, like we were two nervous ninjas on a mission to retrieve trifle.

Owen isn't slowing down, though; he has something tucked into his jacket and doesn't stop briskly walking until he's at my room. I open the door for him and lead him inside.

'What was with all the bending over?' I ask as he unveils a large bowl of profiteroles from under his suit jacket. I immediately forget the question as I squeal.

'Did you get the spoons?' he asks me as I kick off my high heels and jump onto the bed, my aching feet wriggling into the fluffy duvet.

'I'm sorry but when during that mission impossible did you stop to debrief me and give me my orders?' I say mischievously.

'Fingers it is then,' Owen remarks, causing my cheeks to warm for no apparent reason other than I know if Charlie were here right now, she would have perceived that as a dirty comment. But she's not here, so there's no way I'm thinking anything of the sort. Owen sits down opposite me on the bed and places the bowl in between us. I watch as he kicks off his shoes and pulls his feet up to the side of his large frame, getting comfy. I dive into the bowl in an attempt to act natural and ignore whatever ludicrous thoughts are trying to sabotage my brain.

The sweet Italian *crema* inside the delicately light ball of choux pastry pours into my mouth, filling it with the most delectable flavours, and I can't help the groan that emits from between my lips. Chocolate melts onto my fingers and I let it, not wanting to interrupt my taste buds from savouring the current bite – I'll get to the chocolate in a moment.

At some point, I close my eyes, and when I open them, Owen's eyes are grey and glazed over, his lips are just-licked wet and he has *crema* on his fingers. My entire body flames. Hastily, I look to the bowl and claim another profiterole.

'You know, I think I need to kidnap Gio and get him to bake for the shop. There's no way sales wouldn't soar if people got to try these Italian delicacies. Don't get me wrong, I'm not quite sure profiteroles go with fish and chips, but with all the new sweet shops and dessert bars popping up, it would be worth a shot. Maybe British people are bored of fish and chips?' I'm rambling but it feels like safe territory, like if I don't stop talking then I don't have to address the feelings that Owen stirs up in me. But my voice is like peanut brittle, raspy and slightly crackly – maybe he won't notice.

'Did you just call fish and chips boring?' Owen asks when I take a small breath, allowing room for actual conversation and not a monologue from me on the state of England's, or more specifically Ned's, fish and chips.

'Yes, yes I did,' I reply, chocolate dripping down my fingers now as my last profiterole didn't quite make it to my mouth.

I'm not sure if I'm the one that's leaning forward, inching closer, or if it's Owen, but somehow, my bare knees meet his thighs. The heat of his body spears through the fabric of his trousers and sends tingles down to my toes.

'Andrea.' There's a pause, his voice coming out husky. When did his lips get so close to my neck? 'Fish and chips are far from boring.' His breath tickles my collarbone and

I find myself wanting to open my neck up to him and fold into his warmth at the same time.

'Hmm,' I whisper so quietly that Owen has to move closer to hear it. Did I do that on purpose? Yes, I think I did. His eyelids are heavy, his cheeks are pink and a nervous flutter flashes across his eyes.

'Owen?'

'Yes?'

'Are you going to kiss me?' I ask as our noses gently meet.

'Andrea?'

'Yes?'

'Would you like me to kiss you?' Owen asks and his voice is so sincere and sweet that this big bad wolf just cracks right through my brick house.

'Yes please,' I reply.

In one sweeping yet slow and thoughtful motion, Owen's large hand is cupping my cheek and his lips are against mine. Of course he tastes sweet, the vanilla crema and rich chocolate delighting my tongue as his and mine intertwine. My profiterole-free hand reaches into his hair, pulling him closer as our breaths become more ragged, our kiss building in intensity.

'Is this a bad idea?' I ask when we come up for air, foreheads touching. We're both now scrambling to our knees on the bed.

'Probably,' Owen answers, his usual deadpan, a small smirk quirking up on his lips – plump lips I admire for a second before my eyes fall back to his intense gaze.

'It's not going anywhere?' I press, throwing the profiterole back into the bowl before Owen moves it to the bedside table. Then our eyes lock again. My hand automatically reaches back into Owen's hair, roaming down his broad shoulders. His hands massage my neck.

'It doesn't have to go anywhere you don't want it to go; if you want just kisses, it can be just kisses,' he says, peppering them along my jawline.

'No, I mean, we're not looking for relationships, that's not what this is, right?' I want to be certain.

'I don't know, Andrea,' he replies, nibbling my ear lobe which makes my whole body quiver.

I gasp, in shock or in pleasure, I'm not sure. 'What do you mean you don't know? It can't be a relationship, you have to say it,' I urge, desperately; even his hands on my biceps are causing me to sweat in hot anticipation, but Owen doesn't answer right away, he pulls back, seemingly trying to stare into my soul with the look he is giving me.

'OK, yes, no strings attached, it's just kissing, no relationship,' he finally concurs and now I'm back to kissing him, scuttling my knees closer so our bodies are now pressed up against each other and it's like the Italian sun is right above me; no part of my body able to escape the heat.

'Because it wouldn't work out; we're not the relationship, marrying type?' I mumble into his mouth as my hands rake through his silky hair.

'Oh god no,' he groans after a slight hesitation that I ignore.

'Because love is silly.' My words come out slow, in shaky breaths. Again, Owen doesn't reply instantly; he slows the kiss and his eyes flutter open. Mine do the same and now we're just staring at each other, me waiting for Owen to agree, Owen waiting for what, I don't know.

'So, so silly,' he echoes, not taking his eyes off me.

'So this is…?' I question, my chest is flush with his torso, heaving up and down.

'This is…' he starts, then pauses, eyes wandering down over my rumpled dress, bandeau neckline dangerously askew, before finding my face once more. 'This is me helping you.' He gives a slight nod.

'Helping me find cake,' I confirm. 'OK, so you've already helped me; I've got cake,' I tell him, my breath hitching as we both gaze down to his open shirt and the smeared chocolate that decorates both my chest and his.

'Hmm, that's true.' His eyes narrow in thought, tiny golden flecks appear around his irises, a blend of the late-afternoon sunlight and my sandy blonde hair reflecting in his suddenly roguish stare. 'Is there anything else I can help you with tonight, Andrea?' he croaks.

My chest heaves flush against him and I grab onto his shoulders to steady my wobbling knees. 'Yes please,' I say against his bottom lip. 'My dress is too tight.'

'From all the cakes,' he adds, his hands falling to my hips, scorching the light fabric that flows over my curves.

'Please can you unzip it?' I ask boldly, very much liking this confident me who isn't afraid to ask for help or for what she wants.

In lieu of words, Owen's strong, sturdy hands gently move from my hips to my lower back, bunching up the fabric of my dress as he drags them up towards my shoulder blades, stopping when he reaches the zip of my dress. In one swift and careful movement, the zip glides down my back, goosebumps scatter across my skin as my dress falls to my knees and Owen and I fall backwards into the sumptuous quilt, tangled up in each other's limbs.

*

I'm unsure if it sounds utterly preposterous to call yourself delicious but that's exactly how Owen just made me feel. Every part of my body turned to liquid, like I was some sort of gourmet gelato that made him ravenous, yet one touch melted me to nothing but a puddle of delicious soft serve. Yet, despite the threat of my body dissolving under his flaming hot hands, he took his sweet time, savouring me, playing with me and pleasing me.

A flush of heat creeps up my neck. The flames have yet to die down, and I know my cheeks must be a rosy hue when I gaze up at Owen. We've somehow ended up in a cuddling position, my head tucked into the crook of his neck as my fingers tiptoe over his soft stomach and broad chest.

When he glances down at me, tucking his chin to his chest, he smiles so wide that the dimple pops in his left cheek. His smoky grey eyes are back to their blazing seafoam blue with flecks of amber and green, and there goes that wisp of spun sugar in my belly.

'Do you think they'll have missed us at the party?' he asks, lips turning into a small smirk, his eyes ablaze with mischief now, as the greens and blues start to blend together.

'No, not one bit,' I croak. 'It's not like the best man and maid of honour are an important part of the wedding.'

Owen lets out a bark of laughter that vibrates off my still very naked body.

'In that case, do we have to go back? I mean, we have everything we need in here,' he says, voice coming out more of a soft growl. His finger is tracing the curve of my hip, making goosebumps prickle upon my glistening, sweaty skin once more.

'But what about the buffet? Did you see the size of those mozzarella balls?' I argue, causing Owen to chuckle and squeeze my hip. The motion causes fireworks to explode south of my belly button, but truly, the salad the chefs were preparing for dinner looked mouth-wateringly out of this world; I can't imagine the delights Italians can do with miniature food items and how exquisite they might be.

'But we have profiteroles in here,' he counters and I see his eyes trail down from where his hand is squeezing my bottom, down my suddenly clenching thighs, to the tips of my toes.

'But they were wrapping basil leaves the size of my head around slices of beef tomato,' I plead, trying to ignore what Owen's hands are doing to me. Once was once, a one-time thing, it was innocent, two grown-ups letting off a bit of steam. Twice, twice is one too many times, twice is getting caught up in the lovey-dovey emotions of the day. That's not what we agreed upon.

'And didn't you see what they were doing with the Italian sausage? They were cutting it into small pieces and placing them on the fluffiest miniature hot dog buns. Italian sausage, Owen,' I add, shaking his chest playfully but purposefully. We needed to get off this bed. 'Everything we desire is out there,' I finish, more determined as I sit up, crossing an arm over my chest as I look around for where I flung my dress.

'I'm not sure about that,' Owen says, but it's a whisper I only just make out as he follows my lead and climbs off the bed along a rustle of blankets. His enchanting eyes are less intense silvery grey and more British-weather grey, and for a second, I worry that I've upset him. But it's only for a second because the Owen I know is on the same page as me. The Owen I know wouldn't want to snuggle up and get cosy when there is a cheese board the size of my living room on the other side of that door.

'Is everything OK, Owen?' I ask nonetheless, just to be certain.

'Yes, everything's fine,' he answers firmly, though his brows are slightly furrowed, at odds with his mouth that is trying to smile at me as he pulls on trousers. I gaze a little too long at the way they tug over his thick thighs and robust bum. His chuckle causes me to shake my head and avert my eyes.

'Is everything OK, Andrea?' he asks, and I relax hearing the laughter in his tone.

'Yes, everything's fine,' I parrot. That's good then, I concede, hearing my own words. We're both fine. There's no catching feelings, no getting upset and certainly no pang of sadness at the thought of not seeing Owen's bare bottom ever again.

18

The millisecond Owen and I walk onto the terrace, Owen nursing the large bowl of profiteroles, me nibbling the one that's in my hand – because one becomes rather ravenous after sex like that – Alex catches my eye and makes a beeline for me, pushing past anyone that gets in her way. She's walking at a terrifying speed for someone with a broken ankle so I know I'm in deep trouble.

Her eyes drift to Owen, to the bowl of stolen dessert, then to me, and I contemplate, actually contemplate, tripping up her good leg to stop whatever it is she's about to say to me from spilling out of her mouth. I don't do it, of course. I think one trip to the Italian emergency room during your wedding week is enough for a bride to handle; I don't wish to push my luck on how much one best friend can forgive the other.

When Owen goes to speak, she raises her hand to stop him, grasps a firm hand around the crease of my elbow as I'm about to pop the last bite of profiterole into my mouth and tugs me away to a more peaceful corner of the balcony, that is now lit up to the high heavens, like the stars above have attached themselves to the villa's paintwork.

'Lord knows I wanted you to relax this week but did

you seriously just have a quickie during my wedding party?' Alex whispers. I turn to look at her sharply as my stomach plummets and I drop, yes drop, a perfectly baked profiterole on the floor. Fear shoots into my chest with the thought that I have screwed up royally until I notice her lip twitching with a smile and her hazel eyes sparkle with the need for gossip.

'There was nothing quick about it.' Oh my god, did I just say that out loud? 'Oh gosh, I just sounded like Charlie,' I splutter, cheeks flushing crimson. This is too much, even with Alex. I don't do this, I don't get flustered or freely talk about my sex life, but then again, I've never had someone take the time to pleasure me and look at me the way Owen just did, like he was worshipping me. Is that grounds to want to tell your best friend everything? Alex loves telling me what she and Charlie get up to; I mean, her versions are a touch more PG than Charlie's no-frills approach. I could absolutely give you their top five rated vibrators and you know what? I'd be happy to, Charlie knows her stuff, but that's beside the point. Is this what it would feel like to be so fulfilled with your sex life that you can't help shout about it from the rooftops? There's no way I'm comparing Alex and Charlie's four-year relationship and healthy sex life with mine and Owen's afternoon of passion. But Hannah never looked at me as if I were a feast. Was it too much to ask to want to be looked at like you're the prime duck at Christmas dinner?

'Oh my gosh, we can double date, this is perfect,' Alex squeals, jumping up and down the best she can with her one good leg.

Suddenly, the prime duck isn't feeling so plump and juicy.

'Alex, shush, no,' I whisper, taking a step closer to her and lowering my head, 'it was just a one-time thing, OK. There'll be no double dates,' I tell her quickly, unable to help the flicker in my eyes as I look around, nervous about anyone overhearing.

The way Alex's face falls, her nose crinkling, her bright eyes growing slightly hooded tells me I've made a huge mistake.

'Andi, does Owen, my wife's very best friend, know that?' The way she looks at me, crestfallen, and emphasises the word 'wife' makes me lower my head further and nod vigorously.

'Oh gosh, yes, Alex. I'm not stupid. He's not looking for a relationship. I promise, we're great communicators, we just got caught up in the moment and we enjoyed ourselves, that's all.' My knees threaten to buckle as flashbacks of just how much I enjoyed Owen race through my mind but I stay strong.

'Are you sure, because I know I didn't want to admit it at first, but you two have been making quite the cute team this week and you seem to fit nicely together. Are you sure that's what you both want?' she asks, her voice softer now as she rests a baby-pink manicured hand on my forearm.

'Yes, of course that's what we both want,' I nod without hesitation. 'I've got way too much to think about when I get home, what with Mum and the shop, I don't need a relationship, OK, Alex?' I say firmly, giving her a pointed look. I need her to say she understands me and that I'm right.

'Yes, sir,' she replies after a hesitant pause. 'What's going on with Ned's?' she then asks, her eyes boring into mine.

'What? You mean, bar all the usual drama?' I chuckle despite the fear that creeps up my spine.

'God, Andrea, I'm so sorry, with all the wedding stuff, I did it again, didn't I? You said so on the mountain but I was so angry and I always think I can fix everything. What's going on?' I see her eyes slowly fill with water and quickly wrap my arms around her.

'No, no, no, no crying on your wedding day, at least no sad crying on your wedding day. You weren't all wrong on the mountain, we've already discussed that and I appreciate you more than you know for always having my back, but this one's a little trickier than wanting to lend me money or mopping up a wet floor; it's my mum,' I explain, because I know if I don't, she'll spend the rest of the evening preoccupied with thoughts of what it could be.

'Is she OK?' the question flies out of her mouth the second I close mine.

'She's more than OK,' I reply honestly as I look up and spot my mum dancing with Alex's parents on the dance floor, the crinkles around her eyes standing out, not because of stress or worry, but because she's laughing so hard, her eyes are sparkling and her cheeks are glowing. She one-steps to the right and left, waving her arms in the air without a care in the world. Now my eyes are threatening to waterlog. 'She's thinking about letting Ned's go.' Alex lets out a small gasp, so I continue quickly, 'It's OK. Look, we're going to talk about it when we get home, we haven't figured it all out yet but it's not something we should be discussing now. It's your wedding day, Alex. Where's that sexy wife of yours?' I nudge her shoulder. She lets out a soft sigh.

'Anything you need, Andi, you tell me. No excuses, no

saying I don't need help, you come to me,' she says sternly, prodding me in my chest and pressing her forehead against mine.

I chuckle, 'Yes, yes, I promise,' since asking for help hasn't exactly completely backfired on me today. And just as I'm concentrating on squeezing my thighs together, my brain having once again drifted to Owen, the big man himself appears, his hair practically giving everything away. I can't help myself; I'm patting it down and flicking it so his parting falls correctly while he's trying to hand me a plate of warm, crusty bread. Alex sniggers, causing me to stop faffing and take the plate.

Gone is the confident, cocky and sure of himself Owen that knew what to do in the bedroom and then some, and in his place is the Owen that gives Alex a butter-wouldn't-melt smile as his cheeks grow rosy.

He holds up a bowl of cheese that has come from the rotating spit over in the corner and my stomach growls, like it hasn't eaten portions of food this week that could feed me for a month back home.

'Thank you,' I say, picking up a piece of bread. I turn to Alex to ask her if she would like some but she's already hobbling away.

Behind Owen's back, she mouths so only I can see, 'But he brought you a bowl of cheese,' and grins as though she's reciting her wedding vows all over again.

The twinkling lights are very much the star of the show as the night draws to a close. I've managed not to make a fool of myself further by mostly avoiding the dance floor and instead raiding the buffet with Owen all evening, but now Charlie is all but demanding every guest get on the dance floor for the last songs of the evening. For some reason, she's giving me an extremely wicked grin as she does this.

'No one let the maid of honour and best man out of your sights; we want to see them dancing, upright,' she smirks and damn it if Alex didn't tell her. I send her the best evil glare I can muster as Owen simply smiles over his wine glass, seemingly unfazed by his best friend's words.

'You're thinking you broke the wrong one's ankle, aren't you?' he asks, winking at me, a hint of that sexy confidence coming through, which causes that familiar ripple of heat to zip through my body.

'How did you know?' I return, shaking off the embarrassment of Charlie's announcement and the dizziness I feel thanks to memories of Owen and his skilful mouth. People start shuffling around us and Nick pulls us along with him into the throws of humans wiggling and waving their body parts around with abandon.

'Weddings suck,' Owen leans down and whispers into my ear; apparently, dizzy is something I'm not going to escape any time soon.

I clear my throat. 'The hardest,' I croak, which makes Owen splutter on air as he offers me his hand when the loud beat becomes a soft, slow harmony.

I roll my eyes at him. 'Really, get your brain out of the gutter,' I tease, taking his hand. My body somehow relaxes and tenses at the same time when his calloused palms meet my smooth skin.

'My brain wasn't in the gutter, but clearly yours was. Please do share what you found in there,' he replies, cocking an eyebrow while placing his hand gently on my lower back, which instantly transports an electric current to all my erogenous zones under his touch. As we each take a step closer to one another, Owen's broad chest heaves and he lets out a heavy breath. Dancing upright might prove to be a challenge; I can barely form words to reply.

'No,' I manage, slightly out of breath. I promised Alex this, whatever this is with Owen was a one-time deal that is out of our systems now. The spark needs to fizzle out this instant. I can't be doing this whole acting vulnerable and needy thing, especially in front of all these people. What I need is to pull myself together.

'Andrea,' Owen says, swaying his hips against mine.

'Yes,' I breathe.

'You make for a better dance partner than what I'm used to.'

'Is that right?' I muse.

'Yes, the goats don't let me get this close.'

Laughter erupts from me, making me toss my head back. My loose waves cascade down my back, feeling light and free. I sense that Owen could feel the tension in my body and am grateful for this reprise and reminder that he and I make good friends. I can relax around him. I can do this.

The laughter hums in my throat as I move much lighter on my feet now, enjoying the slight evening breeze, when a woman walks over in a glittering silver dress and heels that mean she's eye level with Owen and towering over me. Sadie. The woman who gave Alex her first big break by highlighting her photography in her extremely classy travel magazine. I try not to roll my eyes at her presence, which takes an enormous amount of willpower with the five or so glasses of red that I have indulged in tonight.

'I don't mean to interrupt,' oh she definitely did, it's written all over her sultry smirk, 'is it the best man's duty to dance with all the bride's friends?' She quirks her perfectly threaded brow but doesn't look at me, only her prey. I notice she has her hand elegantly extended to Owen and only when he doesn't take it, does she look to me and give me a once over. I'm used to Owen's pauses by now, the seconds it takes him to process something before responding, but her lips twitch like she can't fathom why he hasn't tripped over his own feet for the opportunity to dance with her.

Whereas Alex doesn't rub glam, independent, successful businesswoman in your face, Sadie gets high off of it. Owning a shabby fish and chip shop and always smelling of salt and vinegar does not put me in Sadie's league, and she knows that.

'I'm so sorry I didn't catch you earlier; I wasn't expecting you to be here,' she croons. Yes, like Alex's best friend in the whole world wouldn't be at her wedding; what kind of ridiculous thought is that? 'I mean, how on earth did you afford the trip?' she pushes, and I feel extremely grateful I've only had the pleasure of meeting this woman a handful of times in the years Alex has known her.

'The best man only dances with the maid of honour, unfortunately,' Owen pipes up with a small smile and a tilt of his head.

Sadie immediately hides her embarrassment by throwing her mound of deep chestnut locks over her shoulders and puffing her chest out.

'Oh well, if you fancy something a little more high-end, I'm around,' she offers before sauntering off.

I'm caught between smugness and confusion as Owen takes my hand and turns back into me and we carry on dancing. I snort but there's a nervous laughter bubbling in my stomach at Owen's lack of decorum. I'm unsure as to why I'm nervous but my chest suddenly becomes a little too tight.

'You said, "it's unfortunate",' I muse.

'It's a little unfortunate,' he tells me in his matter-of-fact way.

'For you or for her?' I ask boldly, somehow matching Owen's honesty.

'For me,' he states, causing my stomach to plummet for whatever reason. 'As we've already established, you are a terrible dancer,' he adds and I feel as though I've just taken my first breath after being submerged in an icy lake. He's teasing me and the hint of a smirk on his lips feels dangerous. I can't have that.

'You can go and dance with her if you want to, Owen,' I say, catching the defensive tone in my own voice. I smile to balance it out, ensure everything is fine and casual.

'I'm dancing with you,' he says.

'Well, you don't have to dance with me,' I argue.

'Well, what if I want to dance with you?' he counters.

My lips betray me and crease at the corners. 'Well, I might not want to dance with you.'

'Well, I think you owe me a favour or three after that Harry Styles performance.'

'Stipulations should have been put forward and made

clear prior to the agreement and the act. Your argument won't hold up well in court,' I say confidently and with a firm nod.

'Is that so? And what would you know about law?' he asks, his eyes beaming down at me when I meet his gaze.

'Hey, I've watched a few episodes of *Suits*.'

'Ooh, so she does know what relaxing is.'

'If your idea of relaxing is watching TV to study if someone can sue you because they claim there's not enough gravy on their chips and gravy, then sure.'

I feel Owen's laughter against my stomach as his own bounces up and down.

'No way,' he exclaims, tightening his arms around my waist where his laughter had loosened them.

'Yes way,' I confirm, adjusting my arms around his neck and ignoring the slight twinge of pins and needles as the blood leaves my fingertips from being held at such a steep, high angle.

'I bet your chips and gravy have the perfect amount of chips to gravy ratio.'

'Thank you, I think so,' I say softly, trying to push down the quell of anxiety that rears its ugly head in my brain at the thought of heading back home to it all. Before my eyes can completely glaze over, a woman with the sweetest button nose covered in freckles and chocolate-brown eyes steps up to Owen and me. She's wearing the most gorgeous chiffon playsuit over her generous curves and is looking from me to Owen and back again. She must be one of Charlie's friends as I can't place her.

'Will you save me a dance?' she stutters politely. She's gorgeous and I'm momentarily stunned that she is asking me and not Owen. I should dance with her. I should spend some time away from Owen tonight, get used to being apart now that the wedding is over. Soon we will be going back to our separate lives, miles apart. He's not going to be there to catch me every time I stumble and I don't need him to be.

I go to say yes but what comes out is, 'I'm so sorry, I'm afraid I'm on best man duty; I've got to keep him out of trouble.'

The woman smiles sweetly. 'I totally understand. Enjoy the rest of your night,' she says and walks away, making me wonder if aliens have intercepted my brain. What am I doing? Owen's hands feel a touch firmer on my lower back, his lips move to my ear; he's leaning in again.

'You said, "I'm afraid",' he whispers, causing me to turn my head towards him, our lips now centimetres apart; he's all dimples and cocky smirk.

'I know what I said. This is all incredibly taxing for me,' I breathe.

'I'm terribly sorry I'm so hard,' he croaks, his voice coming out husky.

'I don't think you are sorry,' I reply, my voice matching his.

I'm saved by the final chorus of the last song. It fades into nothing, getting lost in the black night and the serene sound of the waves lapping against the cobbled beach far away in the distance. Owen twirls me around to a stop and the cool air that fills the space between us knocks some sense into me. Guests begin to disperse, hugging Alex and Charlie on their way out, thanking Will and Gio and taking their tiny, bagged macarons with them.

'I never thanked you for picking up the macarons,' I say

to Owen, clearing my throat and staring up into his weary eyes; his waterline is a touch red, his eyelids heavy with sleep.

'That's OK, you were too busy bashing up brides,' he says, deadpan. I shove him in his soft bicep. He lets out a low groan and rubs where my knuckles brushed him.

'You know, you don't have to save me; I'm a very independent woman,' I tell him, half serious, like I have to remind him of our agreement, of what I keep telling everyone else too, yet I can hear the hint of playfulness in my melody. I have been listening to my family, my friends; I like them being around and am appreciative of their gestures to look after me. But I don't need any more looking after tonight.

'Oh I wasn't trying to save you, no; your pitfalls this week have been highly entertaining,' he replies, and I should be offended but the twinkle in his grey eyes tells me he's ribbing me. I enjoy Owen's humour. It's important to enjoy your friend's humour, be on the same page. Owen and I are on the same page and his tired eyes look like mine feel. It's time for bed and when I say bed, I mean my own bed for sleep. I need to go to and actually sleep in my bed, alone.

19

My arms automatically stretch out to my sides, gliding along the silky sheets like they are searching for something, reaching for someone as the early sunrise streaks orange and yellow flares through my window. My head is a tad fuzzy with a red wine haze but when my fingers come up empty of any soft skin or warm body, I remember that I was sensible last night.

Yes, I had bid goodnight to Owen like I'd bid goodnight to my mother, a kiss on the cheek, a smile and a cheers with a glass of water to show that I was being a good girl. As I flutter my eyelids open, allowing for the light to greet my eyes in steady doses, I contemplate the merits of being a good girl. Being a good, independent, strong woman – who didn't need anyone by her side, or in her bed – wasn't all that I'd cracked it up to being after having Owen as a permanent fixture at my hip over the last few days. And especially not after our spicy afternoon romp in this glorious bed. I squint my eyes closed and take a deep breath with a heavy reluctance to admit that I am feeling the absence of his warm scent and his full, luscious body. I palm my chest where the memories of his weight on top of me make my body heat, and the image of his smooth skin flush against mine make me tingle.

OK, that's enough. I whip the duvet off me and though the Mediterranean heat is already cooking up the villa, stepping out from under the cosy blanket sends a brief chill over my skin and immediately wakes me from my sleepy fog and steamy thoughts.

With no more wedding activities to attend to, the next two days are free of fairy tales and magical bubbles; there's no need for Owen and me to work together or spend so much time side by side. It's back to reality, back to real life, to getting my head on straight and preparing for everything that awaits me when I return home. A home that isn't stunning landscapes or picturesque villas. A home where I only wish the food was as incredible as the food I have tasted here, and a home that is void of Owen, because Owen doesn't live a door down; he lives a hop, skip and a plane ride away, here in Italy.

I twirl the tips of my fingers around my loose hair, toying with the idea of tying it up when a knock at the door makes me jump.

It sounds again but this time, the raps are longer and the tune pricks at my ears like I know it from somewhere. I walk towards the noise and swing it open to find Owen filling the door frame and humming 'Adore You' with a smile on his handsome face. His fluffy not-quite beard but not quite five o'clock shadow highlights his soft jaw and sharp cheekbones and his eyes this morning are a vivid grey-blue. So much for getting back to reality today and keeping my distance; it seems that Owen has other ideas.

'Our excursion starts in fifteen minutes and I wouldn't

recommend pyjamas,' he tells me, his eyes sparkling with enthusiasm and a hint of trouble as he looks me up and down. His tongue subtly glides over his bottom lip, but there's an innocence to his stance, hands in his short pockets, shoulders relaxed, that puts me at ease like he's not here to corrupt my plan, just here to hang out.

'I thought there were no more excursions,' I reply, eyeing him curiously.

'The work of the maid of honour and best man never stops,' he says with a dramatic sigh and shake of his head that causes his hair to fall into his smiling eyes. I look away as my stomach flips and walk towards the bathroom. I don't even have to look in the mirror to know I'm smiling. Then I pause abruptly, remembering my good-girl status.

Turning back to face Owen, I say, 'Owen, I'm sorry, I can't today. I'm needed here at the villa; there's lots to do,' with a determined nod. See, that was easy and Owen doesn't even look that disappointed; his face doesn't change from his laid-back smile. He knows the deal; we're friends, or you could say just two professionals who have been doing their jobs, of acting maid of honour and best man, over these past few days.

'OK, yeah sure, that's no problem. I saw everyone busy on the balcony this morning. Nick and Paula were sat chatting to your mum about how wonderful it is that their daughter is now married, how special it is having a daughter-in-law and how your mum has so much to look forward to. Have fun and I'll catch you later.' His words come out without a hint of sarcasm, just complete pokerfaced, as I've become accustomed to with Owen, but it's the twitch in his dimple and way his eyes glow more blue that gives away his cheek.

'Fine,' I say, suddenly feeling like I have to be as far away from the villa as I can get today while everyone basks in post wedding-day bliss.

Owen stays in the doorway, his eyes scanning the room as I make quick work of splashing my face with cold water, putting on deodorant and a smidge of blusher after brushing my teeth in record time. I wonder for a moment if he's thinking about the last time we were in this room together. I shake away the thought as I step into Alex's cream playsuit that somehow appeared in my bathroom the other day. I love my best friend but right now, I might love the playsuit that little bit more. It's exquisitely delicate against my skin and for once, I feel like I'm wearing the right attire for a summer's day.

I go to twist my hair into a bun but when I see Owen at the door smiling at me with his easy grin, I leave it flowing and slip into my sliders.

'I'm ready,' I say, lifting and then lowering my arms.

'Perfect,' he replies, turning into the hallway, but not before I notice the slight flush in his cheeks.

I skip out of the door and close it behind me.

'What exactly am I ready for, Owen?' The thought suddenly occurring to me as I follow him towards the front of the villa.

'You'll see,' he says over his shoulder.

'I'll see what?' I try again; the control freak inside of me does not like the sound of 'just seeing', yet as I fall into step with Owen, my heart does that racing yet calm beat. As his Owen scent wraps around me, 'just seeing' feels just fine.

★

'It smells,' I tell Owen, my hands firmly in the pockets of my playsuit – yes, it even has pockets, such an absolute winner that I hope it's mine for keeps and Alex wasn't just lending it to me. I scrunch up my face in an attempt to block the smell from entering my nostrils.

'It really does,' Owen says with a laugh, shoving his nose into his shoulder as milk squirts from the goat's teats, which reside between Owen's long fingers.

Michelangelo is standing behind Owen, clapping his hands shouting, 'Bravo, bravo!', and whenever Owen's hands slip, the short, stocky man immediately wraps his arms around Owen's large body, places his hands on top of his paws and guides Owen back to a steady rhythm like a far less erotic version of that scene from *Ghost*.

'I can't believe you brought me here; you're actually putting me off cheese,' I say, unable to take the giggle out of my voice as I watch Owen milk a goat, his knees nearly touching his chin as he sits atop a tiny stool.

'If trips to the bathroom haven't put you off cheese, then I highly doubt this will, Andrea,' Owen remarks before standing up at Michelangelo's arm gesturing. He has a point. Cheese doesn't love me as much as I love it. It's the heartbreak, the unrequited love story no one ever prepares you for as you near adulthood. I instinctively take a step back while Owen cleans his hands on a rather unsterile and raggedy-looking cloth that Michelangelo hands him.

It's not that I'm opposed to getting my hands dirty, far from it, but the smell is becoming quite unbearable, and considering I've already sent one human to the hospital this vacation, I'm unsure of my capability with goats.

'I think it's best to leave this little one to enjoy its day,' I say to Michelangelo, who nods at my English enthusiastically and points to the stool and bucket.

'Unless you know more Italian than you let on, I think you're milking a goat today, Andrea,' Owen says with a slight lean towards my ear as he places his hands on my shoulders, guides me towards the goat and pushes me down onto the stool.

'Is this all part of your mountain-boy aesthetic?' I shoot back, giving him a narrow-eyed glare. My knuckles squeeze together as my shoulders tense. I'm nervous to touch the poor goat's teats. Does it really want me fondling it when it could be off grazing on the hillside of Positano, enjoying the delightful views? I highly doubt it.

'I might live on the mountains out here, but I've never actually milked anything before,' Owen tells me. 'My dad has some land back home, but it's currently just his and my brother's workshop. He looks after the land, planting new trees, looking after the old ones, but there's no livestock. My dad's talked about it and I think that would be a dream of his, but it's a lot of work, and with the furniture having taken off these last few years, I'm not sure it's the right time.'

'That must be lovely to see a future for the land though?' I ask, biding a little more time before I have to touch the goat, and genuinely interested in Owen's world. I love how his often laid-back limbs become more animated when he talks about his family. I only wish I felt that way about the chip shop these days. How I'd love for it to be so busy that I had to turn down other opportunities.

'Oh, definitely. My brother has always talked about being self-sufficient; he'd love to run a fully functioning sustainable farm one day,' Owen adds, almost brushing a hand through his hair, before thinking better of it and looking over his palm. I can't help but smirk at his dorky moments.

'And you?' I question just as Michelangelo comes up behind me and wraps his arms around my waist, guiding my hands towards the goat's privates. I let out a screech as Owen steps back with a howl of laughter. Clearly small talk isn't something Michelangelo cares for when there is a goat that needs milking.

'I'm so sorry,' I whisper to the goat as its warm teats meet my fingertips. I can hear Owen snickering in the background as Michelangelo tugs and tugs. Once the milk starts to flow into the bucket, he lets go and his movement creates a waft of air, sending the aromatic smell of the goat's juices straight to the back of my throat. Caught off guard and my stomach threatening to empty its contents, I squeeze a little too hard and twist my hand so the teat sends a rainbow squirt in Owen's direction, coating the top of his shorts and base of his white tee.

Michelangelo's arms are waving in the air. I hastily let go of the goat, who stomps away angrily, and no doubt in pain, while 'Mamma mia, mamma mia' choruses through the atmosphere. I assume he's yelling at me for wasting the milk as he shakes his head at Owen's soaked clothing and quickly moves the bucket away from my manic, hopping from side to side, feet.

'I'm so sorry.' I bow at Michelangelo as he hugs the bucket to his chest and stalks back towards a small shack.

Owen's face is a combination of amused and slightly upset. One side of his lips is quirked upwards while his eyebrows are pointing downwards, creasing the top of his straight nose. He's holding the hem of his shirt away from his stomach, and if it wasn't for the croissants doing a nervous jig in the base of my belly, there would be room for the butterflies caused by the sight of the soft, light-brown hair that trails from his belly button and disappears into his waistband.

'I saw today going differently in my mind,' Owen says with a chuckle which makes my shoulders loosen a little. I wipe the sweat away from my brow with the back of my hand and meet his gaze. His eyes sparkle more blue in the vibrant sunlight and I feel my stomach slowly settle.

'I'm sorry, Owen, I didn't mean to spoil it. What do we do now?' I ask, hands on my hips as I look around the field of goats where there is not another human in sight. Michelangelo has retired to his barn and doesn't seem to be coming back, and I don't think Owen or I have the capability of figuring out how to make cheese on our own – that, and Michelangelo ran off with the goods.

'Maybe I should have asked the experts about the best cheese-making class and not taken Michelangelo's two Facebook posts verbatim. I can't see a kitchen or a gift shop around here,' Owen says, sounding downtrodden. 'But Will, Gio and Roberta, they've all been so busy this week, and I've never thought to make cheese even after living here for so many years.'

I take a step forward, about to put my hand on Owen's chest, but think better of it when I catch a whiff of him.

'If it's any consolation, I bet Michelangelo makes the best cheese. Thank you for doing this, Owen,' I say sincerely, looking up at him, my neck tilting forty-five degrees. I can't help smile that he thought to bring me to a cheese-making class despite what he knows it does to my stomach. That thought surely can't be sexy, yet here we are. A man who knows how much I love cheese and is willing to accept the consequences. 'How long do we have until the minivan returns to pick us up?'

Owen's eyes widen as he looks from his watch then around the deserted fields. 'Three or four hours.'

'Bloody hell, how long does it take to make cheese?' I gasp. Droplets of sweat are tickling my chest, the sun above the fields unforgiving. We have no water or shelter.

'We can start walking,' Owen suggests, pulling the hem of his t-shirt away from his skin again. 'Sorry, Andrea,' he adds, a grimace etched on his rugged face.

'What are you sorry for? I should be apologising for covering you in goat fluid,' I say, watching his movements and feeling bad that he must be terribly uncomfortable right now, but at the same time, I can't let him waft any longer. 'You're going to have to stop that, Owen; just take your top off. Maybe we should leave it behind as today's casualty; that thing stinks and you wafting it is torture to my nostrils.'

Owen nods and we fall into step down the narrow path, away from the field of goats and what I hope is towards the winding streets of Positano.

'Andrea?'

'Yes.'

'Thank you for coming with me' Owen says, reaching out and putting a heavy arm across my shoulder blades before pulling me into him for a hug. I embrace his sweet gesture and can't resist his cuddle until it hits me.

'Owen,' I shout but it comes out muffled as my face is squished against his chest, 'let me go!'

Owen squeezes a little tighter for a second. 'I thought we were having a moment,' he says as he releases me and I swat at all his body parts.

He raises his arms to protect himself, but he's not aware of my fly-swatting skills during a particular hot British day in a fish and chip shop. Mr Miyagi would be proud of my wax on, wax off motions.

'You need to dispose of that t-shirt, Owen,' I express, switching my hand from Owen to swatting in front of my nose to dispel the rancid smell. He looks around at the open fields and many garden levels that surround us, where there is nothing but lush foliage and the odd goat grazing, not a bin in sight.

'I'm not littering and it's a good shirt, Andrea,' he says as he pulls it over his head and tucks a sleeve into his back pocket, leaving the rest to dangle like a tail. I clear my throat and triple check for rubbish bins. Owen baring his body in public, with sweat highlighting the speckle of body hair on his chest, the sun's rays casting shadows across his curvy hips – I'm biting my bottom lip hard. It's not until I draw blood that I promptly start walking forward, ignoring the small, almost shy, smile on Owen's face as he watches me ogle him.

'I'm not sure that's the right way,' he shouts from behind me. I stop without turning around. I just need a minute or two to cool my flushed cheeks.

'I think it's this way,' he informs me, striding past, his shoulder brushing past me. Now I'm staring at his back, which is somewhat helpful as it shields the sun from my scorching neck, though it does nothing to calm the heat in other parts of my body as I take in the broad back of this mountain of a man.

We start walking up a steep incline, away from a dry patch of land with nothing but browning grass and plumes of weeds, and twist left to another level more full of vegetables, the large leaves sprouting from the rich, dark soil. I let Owen get a few steps ahead before following, the sun, the mix of smells and the flutters he causes in my belly making my head spin.

We fall into a comfortable silence, tainting the Positano air with the heady sour aroma of goat juice and sweat, and it seems to be taking an age to find the road that leads to the villa. I don't remember all these twists and turns when the one-thousand-year-old minivan dropped us off, but that might be due to having my eyes closed and praying the coughing engine didn't give out and cause us to roll off the cliff.

My stomach gurgling and the way the mountain descends into silence notifies me that it must be around lunch time. Italy falls into this beautiful calm when families are sat together to feast. It's quiet, then you get the odd chatter, the rattling of dishes, heavy bowls laden with pasta being set down on the table. It's wonderful. It's even better when you are sat around one of those tables, breaking up fresh bread and scooping up gooey burrata with it instead of getting lost traipsing through what I'm sure are other people's gardens.

The heat and my lack of fitness is making my breathing ragged, so I'm grateful for the quiet. In the moment I promise myself I will never complain about the heat at Ned's again – someone write that sentiment down on a calendar to remind me of my words when I inevitably complain about the British summertime at the shop – that is, if Ned's is still standing by next summer.

On my next breath, I get a sharp pain in my chest and quickly shake my head to get the negative thoughts out of my mind. I don't want them consuming me during these last two days; I'll have plenty of time for overthinking when I get home. Mid-shake, I hear a car backfire and instinctively jump to the side, only to realise it's my wheezing and my own rattling chest producing the noise.

Charlie had mentioned the Italian steps and slopes before but this is ridiculous. I'm starting to feel like I am perpetually leaning. My thighs burn from all the lactic acid build-up that hasn't been released since I had to squat in front of the fridge to keep it from toppling over while Mum fished out a twenty-pound note that had floated behind it.

Stretching my body skyward to allow all the air into my gasping lungs, I don't see the small step up onto a slight pavement and promptly trip. I can now add wailing to the list of noises my body is making.

'Ouch!' I proclaim to no one as the throbbing in my ankle gets bolder and the cuts that now decorate my palms sting my flesh. I twist around gingerly so I'm not performing a downward dog to the scarce passing car and take a seat on the pavement. Lifting my arm to shield myself from the sun, I look around in search of Owen; admittingly, I was half expecting him to be standing over me, arms outstretched to help. I suddenly baulk at that thought: the fact that my brain would even conjure a vision like that. I don't need a knight in shining armour; I'm my own damn knight.

Yet as Owen's hips sway from side to side some way in

the distance, I seem to howl a little louder than necessary as I push myself onto my feet, or should I say foot, as when I put pressure on my right foot, I get a sharp pain in the bony bit of my ankle.

'Ouch!' I cry, louder still, but Owen is oblivious. I inhale and tell myself to get a grip and begin to hobble just as Owen turns around. I can make out the way his face scrunches slightly, then he waves, his giant palm making a rainbow over his head, before he points down at a low, rusty-looking iron gate as if to say, 'I'll wait here'. I shoot him a thumbs up and an extremely forced grin. I can do this; a tweaked ankle is the least of what I deserve after what I put Alex through. A few cubes of ice and I'll be good to go.

Forcing the thought of karma coming after me over the cliff, I put one wobbly foot in front of the other, trying my hardest not to wince each time my right foot makes contact with the uneven ground, and make the walk of shame over to Owen.

By the time I reach him, I'm ready for a week-long nap. The backs of my knees are dripping – keeping my hair down was a terrible idea as strands now stick to my collarbone and chest, and every time they tickle me, I try to pull the loose ones away, only to find that they are attached, making my cranium tender.

'Are you alright, Andrea?' Owen asks, leaning down and placing a heavy hand on my shoulder. For a minute, I'm about to be sarcastic, I can taste the sharp words on the tip of my tongue, but the way Owen is looking at me all innocence and warm, blue-grey eyes, his hair sticking to his own neck, my loose ones now sticking to his hand, I feel my eyes sting and my bottom lip begins to tremble.

'No, I'm not,' I whimper, giving up on pretending for once. 'I'm hot and tired, I need a bath and I just tripped up and twisted my ankle and I don't know what I'm doing with my life.' My brain seems to stagger for a second, like it's trying to figure out what just happened. I just said how I honestly felt and Owen is smiling at me. Why is he smiling at my pain?

'Andrea,' he speaks gently but his tone is kind and the furthest away from condescending. 'Would you like a piggyback the rest of the way?'

Of course I don't want a piggyback; I'm not five. 'No,' I blubber. 'No, I don't need a piggyback,' I say as Owen is reaching out his hand and I am taking it. He lowers his delicious bottom to the ground in a squat position and I'm climbing him.

'Ready?' he asks, wrapping his large hands around my thighs and straightening up. It's algebra-like difficult to keep my mind from remembering what happened the last time he had his hands in the same position. My body gives a pleasant shudder.

'Yes,' I reply, desperate to swim back to the present, yet my head defies me and nuzzles against his cheek like his hair is a fluffy pillow for me to lay my weary head.

'Oh shi—'

'What? What?' I shout, snapping upright, causing Owen to stagger backwards.

'Woah, Andrea,' he calls, like I'm the horse and he's the jockey, but it takes me a second to settle as I come to and register that I'm riding Owen, the villa in the distance and bird poop atop Owen's head.

'Oh god,' I shout while casually wiping my drool off Owen's shoulder with the back of my hand, hoping he's too distracted to work out what I'm doing.

'It's OK, it's OK, isn't it meant to be good luck or something, and we're not far from the house,' Owen tells me. I'm flabbergasted by his nonchalant approach to this devastating situation. If a bird pooed on my head, I would be far more distressed, yet he doesn't complain and troops on. I don't quite nuzzle into him like I had done before; I keep my head at arm's length, no doubt making the steep walk up to the villa that much tougher for him, but his attitude has my arms gripping around his sweaty back that much tighter, because, well, who is this special specimen that doesn't get offended by bird poop while carrying a nine-stone human up a mountain side while the sun is frying his skin?

The butterflies in my stomach are doing nothing to aid in my 'just seeing Owen as a friend' plan.

'Yes, I guess,' I mumble, my voice a little groggy from my however-long nap and swaying thoughts.

'What the hell happened to you two?' Charlie shouts, appearing suddenly from behind one of the large, potted conifers that guard either side of the entrance to the driveway. Alex appears by her side – both of them look divine in their colour-coordinating outfits. Olive shorts and a skinny-strapped white tank top for Alex and an open olive shirt with white linen pants for Charlie. Both their rings sparkling beautifully on their hands.

I attempt to jump off Owen but instead, he bends down slowly, taking his time so I have a simple and smooth dismount instead.

'Cheese,' I say, as Owen says, 'Goats.'

'Goats,' I correct myself as Owen does the same, shouting, 'Cheese!' I dare not look at him for my cheeks are already heating.

'Well, their stories match up,' Charlie shrugs, eyeing us both dubiously. 'Though that doesn't explain your lack of shirt, dearest best friend. Have you two been getting to know each other in the grounds?' she adds with a wiggle of her eyebrows, just in case I didn't know what she was inferring.

But then Alex gasps as she steps forward then backwards, like she was going to hug me but immediately thinks better of it. 'Not smelling like that they haven't,' she informs Charlie sweetly.

'We're going to the club,' Charlie says, taking her wife's hand and walking a safe distance around us. 'You're welcome to join us.'

'But shower first,' Alex chirps with her Disney Princess sing-song voice.

Owen and I both put our thumbs up and wave them off. I don't know whose stomach growls first but suddenly, it's like we're having a conversation through our bellies as we traipse through the house. We utter no words to each other as Owen drops me off at my room. He nods, which I reciprocate, before I sweep into the comfort of my abode.

20

My whole body is tense and it's with great trepidation that I place one pointed toe into the shower, careful not to slip on what feels like my crumbly ankle as I brace myself for the sting of my cuts. I wince, blowing air through my teeth, when they connect with the red-hot rainfall. It's all I can do not to jump up and down to distract myself from the pain, but my ankle sees that that would be a terrible idea as it throbs with each move I make.

Slowly, I begin to unfurl under the blissful stream, unclenching my shoulder blades and relaxing my tight chest. It feels good to wash away today's grime. Looking up at the shower head, I let the water cascade over my cheeks as my mind wanders to thoughts of dinner. Though, while I love the idea of food, which is backed up by my grumbling stomach, there's a small part of my body that might argue for the comfort of the sheets and that I should continue my nap from earlier. As soapy suds weave their way down my chest, I can't help but contemplate whether the luxury pillow that I was tempted to smuggle home draws any competition to Owen's nest of hair and broad shoulders. Following the soap suds with delicate fingers, my eyelids droop heavily and dreamily before I hastily twist the shower to freezing and let out a screech.

Even though I knew it was coming, the blast of icy water makes me gasp like a floppy fish and hop on my one good foot. I reach for my towel, quickly wrapping it around myself and sitting on the edge of the bath to relieve some of the pressure in my sore ankle.

'Bad Andi, bad Andi,' I scold myself for my dark thoughts and shiver in the steamy room. Little goosebumps prickle my skin and I force a deep breath to calm my frazzled emotions. If I wasn't so ravenous, maybe I'd skip dinner tonight and stay in the safety of my room alone, but with each tummy rumble comes a wave of nausea that I know will not be alleviated until I've had a small taste. I make quick work of twisting my hair into a top knot, throw on an oversized t-shirt and pyjama shorts, then slip into my sliders and head towards the kitchen.

The mouth-watering scent of fresh tomato sauce hits me the moment I step inside the place where it's safe to say the magic most definitely happens. It's warm but not scorching, making me think the chatter I can hear from the balcony is continued conversation from lunch time. When I walk out onto the balcony, Will, Gio, Nonna Roberta, Zia Allegra, Nick, Paula and my mum are all laying back in their chairs, broken bread before them, wine glasses, beakers of water and tiny espresso cups spread out across the large table between bowls and plates of scrumptious-looking dishes. A smile forms effortlessly on my face. Italy does it right. Eating is an event. It's a time to pause with the ones you love and savour the food you are eating, take in its flavours, appreciate the time it took to make. The chip shop is always so hustle and bustle, people rushing in for a chip sandwich or chips in a cone to guzzle down. We're fast food to take home or eat on the go; we don't get to see the customers' faces while they're tucking in.

My grandad could talk for hours with his customers; now it seemed no one had a spare minute to chat and I couldn't honestly say it was all on them. With my extensive to-do list always looming over my head, it was almost like I was willing customers to shoot off so I could clean up and see to my never-ending tasks – that, and keep the customer flow going, make room for the next crowd. I can feel another crack form in my heart; I was doing it all wrong.

'Ciao, *bella*,' Nonna Roberta shouts before shooting to her feet and procuring a few extra plates and bowls. I round the table and greet Mum with a kiss on the cheek before Roberta is strong-arming me into a chair. I nod and wave at the rest of the party with a grateful smile as Roberta immediately starts loading a plate with steak in tomato sauce and boiled potatoes and sets it down in front of me. However, she doesn't stop there; next picking up a bowl, she heaps a good three ladles full of a gorgeous-looking penne pasta with broad beans that smell fried and juicy, before adding a full ciabatta loaf to the edge of the bowl. A smaller plate sees that I have at least four different kinds of cheeses at my disposal and a handful of taralli.

'*Grazie, grazie*,' I say, gently patting her hand to signal I've got plenty.

She bows, nodding and waving her hands at me. '*Mangia, mangia*,' she coos before sitting back down in her seat and casually picking up a tangerine to peel. I have a funny feeling the tangerine will find its way to my side of the table in a second.

Taking in my company, I'm pleased to see that my mum

has a dreamy, almost lazy demeanour going on. She's relaxed into her chair, arms outstretched, wine glass dangling loosely in one hand and not a worry wrinkle interrupting the glow on her face. I could get used to seeing her like this. I spike a piece of pasta with my fork and can't help my eyes drifting to the balcony doors. I was certain Owen was just as hungry as me but he's yet to make an appearance. Maybe he's on a call or the goat milk was taking a little longer to scrub from the fine hairs on his stomach.

'Hmm,' I clear my throat and take a bite out of the ciabatta.

'Do we go to Amalfi tomorrow and get you a dress?' Zia Allegra challenges and it takes me a second to register that she is talking to me. Her feet are up and resting over the corner of the table, which I'd have thought blasphemous in Italy but everyone is far too relaxed to care.

'A dress for what?' I reply, covering my mouth with my cut hand.

'For your wedding, no? It's good to be prepared, you no find them at home like Amalfi,' she sings, waving her bejewelled hands in the air, the apricot sun reflecting in her rings and nearly blinding me. I squint my eyes and shovel a rather large chunk of burrata into my mouth.

'I'm not getting married,' I choke on the creaminess of the cheese.

'*Ma*, one day,' Nonna Roberta says dreamily, placing the tangerine segments in front of me.

'It will be better next time, love,' Nick adds with a sympathetic tone, like he hasn't forgotten the last time I dabbled in it either, 'you've just got to find the right one.'

'The one, the two, the three, does not matter, you love,

you're young, you've got all the time,' Zia Allegra says boldly like she's firing up a crowd on *Ant and Dec's Saturday Night Takeaway*.

It's fine, sweetheart, you've plenty of time. If you want to get married, if you don't want to get married, that's fine too,' my mum chimes in with casual support, which I think is all I'm getting.

'*Ma* celebrate,' Zia Allegra booms.

'Such a beautiful ceremony,' Will comes at it neutral, swirling around the red wine in his class.

'I do it again. Simple, elegant,' Gio hums, looking at Will wistfully and I'm not sure if he's talking about their daughter's wedding or their own.

'I just remembered that I need to do something,' I say, standing painfully, having briefly forgotten the hurt in my ankle – I really did need to find some ice. 'Not to be rude but I'm going to take these,' I add, but it seems no one is paying me much attention anymore as they happily reminisce about wedding days gone by.

Balancing the bowl of pasta in the crook of my elbow, the plate of steak on one forearm and taking the cheese plate and a bowl of fruit in each hand, I carefully retreat from the table, not without noticing my mother gazing at me softly. Her eyes are glistening and I can't tell if I've disappointed her or if she's trying not to dwell on how we're different to the rest of the table, how marriage didn't quite work out for either of us. Then she chuckles at something Zia Allegra says and I allow myself to exit.

Walking along the corridor, there's still no sign of Owen, and before I know what I'm doing, I'm knocking on his bedroom door. After a minute, that was probably more like a second, with no answer, I nudge the door with my free elbow and give it a push. It sweeps slowly open, the light from behind me tinging the room with an amber glow, and on the bed rests a mountain of a man with a bath towel wrapped around his bottom half and his bare upper half moving gracefully up and now as he subtly snores.

There's no second guessing my impulsive decision now though, as my limbs suddenly burn with the memory of our earlier hike and both my arms and my ankle protest enough that I make to tiptoe across his bedroom towards his desk to ease them of the weight. Moving as quietly as I can, which apparently isn't that quiet at all – my toe connects with a stray shoe and I can't help question why it isn't by the door, and my knee connects with the ottoman at the end of the bed – I hold my breath to strengthen my core so no plates go crashing to the floor. Bending my knees gracefully as I lower the plates steadily onto the desk, yet they still somehow manage to clatter.

A loud snort mixed with a grunt and half cough bounces off the stone walls and causes me to freeze.

'Andrea, is that you?' Owen asks sleepily.

'Room service,' I reply, stretching out my elbows like I'm about to swing a tennis racket to rid them of pins and needles.

'Oh god, I fell asleep,' Owen recalls, his voice soft and raspy.

I turn around and am greeted by his half naked frame sitting on the edge of the bed, and I'd be lying if I said I didn't have to squeeze my thighs together.

'That's OK, they're having an early dinner or I think it's still lunch; either way, I thought you'd be hungry,' I tell him, averting my gaze to the crumpled clothes on the ottoman. I can't say Owen is tidy.

'Oh, Andrea.' His voice is sleep-rough and warm.

I stuff a piece of cheese in my mouth for distraction and mumble, 'I'll leave this here for you,' and start towards the open bedroom door. Owen promptly stands, towel securely tucked in, not budging an inch – how did he do that? I can never get it to stay up.

'I know I'm a big boy,' he starts with a light chuckle, hand on his stomach, 'but that can't all be for me. Have dinner with me?'

It had been my idea to knock, and I was still starved, having not eaten much around the table, which is evident when my stomach lets out a small plea in the form of a rumble.

'OK,' I answer, twirling right back around and lunging for the cheese.

Owen throws on a large, grey t-shirt and carries the meat and pasta over to the bed, gesturing with a cock of his head for me to follow. I carefully put the cheese plate and fruits down before climbing onto the bed and crossing my legs.

'So, I know your favourite cheese, but what's your favourite movie of all time?' Owen asks, he's twisted a little so his legs are dangling off the bed, as he breaks off a chunk of ciabatta and hands it over to me before pulling a piece off for himself.

I smile gratefully but narrow my eyes in thought.

'Erm, I have absolutely no idea. I always disliked rom-coms growing up, obviously,' I reply with a knowing chuckle. Owen smirks in response. 'But I can't say that I'm much of a horror or action fan either. I'd suggest them to Alex just so I didn't have to sit through a rom-com, but I can't say they were pleasant. I suppose I'd go for a drama, something more real if I had time to watch them.'

'So you're not a movie buff?' Owen smiles, forking a bite of pasta with broad beans into his mouth.

'Not in the slightest, what about you?' I ask, pinching a bean with my fingers. How one could make a bean taste so divine I didn't know. It was fluffy and buttery, a touch salty and slightly charred, and the flavour packed a delightful punch.

'I like a good drama, documentaries too,' he offered, tearing a piece of steak with his fingers. I had forgotten to grab any cutlery bar the single fork.

'It seems we keep eating like this,' I note, wiggling my messy fingers.

'You can't beat a bedroom picnic,' Owen replies, munching on another slice of cheese, his eyes catching mine. The small window behind him allows the light to highlight his features just so. This evening, they shine a brilliant blue with a greyish twinge. His eyes are dangerous.

'If I wasn't so hungry, every part of me would revolt and tell you that this is wrong. Food on the bed? A sacrilege,' I argue, though I'm smiling.

'Does it not taste better when you can use your hands and simply relax?' Owen queries, placing a piece of tomatoey steak atop a small piece of bread and taking a bite.

'That looks good.' I tear at the bread and dip my hands in the sauce to claim a sliver of steak and pop the whole thing into my mouth. 'Suppose it does,' I add when it takes great strength for me to not groan and fall into the cosy duvet with deep satisfaction.

In perfect synchronicity, we shovel palms of pasta and chomp on slices of cheese and make tiny steak sandwiches with the bread until not even a drop of sauce is left on the plates. Owen is right; resting my ankle against the soft, silky fabric while indulging in such a fine meal, I've never felt happier. I can't fault the company either. Owen in a towel, albeit he covered up his glorious chest, makes for welcome viewing.

'What's your happy place?' Owen asks, pulling me away from my partially sinful thoughts.

'My happy place?' I question, leaning back and grabbing the box of tissues from the bedside table for us to clean up.

'When you can't run away from your troubles, where do you go to in your mind?' he explains softly, taking a tissue and wiping his hands.

'A therapist I can't afford in real life,' I offer with an easy-going shrug. I'm not lying; I can't count the number of conversations I have had with her alone in my apartment.

Owen offers a chuckle that I feel in the pit of my stomach, though there's no knowing for sure whether those bubbles are because of the dimple in his left cheek or because when he turns and leans across to the desk to rid the bed of all but the fruit bowl, his shirt rides up, his towel remains low on his hips and the hint of his pert, full bottom comes into view. Would that count as a happy place?

Instead of admonishing me for my lack of creativity and sarcasm, Owen turns back towards me, no words tumbling from his mouth, no further questions or pressure, as I hastily fan myself with a floppy tissue.

His calm and non-judgemental face eases my prickly heart and I find myself speaking. 'At one time in my life, when my grandparents were still alive, I would have said the fish and chip shop was my happy place. I didn't need to be anywhere else. I'd sit at a table with Alex and colour by the back door and we'd eat my nanna's chocolate fudge cake with molten custard or my grandad would whip us up chip butties. It was always bustling with locals, my nanna and grandad's laughter sinking into the walls, keeping the place held up strong. I don't know where I'd go to these days; the chip shop doesn't have the same warmth and whenever I think about it now, it's always the lists of things that I need to do to stop it crumbling and keep us afloat,' I finish softly. I can feel the scratches against my voice box, it's wobbliness leading to a threat of tears. 'What about you?' I quickly ask, clearing my throat in the process.

Owen eyes me thoughtfully and once he seems settled that I'm OK and that I'd be happy to hear his thoughts to get me out of mine, he begins. 'It's hard to beat these mountains. I can be a bit of a loner when I'm working. I enjoy sitting under the olive trees and just watching the sea, watching the fishermen, being at one with nature.'

A chuckle escapes my lips; I try and hide it by coughing into the tissue I'm still fiddling with but Owen doesn't miss it.

'What's so funny?' he asks, but his eyes are sparkling with amusement under the honeyed sky – the baby blues are being replaced by a colour palette of oranges as the evening grows on.

'You sound like you just stepped out of one of those Viking novels or some Scottish Highland erotica – the mountains are my home,' I tease.

'Says you, gorgeous girl next door, struggling to keep her family's business afloat but with her heart of gold, she won't fail,' Owen snorts.

I *pfft* and shake my head. 'If I had a heart of gold, I don't think it would be failing.'

'And if I were a Viking or some sort of romance hero, I'd know how to keep a woman happy,' he retorts quietly, almost as if to himself, and the mood turns slightly solemn until we both let out a heavy sigh and stare at the fruit bowl.

I pick up a grape and pop one in my mouth before throwing one at Owen.

'Oi,' he grunts with a hint of a smirk on his lips.

'I'm going to be adding brooding to your list of love interest credentials in a minute if you don't cheer up. You were supposed to catch it in your mouth.'

I try again and Owen is no better prepared and still misses. After the third try, he starts throwing them at me. I'm giggling so much, I miss the first two but catch the third before laying back on the bed, utterly stuffed.

'It was the grape that did you in, huh? Not the pound of cheese?' Owen chuckles and it's a delicious sound, one that my eyes mistake for a lullaby as they flutter lazily to stay awake. I pat my stomach and stretch into the glorious fluffy quilt.

'How's your ankle?' Owen asks, his grey-blue eyes – more grey now in the evening glow – look from my face and take their time travelling down my body to my injured appendage. Heat floods through me, and I pray that Owen can't see the sparks that I feel dancing all over. He gently reaches out his hand, his calloused palm and thick fingers tracing the bone and curve of my ankle. I squeeze my eyes shut and try with all my might to transport myself to the decidedly different happy place I was talking about earlier, and not the one where Owen casually and comfortably ignites my entire being and blows whatever walls I have built up over my existence to smithereens.

It's like I can see the fragments splintering like dust particles blowing through the air as his thumb rubs gently over the bony bit of my ankle and then the ball of my foot, sending electric currents to parts of me that need not be led into temptation right now.

'Owen,' I breathe and even I can hear the begging in my voice, the want for more, the need to feel his skilled paws all over my skin.

Owen's eyes flicker back up to my face, his breathing is heavy before his eyes grow wide and he snaps his hand back. 'Ice,' he croaks out, 'I'll get you some ice.' He leaps from the bed with one incredibly agile movement, for such a beefy man, and I can't help that the sly part of my brain wishes that his towel had slipped away from his lower half in the process.

I clearly need help. Come tomorrow afternoon, there will be no more bedroom picnics or casual chit chats or partners in crime; it will be back to just me, the lone crusader. As Owen closes the bedroom door behind him, I scoff at myself. He is obviously able to control himself, and good for him. He knows this isn't going any further, that it can't go any further. I had plainly just been hallucinating before; Owen had innocently been looking after me and my stupid body thought it was something else, wanted it to be something else, something more.

But it couldn't be more. It was never going to be more. I wasn't good at being in a relationship but being the lone crusader, that I excelled at.

21

When I wake the next morning, a small, chilly puddle lies around my feet. Patting myself down and sitting up hurriedly, I momentarily panic that I've had an accident only to find a plastic bag and a tea towel by my toes. Ice, Owen had been getting me ice. But though evidence of the ice lays before me, no evidence of Owen having slept in his own bed is visible. One side of the bed remains untouched and wrinkle free.

Had I made a fool of myself last night? Had Owen sensed my yearning and been frightened away? I scrape my knuckles over my face, wiping sleep from my eyes. I should have stayed away from him like I'd planned. I don't know what had possessed me to enter his room, having already spent too much time with him during the day. Time I had told myself would be spent weaning myself off his company. I rub my stomach with the base of my palms, avoiding my cuts, as the thought of being without Owen's company makes my stomach curdle.

That's when I notice his room is tidy, all clothes and randomly placed shoes gone. Searching for the clock on his wall, I desperately seek out the time and fling my body off the bed. The pain in my ankle is no more than a slight throb now which serves me well as I sprint towards the kitchen. I hadn't asked Owen when he departed today or if we were on the same flight but surely he wouldn't have left without saying goodbye and as it is only nine-thirty, I can't imagine him leaving before a healthy breakfast.

Out of breath, I burst through the balcony doors to find my mum, Alex, Charlie and their families, and Owen, in black sweatpants and a crisp white t-shirt, pleasantly enjoying a table laden with every breakfast food going. I almost salivate while gasping for air. I must have slept well last night because I feel thoroughly disorientated.

'Sweetheart, are you OK?' My mum is the first to speak, as I straighten myself up, avoiding eye contact with Owen, and take the empty seat next to Alex.

'You didn't make it to the club last night?' Alex says, looking slightly downtrodden.

I take a sip of freshly squeezed orange juice, feeling every pair of eyes on me. 'No, sorry, you know what I'm like, not much of a club goer, and I'm fine, thank you, Mum. Everyone else good?' I ask, trying to draw the attention away from my dishevelled state.

'You didn't make it to your room last night either?' Charlie questions in a hushed tone, though Owen choking slightly on his coffee makes me think he heard just fine.

I add a dippy egg to my plate as well as a piece of toast and begin to butter. 'Nothing happened, I just fell asleep, in someone else's room,' I say in a tiny whisper to ensure Owen doesn't hear. Luckily Nonna Roberta starts fussing over his plate, adding a healthy portion of meats, cheeses and a small baguette.

'I wish you could all stay longer,' Alex says, thankfully

trusting my answer and moving away from the topic. For a moment, I wonder if she's still sceptical about the idea of Owen and I together. Maybe if we were on our own I would ask, but really there's absolutely no need. Why would I need to ask her opinion on something that is never going to happen? I concentrate on my pushing my toast soldier into the perfectly tangerine-orange yolk in front of me.

'It's been a beautiful adventure,' I say once I swallow my delicious bite. 'Thank you for having me and for all of this,' I tell both Alex and Charlie sincerely. I know they're planning on staying in Italy for a while longer and exploring more of the coast as part of their honeymoon, and as I take in the panoramic view of Positano to the right and the winding cliff faces that run to Amalfi on the left, I can't help the twinge of jealousy that causes my eyes to glaze over the mountains. That old feeling of missing out hits me like an icy snowball. I thought I'd gotten over it a long time ago; I'm not sixteen anymore, I didn't get jealous of my gorgeous best friend, she'd worked hard for the life she had and she deserved every ounce of happiness that came her way.

The sun peeks over the Positano hills, highlighting the multicoloured houses and drenching the pebbles across the beach with a glossy coating. As they glisten lustrously, guiding tourists to the perfect spot to place their umbrellas and towels for the day, I feel moisture in my eyes and hastily look down at my plate, taking great care to slice a juicy red tomato. In a matter of hours, I will be back in Manchester, back in my apartment above the shop, back to work at Ned's while Alex and Charlie literally disappear into the sunset hand in hand. As the heavenly flavours of an incredible

Italian tomato dance on my taste buds, something inside me caves.

I don't suppose I want to be the lone crusader forever. I don't know if I want my dad, my exes, Hannah, to keep winning; would it be too much to hope that one day, I could have a tiny piece of what Alex has?

Then Owen stands and I suddenly find it incredibly difficult to chew.

'This week has been a treat.' He nods around the table, sending a sincere smile towards Will and Gio. 'Charles, I don't know how you did it but you've found yourself a goodun. You two look after each other while I'm away,' he adds, eyes squinting in the morning sunlight that's reflecting off the moka pots dotted around the breakfast table. 'And I hope to see you all soon; it's been a pleasure,' he says, looking towards Mum and me, tucking in his chair at the same time Nonna Roberta jumps to her feet and starts fussing over him, trying to stuff bread into his pockets for the journey, and the whole party joins him in standing to say their goodbyes, which seems ridiculously sweet considering they'll see him again much sooner than I will.

No matter the succulence of the tomato resting on my tongue, my mouth feels dry and my mind feels stupid. Amid the screeching of chairs, patting backs and kisses on cheeks, I urge myself to swallow my food and take a sip of espresso. The rich, brown liquid scalds my taste buds, still piping hot having just been poured, and a whimper escapes my lips despite my best efforts.

'Andi, are you OK?' Alex asks, hugging me from behind, concern drawing her neat brows towards her nose.

'Yes, yes, sorry, the coffee's hot,' I splutter, waving my

hand in front of my mouth. She leans over my back and grabs me a glass of orange juice which I take gratefully. As I'm sipping, she whispers into my ear, 'Talk to him, Andi,' before giving me a small squeeze, that feels more like a choke hold, around my neck.

When I eventually look up towards where Owen is stood, it's like Jesus parting the red sea. Everyone takes a few steps back until the two of us are left awkwardly staring at each other. Owen scratches the back of his neck while mine prickles with the many eyes I feel watching me, waiting for me to say my farewell.

I feel ridiculous, hot and frustrated all the same time. 'Sorry, yep, you're going, OK. Bye, Owen,' I say, copying the others and rising from my chair as they all, bar Nonna Roberta, sit back down. Breakfast and a show it seems I am performing this morning.

'So, Mum, Dad, where are you off to next?' Alex quips to her parents, drawing the attention away from Owen and me. I owe her at least one romantic comedy.

Owen looks around, patting down his pockets, ensuring he has his essentials, and begins shuffling towards the door while looking at me through hooded lids. I automatically start shuffling too, following him towards the exit as Nonna Roberta makes one final attempt to stuff a quarter wheel of Parmesan in his pants.

'So, I'll see you...' My sentence ends abruptly when I don't quite know how to end it. Soon? In a few years? Never? Online? Could we WhatsApp? Video call? Have some sort of long-distance friendship?

'Yeah, I'll see you,' Owen replies, as we make our way out onto the gravel driveway where a taxi is already waiting.

With Will and Gio taking me, Mum, Nick and Paula to the airport this afternoon, I imagine Owen protested at making them do the drive twice in one day, because he is considerate like that – a sweet giant. The taxi man pops out of the vehicle and is quickly and smoothly seeing to Owen's luggage before opening the door and gesturing for him to get in, like there's no time to waste.

Owen stumbles forward, then changes his mind, taking a step back towards me as I take a step towards him, not wanting to let him go without a hug, without breathing in his comforting scent one more time. We stagger into each other; I end up in a sort of headlock before Owen loosens his grip and I'm nuzzled against his chest, breathing him in for the briefest of minutes.

'*Vieni, vieni*, we must go,' the taxi driver announces, climbing into the driver's seat, passenger door wide open.

'Thank you,' Owen breathes into my ear, causing my whole body to tingle on high alert.

Before I can ask what for, he's releasing me and closing the car door and all I can do is watch as the car pulls away. The crunching of the tires along the path sounds strangely like the crumbling I can feel in my chest.

It takes effort for me to move, but before I can, I hear my mother's voice from behind me. 'You two should keep in touch, arrange a cup of tea while he's in Manchester,' she suggests. I rub at the back of my neck and wriggle my shoulders, shaking away any cricks. We hadn't discussed seeing each other while Owen was home; neither one of us brought it up.

'He'll have plenty of family and friends to keep him company back home, Mum. Besides, long-distance stuff never works out,' I say with a shrug as that familiar black velvet drape of anti-romance, anti-love, anti-weddings, anti all of it adheres itself to me like a second skin: comfortable, easy, safe.

I stride towards the house, determination in my bones. This week is over. It's back to work.

Mum doesn't push her thoughts, instead asking me, 'Have you packed?'

'Not quite, but it shouldn't take long,' I tell her as we walk the well-known route towards the bedrooms.

'Why don't you have a bath and get yourself sorted before lunch?' she suggests, a soft, almost sympathetic tone in her voice that I don't care for.

'I'm fine, Mum,' I say sternly, 'but I think I will do that.' I nod, disappearing into my room.

Embracing the luxury of the tub one last time, I allow my head to sink under the red-hot water, washing away the craziness of the week. I try not to dwell on my time spent in Italy: on the mistakes I made; the people I hurt; or cooking gnocchi with fresh ingredients outdoors; the taste of Owen's lips on mine; or his rough, calloused hands, gentle when they roamed my skin; his company; his having my back; or getting through my best friend's wedding and it not being so bad. I try not to contemplate it all as the water laps over my head and I focus on the calmness, the serenity, the nothingness of the underwater.

The week has been a joy ride, a quick dip into the lives of others, a week from some sort of distant dream that I would never have dared to imagine.

Puncturing the still water, I gasp for air, spitting out the soap suds that I manage to swallow coming up. I hadn't had many swimming lessons as a child, and I've never been great at holding my breath, even when I had the hiccups. I'm choking on a few involuntary sips of water as I wipe at my stinging eyes, batting away the droplets from my lashes and heaving in gulps of air.

I quickly clamber out of the bath, desperate for the warmth and comfort of dry land and a cosy towel that practically swallows me whole, and take a couple of minutes to revel in its snugness and soothing qualities. No more reminiscing or distraction, my real life was knocking.

Lunch is another final indulgent affair and despite the dull ache that has settled in my stomach after packing, I remind myself that this life isn't real, and polish off two bowls of pasta with beans, a small plate of prosciutto and burrata, countless slices of provolone piccante and chunks of crispy bread. The fear of not eating like this again anytime soon makes room in my stomach for every delicious bite. And after all that, I'm still accepting when Nonna Roberta sneaks me a prosciutto and cheese sandwich wrapped in a napkin for the road as I kiss her cheeks goodbye.

We're gathered at the villa's entrance; Zia Allegra is crooning that we should visit again as soon as possible as she squeezes Mum and me tight under her large sun hat while Will and Gio pack up the car. With Nick and Paula joining us for the ride back, there's no room for Alex and Charlie, so this is where we're saying bye.

They both squeeze me into an Andrea sandwich. Alex's vanilla scent is mixed with a heavy hint of sun lotion while Charlie smells of the sea salt in the air, her skin bronzed and glowing with pride and familiarity of the Mediterranean sun.

'Thank you, thank you for choosing me as your maid of honour,' I whisper, chin on Alex's shoulder, and I mean it.

'There's no one else I'd trust more to nearly push me off a cliff,' Alex mutters in my ear. I poke her in the ribs, breaking up the bear hug, kiss them both on the cheek and climb into the car.

The cliff faces shine humbly as we sweep around the bends, shadows deepening the greens of the trees that protrude from cracks in the land and those that nestle cosily in well-looked-after gardens. The lemon skins light up the path like natural fairy lights powered by the sun, and the purples and pinks of the wisteria that drape over fences and walls add the most delicate yet bold palate to the Italian scenery. I've lost count now of the times that Italy has made me catch my breath with its soothing aesthetic, clasping me in its loving embrace, making me feel a world away from my uncertain future.

What am I supposed to do when I'm home, when the views of black bins, a constant stream of cars down the main road and a front window in desperate need of re-caulking does nothing to placate my anxiety? The airport draws near; I'll find out soon enough.

I take in the last views of the busy Naples streets, so different to the coast but beautiful in its own way. What would it take to have this every day? Was that even possible? For Alex, sure. For me, I don't think so.

We say our goodbyes to Will and Gio and I leave with them a small card and a little token of my thanks for them hosting us this past week. 'Anytime, anytime, you are always welcome,' they both chirp in unison and it cracks my heart a touch. We're on a different flight to Nick and Paula, so it's more farewells and then it's Mum and I bustling through Naples airport, cramming into our gate. An hour after we were supposed to take off, we are informed our flight is delayed.

I can't help but chuckle at the relaxed nature of the Italians. The airport seems to knock the wind from my sails and sucks the energy right out of me. Mum pulls out a book – Stanley Tucci, *Taste* – and I feel she's got the Italian bug, but my eyes flutter and I simply leave her to enjoy it as I rest my head on her shoulder and we wait.

22

I'm in Positano, the pebbles along the shore are massaging the soles of my feet as the water dances over my toes. Amaretto ice cream is trickling down its cone, dribbling onto my fingers, then a tongue that isn't mine is delicately licking the stickiness away. My whole body feels like it's one with the ice cream, seconds away from melting into a messy muddle. I'm taking my eyes off the treat and meeting the gaze of the owner of the tongue, their blue-grey eyes striking under the unforgiving light of the sun. Out of nowhere, a seagull shrieks and swoops; I duck as it shrieks again and again and doesn't stop shrieking.

'Andrea,' my name along with a jangle of keys breaks into my mind and has me shooting upright. My hair sticking to my cheek from a mixture of sweat and drool. The British heat is stifling, the humidity higher than before we left for Italy.

'What time is it?' I ask my intruder who is carrying a fresh loaf of bread and a carton of milk. 'I thought we're not opening today?' I add, as I try to untangle myself from the damp sheets.

'You can't put a time on the rest of your life,' my mum tells me.

My brows knit in confusion. 'Don't you mean price? You can't put a price on the rest of your life.'

'We're not open but that leak is still leaking, the repair man is coming to see what can be done about the fryer and one of the freezers is making a horrific hissing sound; I'm worried the rest of the food will have spoiled if it's broken,' Mum informs me, ignoring my last remark. The sweat on my body instantly chills as I now thrash at my covers to remove them and spring out of bed.

'Hold your horses,' Mum says, fluttering over to the kitchen and busying herself with making a cup of tea and toast.

'That thing you just said about time?' I question, looking for a clean t-shirt and following her to the small lounge/kitchen area.

'Yes, well, there will be time to fix all that.' She waves her hand around like 'all that' isn't as big of a deal as it really, truly is. 'First, I want to talk to you about business,' she says, handing me a plate of buttered toast.

I take a seat on the couch with barely a word forming on the tip of my tongue; all I can do now is listen. I've been waiting a week to hear her plan. She joins me on the two-seater with her own plate of toast but no tea. When she catches my line of vision to the mugs waiting on the side, she says calmly, 'The kettle won't work. I think it's broken.'

Having not been able to get to the bottom of the noise the freezer was so unapologetically making day and night, the repair man advised that it would be wise for us to purchase a new one and not cook the food that had been sitting in the heat for what he estimated had been a few days already. The fryer, too, was no more.

'Would it be possible for you to dispose of them for us or do you know someone who could?' I ask while he's stuffing papers into his tool kit. I pat at my top lip, the heat unbearable in the tiny confines of the back kitchen. He's pulling out a handkerchief to see to the sweat on his brow.

'I'll see what I can do. Let me make some calls,' he replies, looking up and down my sweaty form and giving me a sympathetic nod.

'That would be great, thanks.' Leading him out through the shop, I wave him off and smile at the one customer that has started lining up for opening time. I wave at the little old gent before grabbing my toolbox and stalking back to the kitchen.

'Mum, will you give me a hand with the fridge, and then would you like to be the one to tell Gregory that we won't be opening for lunch time,' I say as I open the fridge door, checking through the contents. It still feels cool inside, no bad smells or condensation signalling the temperature is broken. I'm wiggling it back and forth on my own so I can shine a torch behind it as Mum walks over, mop in hand.

'Any ideas?' she asks, taking over my position so I can crouch down and take a peek at where the water might be coming from. Heat engulfs me when I duck under the worktop; it's stuffy but nothing seems amiss.

'Nothing, Mum, maybe we'll just have to mop it up and monitor it for now,' I say, slowly standing tall so I don't give myself a head rush.

The stagnant air has me opening the back door, pleading

with the breeze to carry a sweet summer scent through the chip shop, to restore some life into it. The hint of coffee from the town centre's bustling corporate coffee shops tailspins my mind to early mornings on the balcony with Owen, and I hastily snap the mop from my mum's hands for something to do.

'I can do this, Mum. Will you go see to Gregory?'

'Thank you, honey,' she sashays away, hands waving, muttering something about bin bags and the food in the broken freezer.

A week, a week is all I have left. What Mum had proposed a few days ago, the morning we'd gotten back from Italy: make the shop look as appealing as possible, make it sparkle and shine, show off its potential, so that she can bring in an estate agent and get it on the market.

She had told me that morning that she was ready to treasure the good memories but let go of the bad.

She had loved this place for so long, loved the time she had spent cooking with her parents, hearing her dad's boisterous laugh when engaging with customers, her mum's passion for taking care of everyone that walked through the door. But she had resented it too. Resented it when she couldn't go to the park when she was a kid because she had to help peel potatoes or when her mum and dad were too busy to take her, resented it when she had me and my nanna and grandad were too busy to lend a hand, help her with nappy changes or doctor's appointments. Her only respite being to leave me in the kitchen while she took a quick breather around the block. She'd resented that my playdates were always a colouring book and a nearby table, for she became the one that couldn't leave the shop when my grandad got sick.

It hadn't all been bad; she had loved it as much as she might have hated it sometimes too.

'I can't hold onto it any longer, honey,' she'd said, and I found that I understood.

That piece of me in Italy that had been fed up, fed up of letting my dad and Hannah win, it fluttered once again in my chest. I couldn't hold onto it anymore, though I seemed to be gripping on for dear life. Maybe I needed to let go of Ned's just as much as my mum, to be free of this safety net, this life that I was born into; maybe I needed to spread my wings and fly.

'Oh shi—' I cry as I'm transported back to reality and hurtling towards the silver counter. I'd done an extremely good job of the floor, mopping in the same place until it was perfectly spotless and perfectly hazardous.

Air whips out of me as I throw the mop and go gut-first into the cash register with an '*oomph*'.

Mum's head whips up from chatting to Gregory and all I can do is wince.

'Floors are clean,' I wheeze. 'I'm just going to take a minute,' I add, hunching over and backing towards the staircase that leads to my apartment. I desperately want to curl up into the foetal position and let out a cry for my bruised ribs but I try to hold it in. Italy weakened me; I am stronger than this, less prone to daydreaming.

Walking towards the living room, I suddenly hear a rattle and clatter from the kitchen area. I tilt my head upwards an inch and see feet and, 'Arrrrgh!' I'm screaming, all pain forgotten as I reach for an umbrella and launch it at an actual intruder. He startles but barely flinches as the umbrella lands at his feet, before lifting his own head from behind the back of the kettle.

'Owen?'

'Andrea.'

'What on earth are you doing in my kitchen?' I shout, hand on my heart where it's racing at such a high speed, I'm worried about my ribcage.

Owen's cheeks instantly blaze and I can see the sweat dripping down the back of his grey t-shirt, his broad shoulders tense and uncertain now with my arrival. My apartment feels like it just got one thousand degrees hotter as I'm staring at him in his black cargo shorts and black sliders, but I don't want to think about that right now until I know what he's doing here.

'I'm fixing your kettle, ouch... bastard,' he says as sparks start shooting out from the plug socket on the wall.

'I don't need you to fix my kettle, Owen; I can fix it myself,' I say, scratching the back of my neck where my too-tight bun is pulling at the nape, but then I'm chuckling and then I'm full-on laughing. 'Did you just say bastard?' I howl, arching backwards and immediately regretting it as my ribs groan in protest.

'I just got electrocuted, Andrea,' Owen huffs. OK, so I'd seen him angry and disappointed back in Italy, and they aren't emotions I'd like to see on Owen again anytime soon, at least not because I'd put them there, but there's something endearing about his little outburst of frustration. I've never felt like Owen had a guard up but maybe that's because I couldn't look past my own enough to see how he was hurting, how that need to make people happy and be a gentleman shone through. He had always seemed unapologetically himself in Positano but this, this was a side of him I hadn't yet been privy to. He seems agitated and he's showing it.

'Erm, I'm sorry,' I say, laughing off my nervous energy.

'Your mum told me you needed me to fix your kettle and that you were expecting me for tea,' Owen shrugs, fiddling with the kettle for a few more seconds before he tries flicking the switch and the blue light lights up successfully.

I take in his actions before replying, 'Both lies I'm afraid. However, thank you for fixing my kettle, you saved me a job and…' I'm stumbling on the next bit, I wasn't expecting him, but do I admit that it was a pleasant surprise? Am I happy to see him? Looking far too large and ethereal, like he'd come from some high court and didn't quite belong in my tiny space. Before I can get swept up in Owen's rugged charm, a thought occurs to me.

'Owen, did you come all this way just to fix my kettle?'

He's fidgeting with his tool kit now, packing away a few screwdrivers, not looking up while he does so. Then he's standing tall and staring at me, eyes innocent and soft.

'I was having tea with my dad when your mum rang and I can't believe I hadn't thought to come and visit you. I mean, he lives, what, thirty minutes away,' he says, shaking his head in disbelief. My mouth simply opens and closes; I mean, I'd thought about it but hadn't been brave enough to speak.

'Oh, unless, sorry, you didn't want to meet up,' Owen adds, wafting uncomfortably at the back of his t-shirt.

'No, no, sorry, of course not, I mean yes, it's lovely that

you wanted to meet up?' I can hear the hope in my voice, the hope that I want him to have wanted to see me, but my brain is highly aware of its hypocritical dance. How can I want more from Owen if I'm not willing to admit it myself? If I'm not willing to be brave and tell him that his unexpected visit was indeed a lovely surprise. If I'm not willing to make the first move for fear that he doesn't want the same thing?

'Heaven forbid you get through this hot weather without a hot beverage, Andrea,' Owen sighs and there's a teasing in his tone, a smirk playing at the edge of his lips that has my hope flying despite itself.

'You know that's another thing to add to the list, right?' I quirk my brow.

'What list?' His eyebrows rise as we're both standing like we're about to go into battle.

'Your leading man list. You're ticking a lot of boxes. First mountain man, then highlander, now hot handy man, it's quite the list.' I'm grinning, I can feel it, along with the tug I feel towards him, but I don't move from the hallway.

'So, what does that make you? The quirky, hot heroine who doesn't know the difference between a screwdriver and a wrench, who needs a handy man to save the day,' Owen fires back, his grin growing broader, his dimple almost in place, as he takes a tentative step forward.

I gasp, 'I'm utterly appalled by that suggestion,' throwing my hand to my chest in mock offence.

'I don't make the rom-com rules.' That dimple is fully exposed now and I'm dangerously aware of the way Owen's scent is quickly filling up my space as he takes another step towards me.

'Well, maybe you should, you know, like, change them up a bit,' I croak, my words coming out heavy and raspy.

'Hmm, OK.' He's thinking and walking and doesn't speak again until he's leaning on the edge of the archway that frames the kitchen. 'How about, there are no rules. No one-time deal. No comparing the past to the present. No hiding from you because I'm scared. And maybe, just maybe, if love isn't something we believe in right now, how about we start with like?'

Well, I wasn't expecting all that. I'm torn between blaming the summer heat or Owen for stealing my breath away. I can feel it in each little tremble of my fingers, the vulnerability in his features, the magnitude of him opening up to someone like me, because it's there, the part of me that is programmed to close up, run and hide, or worse, the part that would laugh it all off, retort with sarcasm and be done with it. However, there's that hope, that hope from earlier that's thumping hard and heavy in my chest, that maybe what I wish for deep, deep down, can actually be mine.

'Like,' it comes out as a whisper, 'I think I can do like,' I say, absentmindedly reaching towards Owen, my fingers gently grasping at his shirt, to pull him closer so I can absorb the sweet, comforting smell of him that ignites all my senses.

He leans down to reach me, his lips parting as he feathers a kiss across my forehead, down to the tip of my nose, until his mouth meets mine. He's cupping the back of my head when our lips touch and I'm no longer bothered by words or rules; all I know is that I like this, I like Owen.

We're kissing like our lives depend on it, his tongue

toying with, teasing mine, and he tastes sweet like a warm vanilla custard tart but also salty as we are both sweating profusely.

My hands find their way under his shirt, gliding over his soft stomach and up across his broad chest and I'm moving then, walking backwards towards my bed.

'Ouch, ow,' I shriek, breaking the kiss as my ankle connects with the coffee table.

'Are you OK?' Owen's eyes flutter open, glassy and dazed. He's hunching over so that he's level with me. We pause like we're in some kind of football huddle, air straining between the two of us.

'Owen, I need you to be a leading man and carry me to my bed right now,' I say, face firm, voice light.

'It's like two feet away,' he smirks, cocking his head to the side, his floppy fringe falling across his eyes. I reach out and tuck it behind his ear. 'But I do like it when you tell me what you need,' he says, hoisting me into the air with only a slight groan, so I'm able to wrap my legs around his waist, ankles safe from obstructions.

When we cross over the threshold to the bedroom, we're both gasping; it feels like a sauna as the sun blasts through the large windows. I forgot to keep the curtain closed this morning for want of embracing the sunrises like I had done in Italy.

'Owen, is this sexy?' I query, peppering his chest with kisses while trying to remove his shirt, the heat and Owen's scent rendering me daft.

'Everything about this is sexy,' he exclaims, but when I look up, he's wiping sweat from his eyes.

I can't help giggling. It's an Olympic challenge peeling off our clothes but it doesn't simmer the pulsing want and need between my thighs. We're both glistening with sweat, the sheets already damp, but when I look over at Owen, who is now stood at the side of the bed naked, my whole body shudders with hunger. He's looking at me, those blue-grey eyes, more blue now and piercing as they sweep my skin.

'Andrea.' His voice comes out deep and rough.

'Owen,' I counter, forcing my voice to not come out so breathless and completely failing.

'Come here, please.' It's a demand, a demand from Owen, which I am absolutely not used to, nor apparently ready for. My limbs wilt, actually wilt, and for once, I don't argue against what I've been asked to do.

23

'I'll figure it out,' I tell Owen as we're lying sprawled across my bed like starfish, as far away from each other as the bed will allow. The British summertime being a stealer of cuddles and affection post sex. I'm explaining to Owen the plan Mum has for the shop and how she hopes to sell it within the next few weeks.

'I'll move in with mum while I job hunt and see what's out there, which actually saying out loud makes me feel physically sick. I've never had to look for a job, Owen; what happens if I suck at it?' I can feel the whooshing in my stomach, the sheer terror spinning around in my gut.

'You might do, but you also might not,' he replies with his trademark bluntness, which somehow manages to interrupt the terror in my belly with a bout of laughter. 'But seriously, Andrea,' he starts more gently as he turns onto his side. His eyes are intent and utterly gorgeous. 'If you can find something you love, I've no doubt you'll be incredible at it.'

'I just feel like I'm starting from scratch, like I'm behind everyone else, but thank you, I do appreciate that,' I confess, my emotions bouncing around all over the place. Since Mum discussed the plan with me, I haven't quite settled on just one feeling. One minute, I'm excited for the next chapter and the fact that at one point in time, I had only one box to climb into, everything packed inside it, all ready and waiting for me, and now, well now it feels like the world is massive and that there are billions of job prospects but I'm not sure I'm ready or capable enough to do any of them.

And now with Owen here, there's this new feeling that whatever it is that I do, whatever job that I find, I'd just love for him to be close by. It hits me hard then like a storm cloud erupting above my head that that is not an option. Owen might be here now but soon, he will be gone, again.

Sitting up straight, I pull the duvet up to my chest despite the heat.

'Owen, did we think this through?' I ask and instantly know I've said something wrong as his eyes narrow and the blue swirls away into a glum grey.

'Andrea?' He speaks just my name but I can hear the hurt in each syllable.

'But it's just, you know as well as I do that long distance doesn't work. We can't do this from a thousand miles away,' I note, gesturing to the ruffled duvet. 'I won't be able to hug you after a hard day's work and share my morning coffee with you.' The words are tumbling out now as Owen, too, pulls up the security blanket around his torso and sits up.

'It's not ideal and yes, some things might be off the cards but that doesn't mean it won't work,' Owen tries softly.

'Really? But wouldn't you want more, wouldn't you want it all?' I ask, gently. I don't want to hurt him but surely he can see my point of view?

'I like you, remember? I thought I might be getting it right this time, Andrea, that I could make you happy,' he notes, his hair a tangled and shaggy mess. His full cheeks suddenly look a touch gaunt. 'What do you need from me? Tell me what you want, I'm all ears,' he adds, twisting around to face me.

I stand up, pulling the sheets with me, panic filling my chest and making my heart race. How long would he want to make me happy for? How long could I make him happy for? It's all too much. 'Owen, I don't need anything and I don't want anything from you, I can't, you know why,' I stutter, unable to look him in the eyes.

'Your ex,' he breathes, 'but I'm not her, Andrea.' He talks slowly as he gets out of the bed in search of his clothes. I don't stop him, I just watch, feeling numb. I don't want to fight. I know he's not her, he's nothing like her, not in this moment, not in the last few weeks, but relationships change people. 'I'm sorry that happened to you, I, I don't know what to say.' He starts dressing, his head down, defeated, and every part of me wants to reach out and wrap myself up in his scent, but I don't; it wouldn't be fair.

Once he's dressed, he places one knee on the bed, leans forward and kisses me on the top of my head.

'I like you,' he whispers, and I don't find words; I simply watch him walk out of the door.

If my mum is worried about me, she has a funny way of showing it. I've been gone from the shop for a solid four hours and while I'm grateful she didn't burst in on Owen and me mid-catching up, right now I feel that, for some reason unknown to my own brain, I want to talk.

As I traipse to the kitchen, oversized tatty t-shirt quickly thrown on, to make myself a cup of tea in my newly fixed kettle that I don't want to think about, my phone starts blasting Chesney Hawkes' 'The One and Only'. 'Damn it, Charlie,' I say out loud as I reach for it on the coffee table where I left it this morning.

The screen is lit up with a video call from Alex, though I know it was Charlie behind the new ringtone. She's most likely changed hers too, which will be a treat for another time, something to look forward to no doubt.

Alex's tanned, glowing face appears on the screen along with the positively blue Positano sky and I'd be amiss to say that my heart doesn't crack another inch more than it had done just half an hour ago when Owen walked out of my door.

'Andi, why do you look so rough, what's going on?' she asks sweetly the second my face joins hers on the phone. Her brows are furrowing, nose wrinkling with worry. Why is it some people glowed after sex and I apparently looked 'rough'? Life truly wasn't fair.

I stare at my best friend for a moment, her hazel eyes wide with concern.

'Is Charlie with you?' I ask, not brave enough to be quite so honest if Charlie can hear me.

'No, she's nipped out to get some ingredients for dinner. I'm just by the pool,' she tells me. I sigh and sit on the couch, tucking my feet up underneath myself. Kettle long forgotten.

'I think I upset Owen,' I whisper, not liking the sound of those words in the atmosphere.

'Oh hon, what did you do? Wait, when did you see Owen?' Her brows shoot straight into her hairline.

'He came to fix the kettle and we talked and... erm, we

kissed a bit.' I'm mumbling, embarrassment and shame washing over me at what comes next. It had all been going so well. 'And then I basically said why are we bothering when he lives on the other side of the world.' I cringe, scraping my fingers through my knotty hair and getting a delicious whiff of Owen in the process. My stomach tightens.

'Aww, Andi, I'm sorry. Is that how you really feel about him? I mean, Italy isn't exactly the other side of the world and you seemed to be forming a comfortable friendship here,' she asks, taking a sip of something red and scrumptious-looking in a fancy glass.

I flick my hair over my shoulder so I can't smell him. 'Well, yes. How on earth do you keep a relationship going from miles apart? Everyone has needs, he'll have wants and desires and I won't be able to satisfy him.' And that's when it happens again, the vision I've tried to keep at bay for the last four years, the vision that's been attacking my thoughts since Alex announced her wedding, rears its ugly head – Hannah shagging her chief bridesmaid on what was supposed to be our wedding day.

And Alex sees it, I know she does, she sees it written all over my face as she leans in closer to the screen so now it's only her face that I can see – her pores are as clear as crystal. 'Oh Andi, honey, no, do you think that's all he wants from you? Come on, there's more to relationships than that.'

'But it's a huge part.' I'm willing myself to keep the tears I feel readying themselves in my tear ducts at bay.

'It is, yes, but are you telling me that's all you want Owen for?' she asks, turning my comment around, and I get it.

'Of course not, I like his company, I like his bluntness, I like his passion and his ability to live in the now.' I'm listing

Owen's attributes and it's as if my tongue has a mind of its own and it wants to stand up for Owen. When I notice the sheen in Alex's eyes that has nothing to do with the fruit cocktail she's drinking, I stop abruptly.

'You really like him and he must really like you,' she states, her pretty, strawberry-glossed lips smiling broadly.

'How do you figure that?' I protest.

'Andi, two words: Harry and Styles. I don't know many people who would perform a routine with you on the spot to cover your ass.' I grimace a touch by way of apology. We'd performed a couple of dance routines in the shop as kids; she knew when my work was practised and polished and when it was off the cuff.

'And Andi, people only get upset when they care,' she adds.

'He was covering his own ass too and that's what I'm scared of,' I say honestly. 'It's just too much to think about right now, what with moving, selling this place, looking for another job, I need to be an actual human and not a mess before I think about another relationship. He deserves better than that,' I tell her with an affirmative nod, like I've made up my mind.

'All humans are messy, and wouldn't right now be a wonderful time for new beginnings? What if you sell up and take a trip?' she suggests, taking another sip of her snazzy drink, making me lick my lips and wish I had one in my own hand.

'What, Alex, no. I can only hope there's enough left over once we tie up all the loose ends to look after Mum and her place. I need a job, not another vacation,' I explain.

'OK, fair enough, but who says your job can't be in

a faraway land with luscious landscapes, sexy accents and gorgeous mountain men.' She wiggles her eyebrows, leaning back on her sun lounger, I can only assume for extra emphasis. The change of scenery in Positano had been heaven.

'You know Owen is British, right? And that is absolutely not how this is going to work, Alex. I'm not uprooting my entire life for a "like" interest. Why should I have to do that? Why not him?' I argue, pouting so she understands just how much I dislike her idea. I'd seen a few of those rom-com trailers she was always trying to get me to watch and I strongly despised that it was always the girl leaving her life behind for the small-town hero.

'I'm not saying you have to uproot your life or buy a one-way ticket, but just think about it. The chip shop won't be tying you down. Will is already planning your mum's next visit here, so what are you leaving behind exactly?' she says with perfectly great reasoning and logic, and she truly has me stumbled, so much so I shift in my seat, stretching my legs out and putting them up on the coffee table.

'I'm, I'm just not that woman. I don't just buy plane tickets to foreign lands to go after a man,' I tell her.

'Why not? You can be whatever woman you want to be – and I believe a woman who is brave enough to sneak off for a secret liaison at two in the afternoon can do anything,' she says with a sly smirk and a wink, and even though she's my best friend, I can feel the heat rise up my neck, blooming in my cheeks.

'I said we kissed!' I gasp.

'And I said I wasn't sure about Owen, but you know how I know this is different?'

'How?'

'Because everyone always says just follow your heart, but people aren't perfect, love isn't rose-tinted glasses, it's protecting your wants and needs just as much as the wants and needs of the person you're with. It's acknowledging imperfections and deciding whether or not you can fall for those imperfections too. There's thinking involved and you, my dear best friend, are thinking. So, I'm not saying buy a one-way ticket and never look back, I'm just saying, is Owen worth the risk of whatever this could be?'

I'm chewing so hard on my bottom lip that blood mixes with the taste of vanilla custard as I mull over Alex's words.

'Owen's messy, his room at the villa was untidy, and what happens if I don't like Italian winters?' I ask, replacing my bottom lip with my fingernail, chewing anxiously.

'You don't have to live here; you know Owen's British, right?' she retorts brightly, throwing my own words back at me.

'How long are you staying out there now?' I say, curiosity brimming at possibly seeing my best friend again soon if I did take her advice, not that I'm going to.

'I've lined up a few jobs and Charlie is helping Will with a project, so a couple months until my visa runs out,' she explains, adjusting her sun hat and looking the picture of chilled.

Could I find a job that allowed me to travel the world and actually be comfortable enough to treat myself every now and again too?

'Sounds idyllic,' I reply, smiling at my best friend. I don't want to feel jealous of her sunning by the pool; I want to feel inspired. 'So what are Charlie's imperfections?' I ask, a coy smile turning up at the corners of my lips. I'm feeling a little better already, though what I'm to do about Owen, I'm not entirely sure. I've already abandoned Mum for most of the afternoon, I can't possibly chase him down now, and I'm not about to do that until this place is sold and I know Mum is looked after.

Alex *pffts*. 'Not a chance. I tell you them and you'll just store them as ammo for your next sarcasm off.' She slurps the last of her frozen cocktail as my stomach rumbles and I hear shouting up the stairs.

'I would never,' I say dramatically. 'But you did say "them" so she has more than one,' I tease and chuckle at her head tilt. 'Right, I love you, thank you for, well, just thank you for everything but I've got to go.'

'Brush your hair,' she shouts before we end the call and I'm shooting off the couch.

'I'm coming, Mum,' I yell, rushing to get my work clothes back on.

24

The days after Owen left and I had that call with Alex have me feeling stressed like I haven't been since she asked me to be her maid of honour. The ghost of Owen's feather-like kiss lingers on my forehead and every time I feel it, my heart aches that little bit more. I have to admit that I feel like I'm living in a world of 'before Italy' and 'after Italy'. Before Italy, I would have been moving boxes, carrying furniture with great difficulty and sheer determination down the stairs and to Mum's without so much as a thought about help. Sure, had Alex and Charlie been free, they would have come to chip in, but I wouldn't have asked. Now, after Italy, all I can think about are Owen's sturdy hands, his ability to know when I need help without me asking and my ability to actually ask him. I miss our banter and his company.

We've had people in to examine the shop and just yesterday the 'for sale' sign went up. Every time I catch a glimpse of it, my stomach turns with anticipation. The asking price would cover the cost of our unpaid bills with more than enough left over to look after Mum while she travels and for me to tuck into my savings for a rainy day. I won't even consider looking for a new place until I'm secure with a new job. The idea of living a debt-free life is incredibly appealing, though the happy undercurrent of electricity that buzzes through my brain at my life no longer being ruled by Ned's is somewhat offset by the dull ache that sits in my belly as I pack away my grandparents' photos, safely storing them in Mum's loft.

'Do you think somewhere up there, they're looking down ready to smite us for what we've done?' I ask Mum as I step down off the ladder.

'Cup of tea?' she replies, her brown eyes gleaming a little, a soft look on her face that I can't place. She's been a whirlwind of organisation and Miss Clean It this past week; I don't suppose she's actually stopped to take in the magnitude of it all.

Following her downstairs and into the kitchen, I ask, 'Are you OK, Mum? You're happy, right?'

She flicks on the kettle and starts piling jammy dodgers and bourbon biscuits on a plate. It's not gone unnoticed, by me, that she seems to have stocked up on my favourite things from my childhood since my moving back in. As I'm nibbling around the edges of a jammy dodger, I can't say moving back into my childhood home at thirty-four is such a terrible thing.

'Yes, I'm happy, Andi,' she answers after I've consumed one jammy dodger and I'm helping myself to a bourbon. Placing our tea on the table, she takes a seat and picks up a bourbon, but doesn't take a bite yet. 'You know, I don't think it ever gets easier,' she says, shaking her head with a wry smile and dunking her biscuit into her tea.

'What doesn't?' I ask, already eyeing up another biscuit.

She chews thoughtfully before speaking. 'That inherent want to please your parents. I loved them, gosh, I loved them so much and I miss them every day, and like I've told you before, there's always good with bad and bad with good. I loved Ned's, I hope you know that, Andi, I loved it, but it's time,' she explains, waving her bourbon in her hand. 'I can't hold onto the sinking ship much longer and maybe that makes me a terrible daughter, but while it might have been a dream for my mum and dad, it was never mine.' She pauses to take another bite of her biscuit while I decide on another jammy dodger.

'And I guess for the longest time, I loved that my own daughter seemed to enjoy being around me. I never really stopped to question your career path, not in the days when the shop was booming and there was chatter and regulars and laughter. When it was the four of us, you, me, your grandparents, I suppose it sometimes did feel like a dream, and selfishly I thought it was the best place for you,' she finishes on a sigh, her eyes slightly glassy.

'I don't regret that time with you, Mum, or the time I spent with Nanna and Grandad,' I say hastily, not wanting her to be so hard on herself; she did her best as a single mum and the good times she's talking about were really good.

'Oh honey, I know you don't but I wouldn't blame you if you did. I mean, there was that one time, remember in your twenties, when you very nearly launched a battered fish at my head because Nanna was sick and I needed you in the shop? It might have been Alex's birthday; she was having some party. God, Andi, I kept you from so much,' she says, half laughing, half sobbing as she rubs a palm over her face.

I force down the jammy dodger-sized lump in my throat to speak. 'Mum, it's done now. We kept it going for as long as we could, but you're fifty-six; I think you're allowed to follow your own dreams now. I think you've worked hard enough for it,' I tell her, though the uncertainty of what I'm going to do next is still haunting me.

'You're right, we did and I have to believe that they would have been proud of that. It's time you and I make our own mark in this world,' she says, straightening out her back and taking another bourbon biscuit more enthusiastically this time, dunking it with gusto into her tea. Seeing her smile is enough to put my worries at ease, even if for just a little while, just while we drink our tea and eat an entire plate of biscuits, because she's doing what's right for her and I love that. I have to believe that I'll figure out what's right for me.

'Speaking of following in parent's footsteps and the pros and cons,' she says, wrapping her hands around her mug; the August weather has cooled to a delightful twenty degrees.

'Is that what we were talking about?' I ask, taking a healthy sip of tea, not wanting to have this conversation again.

'Marriage, love, it isn't all bad, you know,' she says in a butter-wouldn't-melt tone.

'Mum, name one thing that was good about your marriage?' I demand, my wall having rebuilt itself remarkably fast since Owen left.

'I've told you before – you,' she smirks, like she's just said, 'checkmate'.

'Oh, well in that case, you hit the jackpot. I didn't even make it down the aisle and all I got left with was debt.' I somehow end up chuckling as that relief of what it would mean if the chip shop sells hits me. To be rid of the debt

Hannah bestowed when she and her maid of honour went ahead with our wedding party without me.

'Not just debt, Andi. You got perspective, you learnt boundaries, you learnt what you want and that what you want matters,' Mum informs me.

What I want. I contemplate her words while staring intently at the cream sandwiched between two chocolatey rectangles. Could what I want be a six-foot-one carpenter with a love of cheese, a tell-it-like-it-is manner and a habit of having to touch everything he sees? Someone who isn't overly romantic but naturally sweet in his own way. Someone who's not about luxury and putting on a show but who is kind hearted, smart and simple in the most beautiful way. Could what I want be a plane ride away? And, am I brave enough to go after it?

I stuff half the biscuit in my mouth.

'We've never talked about relationships much. I thought with Hannah that I wasn't allowed a say, as who am I to talk romance, really?' Mum scoffs but she's smiling at me gently.

'You're always allowed a say, Mum,' I offer, wanting her to know that her voice matters and is valued in this world, in my world.

'Hmm, well I've occasionally tried but your sarcastic tendency, I have to say, is a trait you most certainly didn't get from me,' she says with a wanton shrug, like she didn't just drop a Dad bomb on me and proceed to take a bite out of a jammy dodger like it was nothing. I narrow my eyes at her but she simply waves my mute protest off.

'I'm allowed a say,' she repeats my words, winking at me as she does so. 'My point is, Hannah never seemed all that interested in you. I barely saw her in Ned's and she rarely stayed over at your place; why she wanted to get married in the first place, I can't put my finger on it.' She looks thoroughly confused which is doing wonders for my self-esteem.

'And your point, Mum?' I try to urge the conversation on and to a swift end.

'The wedding was hardly designed with you in mind at all and I should have said something but I was too scared that you'd hate me or that I'd ruin something that could potentially be great, but I see it now, my gut wasn't wrong, it isn't wrong and so now I'm saying something.'

'You're saying a lot of somethings,' I reply, feeling every inch of my confidence disappearing as fast as the plate of biscuits.

'I like that man, Owen, Charlie's best friend,' she says boldly as a shiver runs down my spine at hearing his name.

'That's nice, do you want to marry him?' I retort, the sarcasm alive and well in my tone; I can't seem to help my teenage response. Am I proving Mum's point of hating her if she shares her opinion? I don't want to hate her but I'm pretty sure I don't want to continue with this conversation either.

'What happened the other day? I assume it didn't take him, what, three hours to fix the kettle. He left looking slightly forlorn, before you came down in a completely different pair of trousers to the ones you'd been wearing that morning,' she notes like she's been waiting for the right time to show off her best Enola Holmes impression.

'You know what happens when you assume: you make

an ass out of you and me,' I give her a pointed look but it's to no avail.

'Andi, we're talking, come on, I was never very good at this. Help me out,' she pleads, pushing the plate with the last remaining jammy dodger in my direction as a perfectly worthy bribe. My tongue loosens ever so slightly before I groan into my mug of tea.

'I like him, Mum, I do, but I mean seriously, could he have picked a far enough place to live? Italy isn't exactly round the corner.' I take a chunk out of my biscuit. 'I can't just up and move to another country in the hope that a relationship, a friendship might work out; it would be ridiculous,' I add, spraying a few crumbs across the table, which Mum wipes up efficiently with a piece of kitchen roll.

'People do stuff like that all the time. Aren't we going to have a go at being people – I mean, people that aren't tied down to four walls and a deep fryer? And Italy, what, a three-hour flight? Kind of feels round the corner,' she argues, and to give her credit, it's a good point.

'I was partial to the deep fryer,' I return, collecting our mugs and standing to place them in the sink. I need to stretch after filling my stomach with biscuits.

'The thing is honey, if you take a trip back to Italy and it doesn't work out, at least you tried, you went for it and that's brave.'

'And scary,' I counter.

'And is it not just a little bit exciting too? At the end of the day, you know I'll support you with whatever you do. If that's find a job somewhere in Manchester, stay in this house with me until you find your feet, then I'll be more than happy to have you as my roomie, but if it's to take a trip to Italy for another week or so for a shot at building something with an incredibly handsome man and exploring more of what the world has to offer, then I will buy more custard creams for the plane journey.'

I snort at her talking about snacks for the hypothetical plane journey, yet at the same time, I can feel the pulse of excitement humming through my veins at the thought of me doing something so extravagant, and that pulse only quickens when thinking about Owen at the other end, at doing whatever it is I'm going to be doing with him. If he actually forgives me for having sex and then practically kicking him out of my apartment.

'I guess it will all depend on if we can sell the chip shop then, huh?' I say, my hands shaking as I nervously refill the kettle for another cup of tea that I definitely do not need in the heat, but I absolutely need for calming my anxious mind.

25

I'm fiddling with the keys to my childhood home – Mum's two-up, two-down she mortgaged after her divorce from my dad – not far from where my grandparents used to live, while fighting to keep hold of the rather heavy box in my other hand that I have balanced on one knee: the last remaining items from my old apartment, where I spent the morning cleaning every last crevice.

I walk into the kitchen, about to drop the box on the dining table, but grip it tightly, my arms burning with lactic acid, when I notice Mum sitting at the table, staring at her iPhone 3 intently, her cheeks flushing a rosy hue, cups of tea, a notebook she has been scribbling on and a plate of ginger snaps on the wooden surface.

'Mum?' I question, shuffling a chair out from under the table with my toes so I can place the box on the chair.

'Oh, hi, honey,' she replies, distracted, swiping up and down over what appears to be an email. 'The kettle's just boiled,' she lets me know.

What any normal human around the world would do on a scorching August day would be to down an icy pint of water, anything cold, but no, us Brits and our tea – suitable for all weather conditions. I retrieve a mug.

'Good news, bad news, something in between?' I ask curiously, stirring sugar into my milky concoction, as her eyebrows knot a touch more.

'Oh honey, I think we're going to be alright,' she says, finally looking up, her brows unfurling, a smile spreading across her face until it reaches her ears. The light flush and proud beam give her face a young glow.

'What'd you mean? We've already got offers?' Abandoning my tea, I heave the box onto the floor and take its place at the table.

'Three,' Mum informs me excitedly before taking a large, refreshing sip of tea. I reach over to the counter to collect mine. 'I've just been doing some number crunching and of course, thinking about what would be morally sound too; I'd rather not sell to a conglomerate but we'll see.'

My whole body feels like it's vibrating as the words 'we're going to be alright' ring through my brain.

'Three offers, go on, Mum, what are they?' I ask eagerly, desperate to learn more about our future, the future of Ned's.

'OK, there's a lovely family of four who are looking to open an American candy shop, which the estate agent thinks might do well competing with all these dessert bars and growing interest in other cultures. There's an older couple who have always dreamed of opening a pie shop, which, bless them, I'd have to tell them to try their hand at dessert pies if they want to stand out. And then there's a coffee chain looking to expand to that side of town; they believe it's what the city centre has needed for a while.'

Suddenly, my hands feel too hot around my mug and I

have to pick up Mum's notebook and start fanning myself
to cool my overwhelmed forehead.

'The candy shop are meeting the asking price, the couple
are just under and, well, the coffee chain have thrown in 5
per cent more,' Mum then adds, her eyes glazing as she goes
through all the possibilities with me. It's a lot to take in. Only
two weeks since putting up the sign and only a week and a half
of me maybe moping around a touch at the distance between
Owen and me, and only two weeks of self-deprecating job
hunting, and we have actual offers; there is a light.

'Whichever one we go for, Andi, I mean, it will be enough
to pay off the last bits of debt,' she pauses and taps her nails
against her mug.

'I want you to pay off your mortgage. Mum, before you
think of anything else. It shouldn't be too much now; you'll
still have plenty left over,' I say before she can start talking
again.

She breathes in deeply. 'I'd like that, sweetheart, and then
I think I'll need a vacation to celebrate; you can come too,'
she says innocently, smile still etched on her face.

My brain flutters through the Italian landscapes,
visions of the places Alex has told me about over the
years, from beaches to snowy mountains, from lush hills
and vast countrysides, to the Italian lemon groves and the
Mediterranean paths I got to walk, and suddenly, I feel like
my mind is made up.

'That sounds like a plan, Mum,' I say, buzzing with
both fear and genuine excitement. 'And let's go with the
family of four; I think they stand a good chance at building
something wonderful and colourful and new there. I think

our meat and potato pies might have had their moment and I'd hate to see that elderly couple struggle,' I add, picking up a ginger snap in celebration.

'I was thinking the exact same thing,' Mum replies, a sparkle in her eyes adding to the glow on her face.

'I'm coming back to Italy,' I shout, kind of. My voice comes out partially strangled and strained and there's a small chance, hearing myself say it out loud, that I might start hyperventilating. 'I mean, I'm coming back, if that's OK and you'll have me?'

I feel everything but poised and calm right now as I sit on the edge of my childhood single bed, willing a breeze to reach me through my open bedroom window.

It feels cooler out there than it does inside the house; I'm actually considering sleeping in the garden. Yet, I'm staring at Alex and Charlie longingly as they bask in the early-evening Positano glow. They've no need for shawls or cardigans or a fan, their bare shoulders luxuriating in the perfect Italian temperature. The milder evenings around the table had been one of my favourite parts of the week away.

'Yessss,' Alex squeals, nearly spilling her wine.

'Just for another week while I figure everything out and you know, talk to people,' I add, just to reassure more myself than Alex that I'm not crazy; a week trip to Italy is something a lot of people around the world do.

'Is this your grand romantic gesture to apologise to a certain someone?' Charlie asks, sipping her wine delicately, eyeing me over her glass.

'You told her about the other day, didn't you?' I ask, giving Alex a pointed look, making sure to stare at the glowing camera light atop my Samsung S6.

'Don't be mad, wives don't count, like if Charlie says, "don't tell anyone", you know you don't count, so it's fair,' Alex answers, batting her long eyelashes and bringing her sun-kissed cheeks to the forefront so I can see the innocence behind her eyes. I only tut.

Charlie tilts her head from side to side like she's finding the truth in her wife's words, then pops a small kiss on the tip of her nose. I'm rolling my eyes before I can help myself.

'I didn't exactly choose the right time to freak out,' I confess, pinching the duvet between my fingers.

'Yes, I'd say maybe freak out before the man has bared his bottom and let his guard down,' Alex considers.

My stomach falls as fast as one of those fairground rides that hang in the air and then plunge to the ground.

'Well, we did agree to just liking each other first and I mean, I like Harry Styles, doesn't mean dating him would be a good idea.' I hear my voice creep up an octave.

'I think Harry is always a good idea,' Alex says as Charlie mumbles, 'You're a good few years older than him, but I won't judge.'

'Not the point,' I say, pulling them back on track.

'No, the point is, you're coming back to Italy, you're going to tell Owen how you feel and go from there, that's all any of us can do and no matter how it goes, you have us,' Alex says dramatically, like she's coaxing a revolution.

'She's right, no one knows what the future holds but he's a good guy, one of the best, actually,' Charlie's voice softens.

'And you're not bad,' she adds, slight smirk tilting up the corner of her mouth.

'Right, I'm doing it. I'm really doing it,' I announce before my confidence takes a dive.

'Woohoo,' Alex cheers.

'Come get him,' Charlie shouts.

I stand up from my bed as if my plane is about to take off any minute when the reality is I've not booked it yet and I'm still very much in my tatty pyjama shorts and old Care Bears tee, sweltering in my teenage bedroom. But for a moment in time, I feel as though I could very well be starring in my own rom-com. How I feel about that is somewhat undecided when a wave of nausea hits me. I shake it off, walking to my cupboard and retrieving my one suitcase that I have only just unpacked.

'Right, I best pack and book my flights. Love you both,' I say to my little screen, pushing through the swirly commotion in my gut.

'OK, you got this, we love you too, send us the flight details once you have them,' Alex says before hanging up.

I stare at the suitcase for a minute or two before heading downstairs to speak to my mum and see if she's happy for me to accompany her on her own trip back to the Amalfi Coast.

26

'Can I borrow the kitchen and the upstairs terrace this evening? Do you think Will and Gio will mind?' I ask Charlie as I slip into the car at the airport when they pick us up. My heart hasn't stopped racing since we boarded the plane to Naples from Manchester late that morning. 'Will you keep Owen busy?'

'Someone had too many coffees this morning,' Charlie comments as she pulls out of the airport, narrowly missing three cars coming at her on the roundabout. 'But I'm sure that won't be a problem; Dad's working late today, Papa is having a rest and Nonna Roberta is cooking, so you might just have to sway her,' she informs me.

'We can keep Owen busy. I mean, he's been mostly in his workshop till late these days, so I don't suppose he will be back from the beach till evening,' Alex says, passing me a bottle of water that I gratefully take. As much as I love the Italian views, my adrenaline mixed with the curves in the road and the speed and lack of care from Italian drivers is making my stomach queasy. 'But we'll get him to you.'

'Thank you, I appreciate it. I promise I won't get in Nonna Roberta's way, and I'll tidy up. Is it OK with everyone if we stop at the store before we get back?'

'It's fine with me, honey; I wanted to pick up some flowers and wine for our hosts,' Mum says with a warm smile, though she's looking a touch peaky as Charlie rounds a rather severe bend. I pass her the bottle of water.

'Can do,' Charlie says with gusto as she plays chicken with a blue Mini down the narrowest street I've ever had the displeasure of experiencing.

'Thank you,' I say before putting my head between my legs. With my mind running down a menu and a speech for Owen and my stomach clutching onto its contents for dear life, I feel as if I'm starring in *Mission Impossible* and *The Fast and the Furious* blended together.

Nonna Roberta is more than happy for me to work alongside her in the kitchen. Upon arriving, she was impressed with my plan and my menu and told me that her kitchen was my kitchen.

I'm slicing squid into rings after having it cleaned at the fishmonger when I catch Roberta out of the corner of my eye adding more parsley to the tomato sauce I have bubbling on the stove next to her sizzling pan of mussels. I can't help but chuckle and can't quite believe that I am cooking alongside her with such beautiful ingredients. It's incredibly difficult not to eat everything as she and I are cooking; it smells too good.

As if reading my mind, suddenly there's a piece of bread hovering at my lips as she says, '*Mangia, mangia*.' I let her pop the bread into my mouth and groan at the flavours that hit my tongue. She's smiling at me when I look around, searching for what she just fed me.

She's chuckling, pointing at the pan of mussels. 'Juice,' she shrugs.

What on god's green earth? All I saw her put in that pan was olive oil, garlic, parsley, water and slices of lemon. I shake my head and get back to focusing on my calamari rings, while on the bench behind me, Roberta starts peeling potatoes.

When I'm ready to fry off the rings for a few minutes, she appears next to me again, tugging on my elbow to stop me. '*Aspetta*,' she says, telling me to wait while she throws small chunks of potatoes and parsley into the hot pan first.

'A few minutes, then you put the fish,' she explains with a happy nod. I return the nod and wait for the potatoes to turn golden, stirring them occasionally so they are browning on all sides before tossing in the rings for roughly four minutes. As I pat my sweaty brow with some kitchen roll, I catch the time on the clock. It's just gone seven and I know Alex and Charlie won't be able to hold Owen off for long. I'm certain he'll smell Roberta's mussels and come running.

Quickly, I send Alex a text to let her know I'm nearly ready and to tell Owen that dinner will be on the second terrace tonight when a wave of panic washes over me that I haven't even set a table. I excuse myself from Nonna Roberta with a quick explanation and run for the veranda.

I'm leaping up the last step when I notice the flickering of the twinkly lights left over from Alex and Charlie's wedding, in addition to candlelight as candles burn in the centre of a beautifully decorated table kitted out with table cloth, napkins and glasses of wine.

'Oh god,' I stutter.

'It needed a little romantic flourish,' Alex tells me sweetly as she scatters handfuls of rose petals across the floor.

'Oh, OK, yes, thank you, thank you, that's enough now though, it's not a proposal,' I say, swatting at a few petals and trying to take the box off her.

'It's a proposal of sorts,' Charlie butts in.

'I think I'm coming down with something,' I choke. My forehead is feeling suddenly clammy.

'It's just nerves. Come on, you've got ten minutes until he's here; we'll leave you to it,' Alex says, tucking a strand of hair behind my ear and patting my forehead with her floaty sleeve.

'I'll go and get the food,' I stammer, feeling slightly dazed.

Back in the kitchen, I remove the spaghetti with tomato sauce and fried calamari that I had left simmering off the stove, cover it and place it on a large tray along with plates of burrata and prosciutto, a basket of bread and a salad.

Being so careful to watch my steps while carrying the heavy load, I get back to the terrace, but not before Owen has arrived.

He's caressing the table cloth, passing petals through his fingertips with an understandably befuddled look on his face. I take a step toward the table, the plates and bowls clashing slightly, which causes him to startle. His features grow more confused when his eyes meet mine, though they light up brighter than I have seen them before. His hair is sweeping to his left, his five o'clock shadow is slightly scruffier than the last time I saw him and he's wearing his trademark baggy grey t-shirt but with black linen trousers this evening. He looks cosy and snugglable and the sight of him again threatens to topple the tray of food I'm carrying as my legs tingle, jelly-like.

I blink away the want to wrap my arms around him, opening my eyes and focusing on getting the food to the table that Alex and Charlie set up next to our dining table.

Owen hasn't taken his eyes off me – I can feel his stare sending goosebumps up the back of my neck. He also hasn't said a word. My stomach growls from the mixture of the aromas arising from the tray and nerves.

'Hi,' I mumble, turning to face him once I'm free of the heavy load.

'You came back,' he croaks, eyes grey, crystal and piercing.

'I made dinner,' I say, my voice coming out a touch dry and raspy. I'm anxious and gesture for him to sit as I plate up.

His mouth parts, maybe a little gobsmacked – I hope in a positive way – and he takes a seat, pulling out my chair first so it's ready for me and then sitting down. I fill his plate with spaghetti and juicy calamari, then place a side plate of burrata and prosciutto beside him before doing mine and then adding the basket of bread to the middle of the table along with a bowl of fresh chicory and apple salad with an olive oil and balsamic vinegar drizzle.

'You did all this?' he asks, and I simply nod for all the words that are spinning around in my head aren't quite forming coherent sentences.

'Burrata for your thoughts,' Owen says, easing my mind. I nod again as we simultaneously slice into our fresh, creamy burrata and slowly dig in. I savour the freshness of my first bite and take in the man before me, realising that he's more than I ever thought I wanted or deserved in a partner. A man who offers me cheese when I'm nervous. Finally, I spill my feelings.

'I like you too,' I announce, 'I really *like you, like you*. I should have said that three weeks ago, but Owen, I'm thirty-four I have no job and I live in Manchester. You're a beautiful man with worldly experience, who is exceptional at his craft and who currently resides in Italy. I have no idea how this is going to work but I do know that I want to work for it.' The words rush out and I'm now breathing a little heavy. Reaching forward, I lift my glass and take a large sip of water, not ready for the wine just yet.

'Did you make this cheese?' he asks, and he's smiling. My shoulders loosen.

'I made the bread,' I offer with a shrug, but I'm smiling too.

'If you made this bread, I think I might be in love with you,' he blurts, scoffing a big chunk of it. There's a slight red flush creeping into his cheeks. I don't know if he's grinning because of me expressing my feelings, because of what he just said or because of how insanely good the bread is – if I do say so myself.

'You came all the way to Italy to tell me that you like me,' he then says after finishing off a bite that he dipped into the burrata.

'Well, it's not really that far,' I start before Owen starts chuckling. 'What?'

'Andrea, you know you're a rom-com waiting to happen,' he tells me, dimple popping, eyes shining.

'Take that back,' I demand, shaking my head and

breaking off a piece of bread, copying him and mopping up my burrata with it.

'I'm sorry I walked out of your apartment without really finishing our conversation. I just didn't want to face it or hear why you couldn't do this, but that was wrong of me. That feeling like a failure or not enough, it was too much in the moment, I didn't want to go through it again, but that wasn't fair on you,' he says, face suddenly solemn, happy dimple disappearing.

'I appreciate that, but Owen, I was the one that froze. I wasn't talking and you walking out was the wake-up call I needed to make a few changes – that, and Mum selling the fish and chip shop,' I confess. Yes, what he had done was painful but I hadn't made it easy and I can admit to my foolishness.

'So, you're not mad at me?' Owen asks, reaching across the table and taking my free hand in his. I let him and the feel of his skin against mine reassures me that I did the right thing coming here.

'I'm not mad at you,' I say, watching him rub his thumb over my palm. 'Are you mad at me?'

Owen shakes his head and squeezes my hand tighter. 'For what?'

'For having sex with you and then telling you what was the point?' I explain, scrunching up my nose at how cruel it sounds out loud.

'Would every argument we have lead to spaghetti and melt in your mouth calamari?' Owen questions and I can see the sparkle back in his blue-grey eyes.

'Would it make everything better?' I ask, feeling a blush

now creep into my own cheeks as I twirl spaghetti onto my fork. Owen answers with a broad smile that adds extra glitter to his eyes as he takes another bite, and I take that as a yes.

We eat in a comfortable silence, only our groans and moans of satisfaction adding harmony to the Positano beach waves and clashes of knives and forks and chatter that can be heard along the mountaintop, until we have demolished the plates before us.

'Do you think you'd still like to do something with cooking, Andrea?' Owen asks after wiping his mouth with his napkin and leaning back in his chair.

I copy his movements and squint my eyes in consideration. 'I haven't really given it too much thought. Being in the kitchen today was fascinating. I love all the homegrown and locally sourced produce, it's inspiring to cook with, and I haven't felt that inspired about food in a long time.'

Owen chuckles and smooths the shirt over his round stomach. His plate looks like it has just been washed after he mopped up all the sauce with the last of the crusty bread.

'What are you thinking?' I ask, as I start to load our plates onto the tray.

'You still sound so passionate about food, and Andrea…' He pauses to lean forward, making sure to catch my eyes. I stop twisting in my seat and leave the cutlery alone. 'You're a smart, funny, weird, wild and loving thirty-four-year-old, who can do anything, and I know that sounds like a cheesy Hallmark card.'

'Does it though?' I tease cockily, my nose feeling a tad prickly.

'But I mean it, you're honest and frantic and I love having

you next to me or just knowing that you're going to be a part of my day,' he finishes, his eyes looking more glassy than before.

'You didn't see me at the chip shop the last few years; as sour as a lime, I was. And that's the thing, Owen; I don't think I could open up a café or a restaurant. The thought of four walls, bricks and mortar all over again makes me feel claustrophobic. I mean, look at us having dinner out in the open air,' I reply, shaking my head and chuckling.

'And you suck at taking compliments,' Owen adds, his chuckling melding together with mine. Then he tilts his head from side to side, his lips pursed together like he's thinking. 'Shall I go and get dessert?'

'You made dessert too?' he asks, standing to help me clear the rest of the plates. 'What are you doing to me, woman?'

I let out a laugh. 'Thank you,' I say, taking the tray from him. 'You wait here,' I add, wanting to surprise him with the pudding.

I quickly zip down the steps and to the kitchen. Laughter flutters in from the kitchen terrace where everyone is tucking into Nonna Roberta's mussels and pasta. The sound makes my whole body feel like it's floating.

Once I have the cheesecake in my hands, I glance outside. Mum catches my eyes and sends me a wink.

I feel an eye roll coming along but shoot her a small smile instead; the night has been too beautiful to ruin with my sarcasm.

Back on the upstairs terrace, Owen is fiddling with his napkin. When I appear, he stands and comes to help me unload the bowls, and pops the cheesecake in the middle of our table.

'Oh my god, this smells incredible,' he comments as we take our seats.

'Lemons from the garden and limoncello from Roberta's secret stash – the strong stuff,' I tell him, cutting two big slices and serving us both, the citrusy aroma of Amalfi lemons dancing in the air around us.

I find myself waiting for Owen to take a bite first. It's been a long time since I laboured over a dessert so I'm anxious to know if it's any good. He swallows and if I needed confirmation of the way to this man's heart, it's there written all over his smiling face. The blush in his cheeks tickles his ears pink and his eyes flicker closed for a moment or two.

'You should open a food truck,' he states, eyes opening and piercing into my own as I take my first bite. My eyelashes flutter as the zesty rind of the Amalfi lemons delights my tastebuds. I made this. I actually made this and it tastes like heaven.

It takes me a moment to register what Owen just said, then, 'A food truck?' I question, mumbling through my spoon as I'm eagerly shovelling another bite into my mouth.

'Then you don't have to be tied down to one place. Permits allowing, you can travel anywhere you'd like, park up, see and serve the world. Also, this cheesecake should be on the menu,' he tells me enthusiastically, scraping up the biscotti crumbs left on his plate.

I don't think I've ever felt so light, floating on all the compliments Owen has given me tonight.

'A food truck,' I test again on my tongue, making sure I heard him correctly, 'it sounds so extravagant, carefree and utterly free-spirited. You think I could have a food truck?'

'You love fresh ingredients. You source the food locally in the morning, prep for lunch or dinner or both, you could do festivals, the possibilities are endless. You don't even have to do British food if you need a break from fish and chips; you could be an Italian food truck, inspired by the produce here.' Owen's grinning, his words coming out fast and full of passion and excitement; it's hard not to get caught up in the idea.

I take my time licking my spoon clean of cream cheese goodness, watching Owen eyeing up the rest of the cake, while I let the idea linger in my brain a little longer. I then finish my last bite and cut two more slices. Owen's face lights up like the finale of fireworks on Bonfire Night and pushes his plate to where I'm holding up another piece for him. We sit in silence devouring our slices while I continue to let Owen's word ruminate in my mind.

Before I can argue whether I'd be any good in a food truck, or place a barrage of obstacles in my way that prove someone like me couldn't possibly take such a bold leap, Alex and Charlie bound onto the balcony.

'Nonna Roberta said there was cheesecake and I'll be damned, Owen, it's so good to see you out of your moping cavern,' Charlie shouts into the evening. My stomach flips when Owen's cheeks turn bright red; he really was sad without me. *I wasn't much better off without him either*, I think to myself before cutting two more slices, which Alex and Charlie both pick up with their hands like they're eating a slice of pizza. I wonder how much white wine Roberta put in those mussels, but one look at the sparkles in both Alex and Charlie's eyes and the competent way they both move around the balcony indicates they are not drunk but simply happy, high on life, no doubt still riding their wedding wave and their beautiful life currently here in Italy.

The magic of this country once again wraps me in a warm embrace and as Charlie locks Owen into conversation, I let the evening drift on, savouring the night with my friends and a man that I have really, truly come to adore.

Before I know it, I'm standing outside my familiar bedroom with Owen gently caressing my cheek.

'See you at breakfast,' he says softly and my heart tugs, it actually tugs like a flipping romance novel. I don't feel the need to rip Owen's clothes off, though desire burns in my belly; tonight, we have time. Over the next week, we have time. We may not have planned what comes after that, living in two separate places, but we've committed to each other and time feels like such a wonderful thing.

I smile lazily, laying my head against his chest for a hug. Owen wraps his large arms around me and squeezes me tight.

'See you at breakfast,' I reply. We can take it slow, let tonight's conversation sink in before rushing this thing.

Owen drops his head and kisses me sweetly on the lips, and he tastes of lemons and sugar and home.

27

'So you peel the artichokes really small?' I ask Nonna Roberta as she pulls and tugs at tough artichoke leaves.

'*Si, si*,' she replies as I pick up one beautiful, hearty artichoke and copy what she's doing. Meanwhile, Owen has taken to following Gio around the kitchen. Bowls scatter the surfaces, each with tea towels laid over them. Every few minutes, Gio will lift one up and explain to Owen what kind of bread it is and where it's up to in the process.

'*Addesso*, put in here,' Roberta informs me and I quickly draw my attention back to the task at hand and not how gorgeous Owen looks with a tea towel draped over his shoulder and flour all over his nose.

I place my plucked artichoke hearts in a bowl of water, moving them around with my hands to clean them as Roberta pours olive oil into a frying pan. With one wave and point of her hand, I'm dicing up garlic and adding it to the pan before she places a bush of parsley and basil in front of me on the chopping board.

If the kitchen didn't already smell divine with the bread that Gio and Owen have been baking all morning, now with the garlic sizzling in the air, the kitchen doors wide open, letting in the day's breeze, and the parsley and basil that wafts into the mix as I break it up, it smells utterly out of this world.

All I have done since arriving in Italy for the second time is cook alongside Nonna Roberta, Gio, Will and Owen. Three days have absolutely flown by as I've focused on learning how to make the most magnificent Italian food while the thought of a food truck snuggly sits at the forefront of my mind.

I feel a life away from fish and chips, though to pay homage to my grandparents, I'd love to make a version of fish and chips, maybe with an Italian twist and add that to my menu. Listen to me, thinking about menus. Owen dropping a kiss on the top of my head while spinning around me with a baguette fresh out of the oven, alerts me to Roberta's motioning to the artichoke hearts and the pan. I nod, pushing my menu dreams to the back of my mind, or at least I try to, and add the artichokes to the pan, resulting in a deeply satisfying sizzle.

My mouth is drooling as I stir the juicy Italian delicacy while Owen slices the still-warm baguette by my side. Every few seconds, we make eye contact, and my heart feels like it has suddenly sprouted white, fluffy wings. I'm dreaming bigger than I've ever even known how to dream; with Owen, with the tempting idea of having my own restaurant on wheels, and surprisingly, it doesn't feel so scary when I'm looking into those blue-grey eyes that are sparkling back at me with hunger and warmth.

A bustle of commotion snaps my attention away from Owen as Will wanders into the kitchen with shopping bags and my mum in tow. He spent the day showing her the secret passageways and less touristy spots of Positano, and by the looks of her glowing features and tanning cheeks, she's had a wonderful time. Mum practically waltzes over to me, giving me a peck on the cheek, before she and her bright sunflower-yellow sundress are being ushered to the dining table.

The weather is still glorious, the sun unrelenting in the clear blue skies, but the air feels fresh and citrussy, and the vibrant colours of Italy make it bearable. I'm growing accustomed to the sun's toasty grip on my shoulders and I don't think I'll ever tire of enjoying food outdoors in the sunshine.

Once my artichokes are beautifully golden, I'm on lemon-chopping duty while Roberta is pouring spaghetti into a large serving bowl.

Reaching for the olive oil, I assist her, drizzling oil over the spaghetti, then some fresh lemon juice before adding in slices of lemon, a sprinkle of salt and pepper and on top of that, the main attraction: the artichoke. At this point, I feel I could devour the entire bowl, it smells so good.

Nonna Roberta smacks my hand away from an especially juicy-looking piece of artichoke and picks up the heavy bowl like a warrior to place it on the table. It leaves a trail of mouth-watering perfume that is turned up a couple of notches when I see Owen cooking circles of dough in a deep frying pan.

'What are you making?' I ask, walking over to Owen and Gio's station by the stovetop. Gio is standing by Owen's side, showing him how to flatten the balls of dough ever so slightly before popping them into the sizzling oil.

'Pizza fritta,' Gio tells me with a broad grin.

'Oh my god, that's...' I start.

'Fried pizza,' Owen finishes my sentence, his grin even wider than Gio's. The smell coming out of the pan is irresistible; there's a sweetness to the frying bread that is awakening my taste buds and I've not even put it in my mouth yet.

Once both sides are golden, Owen places the breads onto a serving platter. Gio gestures to a bowl of cheese and then a pan of sauce that is simmering on the back of the stove and I'm back in action again.

With Gio's nodding, I place a spoonful of tomato sauce in the centre of each bread and then add a slice of mozzarella on top.

'*Brava*,' Gio cheers, adding half a leaf of basil atop each one. 'You try,' he says, allowing Owen and I to dig in before we reach the table. 'To see if it's good, no?' he chuckles.

I pick up a pizza fritta and Owen pinches the other side as we pull it apart. I hold down the perfectly melted mozzarella on my end so that Owen and I get a fair bite each.

We're blowing the food while it's in our mouths, wafting our hands in front of our faces as if it's going to help, but I can't stop chewing, and though I'm sure I've burnt my tongue on the lava-like sauce, the flavours – the warm, buttery taste of the soft, fluffy inside compared to the slightly saltier and crunchier golden outside – are nothing but outstanding and worth my current pain. I can imagine people under an awning, rain or shine, fingers dripping with sauce and juices as they bite into these fresh out of the fryer. A piece of Italy in Manchester maybe. Could I really do that, be the one to give that to them?

'Good, no?' Gio says, finishing preparing the rest of the platter while Owen and I are otherwise occupied. 'Italy's version of fast food,' he adds, before carrying the tray outside as Roberta comes rushing in waving her hands at the fridge and Owen and me.

'Sorry, we're coming,' I say, taking off my apron and quickly wiping my hands and the counters down, ensuring everything is turned off, while Nonna Roberta piles prosciutto wrapped in fresh brown paper into Owen's cradled arms, in addition to a huge block of Parmesan.

I've never had a dinner here that's been without cheese and the finest salami and prosciutto, and I'm not complaining.

Tonight is a smaller affair: Owen and me, Will, Gio, Mum and Roberta, as Alex is still on a shoot, to which Charlie accompanied her. This table has grown happily familiar and comforting and my whole body instantly relaxes as I settle into my chair. My hair is tied into a bun, but not its usual tight grip; instead, it's loose atop my head, allowing my shoulders to catch tonight's light breeze in my strappy summer dress.

I may have treated myself to a couple of dresses from a boutique in Positano yesterday with Owen's help.

The chatter is going strong with everyone helping each other plate up. Owen fills my plate with a generous portion of spaghetti and artichoke, and my stomach rumbles at the sight of it. I fill glasses with water and when everyone has full plates and is armed with pizza fritta at their sides, we dig in and a big quiet descends.

The artichoke melts in my mouth yet it's hardy and meaty, the lemon and garlic seasoning it to perfection, and I can imagine feeding people bowls of it on a sunny day, albeit the Manchester sun being a little different to the Amalfi Coast's brightly burning orb.

'This should definitely be on the menu,' Owen says, after swallowing another bite of pizza fritta. I smile at the fact that he hasn't stopped thinking about the food truck either.

'I was just thinking the same thing,' I tell him, placing down my fork and picking up my own pizza fritta.

'What menu?' Mum asks from across the table, chewing thoughtfully on her spaghetti.

Owen looks at me, like it's my dream to share with her if I wish, and I feel my insides turn squishy at his attentiveness. Taking a small sip of my water, I clear my throat.

'Owen suggested that I open up a food truck. I could cook whatever food I'd like to and I wouldn't be tied down and, I'm, well, I don't know, I was actually thinking about it,' I say, the words rushing out fast like I have to explain myself and my ability to the table out of pure nerves.

I'm nibbling on my pizza fritta while Owen beams at me proudly and I'm waiting for my mum, or anyone, to say something.

'I think that's a fabulous idea, honey. Wow, you'd get to do it your way, build your own legacy,' Mum quips, raising her fork in the air like she's toasting me.

'I don't know about a legacy; I'd have to see if people like it first,' I say, anxiously chewing on my bread.

'You cook with the heart; people will like it, you'll see,' Gio chimes in.

I didn't see Will get up but suddenly, there is wine in my glass and everyone is raising theirs in a proper toast now.

'To new adventures,' Will says.

'To food and *famiglia*,' Nonna Roberta adds, sending a wink my way.

We all take a sip and I can feel the heat rushing to my

cheeks at the belief everyone has in me. Owen reaches for my hand and gives it a squeeze.

'Thank you,' I whisper, unable to believe that for the first time in my life, I'm taking the lead, I'm choosing my next step, a road unpaved for the likes of me. I can't quite believe I'm sitting on a balcony in Italy talking about opening up my own food truck and not simply sat back witnessing someone else's dream unfold. It's actually my own, me, the leading lady in the story. Did I just refer to a rom-com?

I shake my head and hear Owen chuckle. Looking up, I catch his grey eyes. 'What's so funny?' I ask with a playful pout.

'I'm starting to think you have Hallmark actress written all over you,' he teases, and my laughter barrels into the night.

28

It's my last morning in Italy and compared to the last half pleasant, half anxious morning I had the week Alex and Charlie got married, this one is most definitely 100 per cent pleasant and wonderful due to the fact that I have Owen's arms wrapped tightly around me as I nuzzle into his chest under the lush, fluffy duvet.

The early-morning sunrise is sending streaks of purple and orange through the small windows, and though visions of a food truck and big dreams dance in my head and await me in Manchester, my heart tugs with the lure of wanting to stay right here in this moment.

A kiss grazes my head, alerting me to Owen stirring too. I squeeze him a little tighter.

'When will I see you next?' I ask into his warm, soft skin.

He croaks, clearing his throat. 'I think it's my turn to head back to England. I'll plan it soon, I promise,' he whispers into my hair, making the back of my neck tingle.

'OK,' I whisper back, allowing myself to feel vulnerable. With Owen, I feel safe and like myself. Though I don't tell him that I don't quite know how I'm going to run a food truck without him by my side, I do say, 'I'm going to miss you.'

'I'm going to miss you too, very much,' he replies sweetly, tightening his grip around my body and kissing my head once more. 'Should we go and get breakfast?'

'My favourite kind of question,' I say with a smile, arching backwards and tilting my head so I can see his face. 'Yes please.'

He returns my smile and we begin to rustle the sheets. Reluctantly, I pry myself out of Owen's embrace, step into my slippers and shuffle into the bathroom where I throw on a baby-blue playsuit, splash water on my face and brush my teeth. Owen is a few steps behind me, copying my actions, sporting a casual pair of black shorts and signature white tee in place of a playsuit, though I'm sure he'd look good in dungarees.

The villa is resting peacefully as Owen leads us towards the exit.

'Are we not having breakfast on the terrace?' I query, taking his outstretched hand.

'I thought we'd try something new today, a special last breakfast, if that's OK with you?' he asks, stopping abruptly to make sure I'm happy with his decision.

'That sounds interesting. What consists of a special last breakfast?' I ask, skipping a little now to propel us forwards once more.

'You'll see,' Owen says beaming down at me and continuing his large strides.

'Oh my god, how have you been keeping this place from me? I've been in Italy a total of two weeks, albeit not consecutively, and you didn't think to bring me here,' I say, mock flabbergasted and with a mouth full of coda di aragosta, a lobster tail pastry.

Owen is chuckling and has paused consuming his first pastry in our tray of about ten. I couldn't pick one.

'That first week you were here, you were far too busy with wedding sabotage and schemes for me to even think of pulling you away,' he says, raising his eyebrows.

I splutter on the delicious Italian custard filling in my tail. 'Excuse me, I'm not the only one who forgot to write a speech,' I retort, wiggling my eyebrows back in jest. Owen snorts and shakes his head before taking a healthy bite of a rather scrumptious-looking rum baba. The rum glistens in the beautiful early-morning sun as Positano is waking.

'Touché,' he says simply, wiping the syrup as it drizzles down his chin.

'If you could actually have a hand in planning your own wedding, what would you do?' I ask Owen curiously, feeling relaxed and at ease as the custard transports my tastebuds to heaven.

'Hmm,' he replies after a long and thoughtful bite of pastry. 'You first. What would you do?'

'No wedding favours,' I chuckle before licking my fingers free of pastry flakes and custard.

'No fancy suits or dress,' Owen counters.

'Pyjamas, and no big, grand wedding venue,' I add, eyeing up the selection of pastries for which one I'd like to try next.

'Maybe the goat shed, and no pigeon.'

'Or vegan sausage,' I concur, scrunching up my nose.

'McNuggets and cheeseburgers.' Owen wiggles his eyebrows.

'Hmm, before I came to Italy, I'd have said yes, delicious,

easy, I don't have to think about cooking it, but now, not so much,' I say honestly.

'So, I mean, Italy,' Owen starts.

'Seems like the perfect place for a hypothetical wedding,' I finish, hand on a lemon tart, resisting the urge to scratch at the back of my neck.

'Well, it has everything really: stunning views, simple elegance.'

'And all the mozzarella, burrata, Parmesan, caciocavallo, basically all the good cheese one would want for a celebration,' I add.

'It would be the best hypothetical celebration – I can picture it now,' he notes, his cheeks flaring a ruby shade of red behind his sfogliatella.

It's hard to stop the blush creeping into my own face. My ears feel hot and I don't think it has anything to do with the sun warming my neck. I can picture it too, but how on earth did Owen and I get on the topic of weddings?

'So, what's next on your work calendar?' I ask, steering the conversation away from imaginary weddings.

Owen chews his flaky, shell-shaped pastry thoughtfully and then swallows. 'I have a couple of holiday-goers ornaments to finish. They're popular this time of year. Most tourists are spellbound by the coast and want mementos to take home. And I'm finishing a bespoke coffee table for one of Will's clients, then I'll see what comes along,' he tells me, picking at the crumbs falling from his breakfast.

'They take a piece of you home with them,' I say wistfully, without thinking, wishing that I could put Owen in my suitcase. I quickly blink away my soppy thoughts and take a large bite from my lemon tart, casting a sweeping look across Positano – the colourful houses resting snug against the mountainside, the pebbled beach that hurts when the tiny stones get between your toes, the gelato shops, bakeries, pizzerias – it's enough for my eyes to sting with tears lurking in my tear ducts.

One week away from my comfort zone, that's all it had taken, and my life is now on a completely new path.

'I don't think I could ever tire of eating lemons from the Amalfi Coast,' I tell Owen with a soft sigh, sniffing a little to restrain my tears.

'They're so good, they bring tears to people's eyes,' Owen teases, wiping his hands on a napkin.

I roll my eyes at him as he swipes at my last bite. I mock protest by standing up, hands on my hips, walking to his side like I'm going to fight him for it when he pops it into his mouth and pulls me onto his lap.

My stomach is full to the brim of Italian pastries and espresso, my arms snug around Owen's neck. I rest my head against the top of his as we watch a couple of Vespas fly by and a bus unload a group of people – a mix of locals and tourists.

'I like sharing food with you,' I whisper in Owen's ear, feeling joyful at the beautiful experiences food has given me while I've been in Italy.

'I like sharing life with you,' Owen replies, and I'm lost in his blue eyes which are seemingly reflecting the clear sky this morning as their grey is less prominent, and then my lips are meeting his, and as I've come to know, he tastes sweet, like lemons, vanilla and sugary espresso.

After some time of complete and utter out-of-body

experience, our delicate kisses come to a stop and we pull apart slowly.

'What have I become? I say, kissing him gently on the cheek. He grips my waist a little harder and gives it a squeeze.

'A hopeless romantic, making out at breakfast while the glistening Positano sea sparkles in the background, without a care in the world for PDA,' Owen replies, smiling so big, his dimple pops.

I swat at him and climb off his lap, looking over our table; we've drained our coffees but four pastries remain.

'Should we take these back for the others?' I ask.

'You read my mind,' he replies, the sparkling sea dancing in his eyes.

'Have you got everything? You'll come back soon,' Alex says, squeezing my neck so tight, I think my head might pop off like a dandelion.

'I think I've got everything and then some,' I reply, gasping a little for air and referring to my suitcase that is most likely going to weigh more than the baggage allowance considering the amount of cheese, Italian sausage and artichokes, among other delicacies, that Nonna Roberta forced in there. 'And you've got to come back to Stockport soon; I can't have lost you to Italy already,' I add, trying to force down the twinge of sadness I get in the base of my throat that I'm literally leaving my only family and closest friends behind. But there's also a buoying excitement in leaving this time. Despite the fear of missing everyone and not knowing how

I'll cope without Mum or how mine and Owen's newfound relationship is going to handle the distance, I have hope in my heart for what lies ahead. Something big is waiting for me when I get home and those somethings here mean that Italy doesn't feel so far out of reach like it once did.

'I will, I will,' Alex says, giving me one last squeeze. 'You bet I want to be the first in line when you open your food truck window,' she beams, making my stomach flip. Charlie pulls me in for a hug before Mum, Owen and I are jumping into the car, with Will driving. Gio, Roberta and my best friends wave us off.

The car journey passes quickly with Mum reminding me to take pictures of everything, to make sure to look over the food van, to negotiate a good price with the seller, make sure I cut the grass and to message if I need anything, anything at all. All while Owen keeps such a firm grip on my hand that I can't tell if it's my palms that are sweating or his, or both.

Once again, the airport is a sharp contrast to the serene surroundings of the Amalfi Coast, and the hustle and bustle snaps me out of my sleepy trance, safe in the back of the car clutching onto Owen. I can do this. I brush on a big smile as I let go of Owen's hand and we each exit the vehicle from opposite sides. Wiping my hand on my playsuit, I shout to Mum, not wanting these goodbyes to be too teary.

'I'll make sure to keep the house clean and stocked up on biscuits.'

'Remember, if you need anything at all, just ring and I'll come back,' Mum replies, squashing my face between her palms, and I'm grateful that hers are cool and not sweaty. I'm aware opening up my own food truck is not going to be easy, but she's spent her life helping others live their dreams;

it's time for her to do her own thing and for me to see what I'm made of. So I wrap my arms around her tight.

'I will. Now you remember to see every inch of Italy and only come home when you've tried a dessert from every region,' I say with a smile.

'That is a challenge I will happily help your mum with,' Will pipes up, sneaking in a hug once my mum has let go. 'I'll look after her,' he adds in a whisper, making my heart relax ever so slightly. It immediately seizes up again when I think of my next and last goodbye.

I turn to Owen, shuffling my backpack strap back onto my shoulder, doing my best to keep my smile in place when I notice him retrieve a rather large suitcase from the boot of the car.

'But I have my suitcase; I don't think they'll let me take anymore,' I say with a tremble in my voice, starting to panic about sniffer dogs in the airport and going through customs.

'Oh, this thing, it's not for you,' Owen comments, pulling out the handle and walking to my side 'Are you ready to go?' he asks. My face contorts into a befuddled expression, my nose scrunching up so tight, it's starting to tingle.

'I'm ready yes, but what? I can't take...' My words trail off as Will and Mum climb back into the car, waving giddily at Owen and me. Owen takes a step away from the car towards the airport and I about lose all composure and shed every last bit of my 'I hate rom-coms' persona.

'Owen, where are you going?' I mumble, tears already springing to my eyes. 'What about your coffee table and your holiday pieces?'

'I finished them while you were gone those few weeks,' he replies, gently taking my elbow and walking us to a less packed area of the pavement and away from being an obstruction to travellers. 'I mean, you're going to need a sous chef and someone who doesn't mind being cramped up in a tight space with you all day, and someone to taste test your incredible cooking, and someone to maybe just be there to triple check all your DIY because I know you can do it yourself but it helps…'

Owen doesn't get any more words out of his mouth as I'm pulling him down towards me while standing on my tiptoes, and pressing my lips against his with an aggression I didn't know I possessed.

My tongue tingles with the sweet taste of limoncello – that Roberta insisted we needed after lunch for the journey – and the salty taste of the tears that are streaming down my face.

My suitcase falling over, the handle digging into the back of my knee, causes me to buckle and pull away from Owen. Both breathless, we burst out laughing with him gripping my waist tight so I would never have hit the ground.

'Oh my god!' I exclaim, not a care in the world as to who is listening or how many people turn in my direction. 'We're kissing in an airport,' I gasp, still laughing as I look into my favourite pair of eyes.

'Oh my god,' Owen shouts, 'we are such a cliché.'

Epilogue

'You're absolutely killing it with those lasagne pots; we're all out and it's not like anyone needs warming up today,' Owen tells me from where he's chopping up artichoke for our artichoke and Parmesan salad. He's not wrong; it's the middle of August in Stockport and we've been blessed with another heatwave.

Inside the food truck feels like a blazing hot infrared sauna, yet strangely enough, my knickers sticking to my butt cheeks isn't dampening my mood as I serve slices of lemon cheesecake to two waiting customers.

'I can't take the credit; Zia Allegra's recipe is gold,' I reply with a slight twist over my shoulder as three friendly faces step up to the window.

'What can I get for you today, boys?' I ask, my smile broadening at Stefan and his two kids, regulars of our food truck. 'Would you like something new or are we sticking with our favourites?'

'Hmm,' George says, scrunching up his button nose and wiping his white-blonde fringe out of his eyes. 'Please can I get the pizza fritta with tomato and cheese and...' he pauses, and for a second, I think he's finished with his regular order.

'Italian sausage,' he breathes out. and though I don't show it, my heart is doing a tap dance.

'Of course you can, that's a brilliant choice. My mum only just brought back some fresh Italian sausage that I think you'll love,' I say, not overly dramatic. I don't want to make too big a deal of this momentous occasion as I don't wish to scare him or make him overthink his decision. George and his brother Rory have been ordering their pizza fritta with cheese and tomato since we opened last November. For him, trying something new is a big step and I'm so proud, but too much attention might put him off. I'm so pleased when Rory steps up, copying his brother's order in a show of support.

Stefan then comes up to the window while the boys go and find an empty picnic table. His round cheeks are bulging red with a smile that's lighting up his whole face.

'Thanks, Andi,' he says kindly.

'No problem. I think you did great stepping back and letting him choose, good call,' I reply, thinking back to a few months prior when I'd rambled off the new menu items and Stefan had pushed George to try something different. The two of us combined resulted in an extremely overwhelmed child and I'd felt awful. It had broken my heart and made me pay closer attention to each individual customer and their needs.

Some people ask about the menu, others happily choose off the chalk board. Some make conversation, others give me an encouraging smile, get their food and go about their day. We've served a beautiful kaleidoscope of people from our spot in the bustling Stockport Market and I am loving every minute. Familiar faces return each day or week, and new faces appear all the time; both keep me filled with hope and excitement.

'I'll try that artichoke and Parmesan salad please; need something light for today I think,' Stefan says before paying and joining the boys as I set to work.

'One salad, please, chef,' I say to Owen as I hip check him when he swivels past me, taking my spot at the window to deliver two fresh salads to waiting customers.

'Won't be a moment,' he calls out merrily to the next in line, then he's by my side plating Stefan's salad while I pull two sizzling, crispy on the outside, fluffy on the inside pizza frittas out of the deep pan and sauce them up. I allow the Italian sausage to golden on the stove before wrapping up George and Rory's lunch and calling for Stefan.

Owen tickles my ear with a kiss as he hands me Stefan's salad bowl and I pass all three dishes over.

'*Buon appetito*,' Owen and I say in unison.

'Your salad is a hit,' I tell him quickly before we each take another two orders. It was Owen's idea to add the salad, as well as a delicious, simple and elegant prosciutto and chicory cold sandwich, to the menu during these hot months. He also had the brains to suggest a dessert fridge so we can make things in advance and simply have them on hand for customers, and stick to a small menu so we can whip up the main meals fresh as we go.

It's hard to say what items are our most successful as we've been selling out consistently since around Christmas.

November was touch and go while we tried to get the word out and give away free samples in the rain. I'd had moments where the vision of an empty chip shop on a lonely hill edged its way into my mind but Owen kept the positive ball rolling, as did visits from Mum, Alex and Charlie. On those visits, they were never empty handed, delivering the most wonderful produce that had my heart craving Italy and my passion soaring – thrilled to be sharing our food with the locals and bringing them a taste of Italy.

Mum was making good on her challenge of trying a dessert from each region and brought me back one when she could. I'd so far had a lemon cannolo from Sicily and a slice of buondino di riso from a trip she took with Will, Gio and Zia Allegra to Tuscany back in April.

'You were right about adding slices of lemon,' Owen tells me. Our conversations throughout the lunch time rush tend to go a bit like this. I'll say something and then twenty minutes later after taking orders, cooking and conversing with customers, Owen will reply, or vice versa.

At the risk of sounding like a soppy romantic, each day with him by my side has been one funny, delightful, happy adventure. Even the wavering start didn't seem quite as dire with Owen on board.

He still works on his own crafts, and Mum's house has accumulated a bunch of tools, random materials and planks of wood over the last couple of months. When Mum ventured back to the UK in spring, Owen popped back to Italy for a fortnight to work with Will on a piece that he could not pass up on. Will had wanted his best craftsman on the job for it.

Now, as the lunch time rush comes to an end, Owen pops a spoonful of lemon sorbet into my mouth once I've finished wiping down the counters and turn to face him in our tight quarters.

The chill of the sorbet mixed with the slight sourness of the lemons instantly cools my cheeks.

'Are you ready for our vacation?' he asks me giddily before spooning some sorbet into his own mouth.

I smile with a mixture of nerves and excitement and open the back doors of the truck to allow some air to sweep through the van.

After the whirlwind few months that followed our return from Italy – acquiring the food truck, preparing the food truck, learning to cohabit for the most part when Owen wasn't at his dad's, getting our permits, getting Mum's kitchen inspected and preparing our menu – Owen had suggested we book a holiday, to put it in the diary no matter what and to give us something to work towards.

If there's one thing he has learnt from living in Italy, it's the work-life balance. That resting is important and family time even more so. It is something I'm coming to understand, especially when my feet are screaming at me in agony and my pores are in need of respite from the steam in the cramped van, but still, the idea of closing the truck for a week when it's booming terrifies me.

'I think I am,' I reply, feeling the tightness in my calves from standing all day when I shift uncomfortably. 'And you're sure we'll still have customers when we get back?' I can't help but ask, letting Owen in on my anxieties. He eases them by feeding me another spoon of sorbet.

'I believe they'll be queuing round the block ready to see you again, dying for your mouth-watering cooking,' he tells me, his mesmerising blue-grey eyes warm and sincere, though my own eyes threaten to roll despite my shoulders loosening considerably.

'I can't exactly say it's a terrible chore, all these breaks to Italy,' I reply with a playful smirk.

'That's my Andrea, always positive,' he replies, dimples popping, his eyes swimming with cheek.

I grab the spoon from his hand and help myself to three spoonfuls of sorbet without giving him any, which resorts in Owen tickling my hips until I surrender.

'No, no, no, that's not fair, take it, take the sorbet,' I scream, laughter echoing around our metal dream.

'Owen, where are you? I can't see a thing!' I exclaim, hands out in front of me trying to reach out and touch something, anything that will balance my equilibrium.

'That's the point of a blindfold, Andrea,' he retorts bluntly, but I can picture his slight smirk and dimple.

I can smell the saltiness of the Italian sea, mixed with the fruitiness of my sunscreen and dinners being cooked along the coast. There's no mistaking the crispy woodfire dough and sweet aroma of tomato sauce and cheese. Mmm, someone's making pizza. My stomach grumbles and I hear a faint chuckle from Owen somewhere in my vicinity.

'Can I look yet? Is there food?' I ask, settling with standing as still as can be with my arms out like a scarecrow so I can give myself a strong base and won't fall down or into anything.

'Just one second,' comes Owen's gentle voice suddenly next to my earlobe, making me simultaneously jump and shiver all over.

'Oi!' I shout, trying to swat at him but only swiping at air as his large frame is now behind me.

'OK, are you ready?' he asks, placing one warm hand above my hip and using one to gently tug at the blindfold. The gorgeous smell of pizza is replaced by his delicious Owen scent and it's a challenge for me not to turn around and bury myself in his chest when the blindfold falls away.

I let out a gasp as the small hut comes into view. It's lit up by a couple of rusty lanterns and a haphazardly draped string of fairy lights.

There's just enough room for me to manoeuvre past the two large work benches. One of which is set out with huge slabs of clay, like Owen is about to instruct a workshop, and the other is covered in a linen table cloth and bearing a picnic basket with breads, cheese, salami and olives spilling out.

'Oh my goodness, Owen, how are you just showing me this now? It's incredible,' I say, taking in piece after piece of stunning sculptures that are dotted around on the high shelves around us.

'We've been a little preoccupied on your last two visits, but I wanted to show you where I'm working when I make my trips back here, so you don't miss me too much,' he says with a shy smile, the rosiness in his cheeks lit up by an amber lantern.

'I always miss you too much,' I say with a sigh, tracing my hands over two beautifully carved wooden fish. 'Don't you miss working in here, being here all the time?' I ask, the question falling out of my mouth before I can stop it.

Owen shakes his head. 'I'm grateful that I get to do both, and besides, the food truck has something that this workshop doesn't have – well, except for tonight,' he says, taking a step forward so he's behind me again, nuzzling into my neck.

'What's that?' I breathe, closing my eyes.

'You,' he says simply, his warm breath tickling my neck.

'What a nerd,' I scoff, teasing him before turning into his embrace. 'Owen?'

'Andrea.'

'Are you going to teach me how to sculpt? Is this like a date?' A small giggle escapes my lips.

Owen releases his hold on me and untucks the stool from under the work bench, gesturing for me to sit down.

'Why, I think it is. We sleep together, we work together, we've schemed together, we've even wedding'd together, but I do believe this is our first official date.'

'Wow, so no talk of work allowed, no Alex and Charlie interruptions, no one else around, just us?' I ask, taking my seat, Owen standing tall behind me. He leans down so his chin rests on my shoulder and we are cheek to cheek.

'Just us,' he replies, a touch hoarse.

'Owen...'

'Andrea.'

'I think I'm passing "like",' I tell him. My head immediately begins throbbing, unable to comprehend the words that just came out of my mouth, but my heart is fluttering as fast as a hummingbird, like it's doing a merry little jig. I'm thankful I'm sitting down. Owen and I have been taking it slow this past year, not wanting to put any pressure on ourselves, but tonight, I feel it. I feel it in every part of my body. I love him and the 'L' word isn't scaring me the way it once did.

'I hadn't even got to my homemade lemon-custard-filled zeppole,' Owen replies, his nose caressing my cheek now.

'You made zeppole?' I inquire, heart leaping harder and faster still.

'Well, nothing says I love you like homemade lemon-custard-filled zeppole,' he notes, twisting my legs so I swivel to face his handsome features and those hypnotic, grey-blue eyes.

'I love you too,' I say as Owen peppers kisses down my nose until he reaches my lips. His are soft and plump and forever tasting of vanilla and sugar.

'You haven't even tried them yet,' he whispers, pulling away slightly.

'I somehow think they will be perfect,' I mumble, eager to get back to kissing him, and to eating some olives and bread.

'There's no such thing as perfect,' he deadpans, and I pause our kiss, leaning back so I can see his face. Tilting my head from side to side in thought, I stand up and take his hand towards the picnic basket – art will have to wait.

'That's true – I mean, someone once told me that nothing lasts forever and we all die in the end,' I can't help but smirk recalling the very first words I heard from Owen's lips.

'Uh, how unromantic and disgustingly cynical,' he replies, mock aghast, his dimple lit up under the soft lights.

'I know, can you believe that?'

'I'm appalled.'

'But you know what? I'm rather enjoying this ride to death with you by my side,' I say, resulting in a large bark of laughter from Owen that nearly has me choking on an olive. I love the sound.

'I might have to revoke your Hallmark leading lady

status. Now put down the olives, stop talking about death and kiss me,' he says, closing the gap between us.

'Fair enough, but you're getting better at leading man,' I tease, before cupping his face and doing exactly as he asked.

Acknowledgements

I have so much love and gratitude for the amazing team at Aria who come together to make sure my books are the best they can be. My editor Bianca, I love working with you. You have a way of making me believe in myself that gives me the confidence to keep writing. I always love talking about my stories with you and hearing your ideas. Your guidance has been wonderful and forever inspires me. You are the best.

To the incredible Meg Shepherd, Emily Champion, Jessie Price, Charlotte Hayes-Clemens, Emily Reader, Zoe Giles, Jo Liddiard, Amy Watson, Ayo Okojie, Vicki Eddison, Anne-Marie Hansen, Daniel Groenewald, Rachel Rees, Karen Dobbs, thank you for all that you have done and continue to do, for not only *The (Anti) Wedding Party*, but for all my other books too. You are all brilliant and I am forever grateful.

I'm sending nothing but ginormous hugs to every single person who has ever picked up a copy of one of my books, shown their support through social media, left reviews or passed on my stories to family and friends, it truly means the world to me when characters of mine connect with you and you have enjoyed what I have written.

To all my amazing author friends who continue to inspire me daily, thank you! I love you all. Keep being your incredible selves.

Mum and Dad, thank you for always going above and beyond with your love and support. I don't think I'll ever find the words to express how much I love you both and how grateful I am to you for all that you do. Writing this book has had its challenges, but your care and all the ways you look after me helped every step of the way. Thank you.

Jen, I don't think I'd have a book if it wasn't for you. You helped me get unstuck and figure out what I was writing. I can't thank you enough for listening to me ramble about this book and for making me see... 'it's not complicated'. I love you endlessly and hope you enjoy this one.

Kelly, thank you for always reading my books a gazillion times before the rest of the world and for both being honest and critical and my biggest cheerleader. When you and Jen enjoy it, connect with it and it makes you smile, that's all I need, I'm happy.

Dan, thank you for talking about Manchester chip shops and book ideas with me for hours at a time, for listening to me explain (often too loudly) about the writing process and my dreams, for always making me laugh and being ready with cuddles when I need them. I'm grateful and excited for the next chapter with you.

William, you are sleeping in my arms as I write this. Thank you for inspiring me like I've never known before. I hope to make you proud of your Mummy. I love you beyond measure and look forward to guiding you in following your own dreams as you grow.

I've written my books through so many joyous moments

in my life, but also through grief, divorce and loss, and I feel that all the characters have played a special part in my life, for which every book leaves its mark on me and is incredibly treasured. This book I have written during pregnancy and I just want to shout out to all the awesome humans out there who have been pregnant, are going through pregnancy or the pregnancy journey and the ups and downs, and say: you are incredible. You are beautiful. You are superhuman. I'm thinking of you and sending all my love. Also baby fog is very real; be kind to yourself.

About the Author

LUCY KNOTT loves nothing more than curling up in a cozy writing spot, with coffee and biscuits on hand, and writing the day away.

She loves love in all its forms and adores writing warm, happy stories full of romance, sibling bonds and best friends who know each other inside and out. You're also guaranteed to find the most delicious food in her books, with Lucy being a lover of Italian food and anything and everything sweet.

When not writing, Lucy enjoys spending time with her family, her partner and their baby boy, cooking her Nanna and Grandad's Italian dishes (that you can find in her and her twin sister, Kelly's cookbook, *Fame Da Lupo*), baking all kinds of cake and cookies, and getting lost in a good book.

You can find Lucy on X, Instagram and TikTok:
@LucyCKnott